SEATTLE WHALERS HOCKEY ROMANCE

ALL THE WAY

Emily Bunney

4 Horsemen
Publications, Inc.

4 Horsemen
Publications, Inc.

Published By: 4 Horsemen Publications, Inc.

4 Horsemen Publications, Inc.
PO Box 417
Sylva, NC 28779
4horsemenpublications.com
info@4horsemenpublications.com

Cover by Niki Tantillo
Typesetting by Valerie Willis
Editor J.M. Paquette

Library of Congress Control Number: 2021936206

Audio ISBN: 978-1-64450-212-9
EBook ISBN: 978-1-64450-213-6
Paperback ISBN: 978-1-64450-214-3
Hardcover ISBN: 979-8-8232-0684-6

Dedication

*I'm dedicating Nate and Beth's story
to my gorgeous hubby and all the other
sweet, funny guys out there.*

Table of Contents

Trigger Warning

This book deals with domestic abuse and violence, anxiety, death, and grief. As with all the Whalers books, there is plenty of fun, sexy times, and banter, but please be aware if these issues are triggers for you, and proceed with caution.

PROLOGUE

Nate

"**F**ailure is what, Nathaniel?" my father barks in his deep Okie accent, the smell of pipe tobacco and sweat making my nostrils flare.

"Not an option, Sir," I repeat in the strongest voice my seventeen-year-old self can muster.

"That's right." He holds my shoulders tightly, so tightly I can feel his fingers pressing into my muscles even through my hockey pads. "This is the big game. The one you've played all season for. You've played with the flu, with broken fingers and bruises. Make that count. Now get out there and bring home the win!"

Even though, at seventeen, I tower over my father by six inches without skates and probably outweigh him by fifty pounds, he's still the most intimidating man I've ever met. He's the disciplinary force in my life, and he runs his family like he runs his new recruits at Fort Sill Army Base. He's a Drill Sergeant, and that role doesn't end when he walks in the door at the end of the day.

It's the biggest game of the season, and we're favorites to take home the State Championship. My father managed *to talk his way into the locker room (he and Coach are hunting buddies), and he's giving me another one of his "pep talks." However, unlike our Coach, his talk contains thinly veiled threats that should I not play until I bleed, it won't be good enough in his eyes.*

I listen intently as I've learned to do over the years. When you get clipped round the ear enough, you learn to pay attention. I nod in the appropriate places and grunt my responses, but right now, I'm in my head, replaying Coach's rousing, inspirational speech that he delivered not ten minutes ago.

"Now go out there and make me proud." He slaps my broad padded back and sends me off down the tunnel, painfully aware that no matter what I do, that'll never be the case.

As I clomp toward the ice, there's one thing my father will never know. I don't play to make him proud; I play for my team, for my Coach, and for her.

1

Beth

These hockey boys have interrupted my chaotic packing, and now they're bringing all this drama to my doorstep. Jesus, they're worse than high school chicks. I have three big, burly Whalers hockey players chattering away when I have things to do.

"Beth, baby. Please listen to him. I swear it'll all make sense." Nate gives me his best sad face, jamming his big foot into the doorway. Nate Halsted: Seattle Whalers defenseman, sexy, tall, and my Achilles heel.

"Why should I?" I ask, spitting my venom and narrowing my gaze in Matt's direction.

"Because the kid isn't mine, and my ex is a spiteful bitch," Matt growls. "Beth, I'll do anything. Please just tell me where Mila is."

I pause, drawing this out because watching Matt Landon, hockey douche and Whalers center, bounce around on the balls of his feet with pent up frustration is too much fun to waste. He hurt my best friend and roommate Mila Bennett more than I can bear. But his story seems plausible, so I suppose I can give him the information he needs. Not for him, though. For Mila. When things were good with them, she seemed … happy.

I can't understand this desperate need to chain oneself to another person, but whatever.

To each their own.

"Fine, but I don't want anything from you." I jab my finger in Matt's chest.

I whip around and fix Nate with my most frightening stare. "I want something from you."

He looks momentarily stunned, and Bugs, the Whalers captain, chuckles behind him. Then a slow smile spreads over his ridiculously handsome face.

"Anything you want, princess." He drawls it out in his best Midwestern, wholesome, good guy voice.

Good god, it hits me right in the clit, and I squeeze my thighs together to fend off my arousal. The memories of our night together are always so close to the surface, especially when we're in close proximity.

"When you two finish eye-fucking each other, maybe you can tell me where Mila is?" Matt barks in frustration, slapping his hand against the wall.

Poor guy is frustrated. Sorry not sorry.

I drag my eyes away from Nate's bright baby blues and glare at the man who "loves" my best friend. "She went to New Orleans. She had that free vacation so she's using it for Bye Week."

"Thanks Beth. I owe you." He plants a quick kiss on my cheek, and he and Bugs take off down the stairs, leaving Nate and me alone.

"Actually, *you* owe me, so get your butt in here and you can start repaying your debt." I cock my eyebrow and beckon him with my finger, standing to one side so his huge body can squeeze past me.

"C'mon, you must weigh like two hundred pounds. Harder! Harder!" I moan through gritted teeth.

"You know this wasn't what I had in mind when you asked me to repay my debt." Nate chuckles as he bounces his huge frame on my suitcase while I try to zip it shut.

"Done," I cry triumphantly, standing up and putting my hands on my hips. I'm only going to L.A. for three days, but I've got a few fancy parties to attend so I need plenty of wardrobe choices.

It doesn't help that I'm a chronic overpacker.

"So that's it? We're good?" Nate asks, standing up to his full six feet seven inches of delicious man muscle. I must admit, as annoying as he can be sometimes with the lovey-dovey shit, he is by far the hottest guy I've ever been with. I would say dated, but I don't date.

"Oh baby, you haven't even come close to repaying me yet." I smirk, drawing my favorite Japanese kimono closed more tightly across my naked breasts. I could easily get Nate to pay me back in the most pleasurable way possible, but I'm not sure I want to blur those lines again.

Nate's eyes darken with desire, and he takes a long stride toward me, his huge hand coming to the back of my neck, drawing me close so my breasts graze his chest. For a moment, I allow myself to be pulled in by his hypnotic blue eyes and wholesome smile, lost in sexy flashbacks of his thick muscular arms holding me close and his trim hips thrusting against me …

No! Focus, Beth.

"Whoa, there cowboy," I whisper in a raspy voice. "That's not what I mean." I reach around, removing his hand from my neck and taking a step back.

"C'mon Beth, you know it'll be fantastic," he whispers huskily, licking his full lips and letting his eyes momentarily drop to my cleavage.

"You're wrong," I reply quietly. "It would be epic. But I have something else in mind."

I dodge around him and head for the living room. There are way too many horny memories in this room, and a change of location is needed. Fast.

Once we're safely in the living room, Nate props up against the counter and drinks a bottle of water while I perch on a stool.

"I have to go to L.A. today." I cross my legs but keep a firm hold on my kimono as Nate's eyes flash at the movement. "Andre and I have a meeting with a big-time director to do the hair and makeup for his next movie. But before the meeting, we're attending a fancy benefit he's throwing, and I want you to come with me."

Nate scratches his hand through his wavy, sandy blonde hair and scrunches up his face. "You want me to be your date?"

"Kind of," I reply. "The director in question is a Seattle native and a huge Whalers fan. If I show up to his benefit with Nate Halsted, I'm sure to get his attention and have an advantage in negotiations."

"So what, I'm your arm candy?" He gasps, his big hand fluttering over his chest. "I'm a person, you know, not a piece of meat." Then he flicks his imaginary hair over his shoulder in fake disgust.

God, this guy cracks me up.

"That's about the size of it, pretty boy." I chuckle. "You're free, right? Bye Week has started?"

"Sure, I have a team debrief this afternoon, but then I'm free as a bird for five days."

"Great. I'm flying out in a few hours, but as long as you can get to L.A. by tomorrow night, we're on." I hold my hand up and we high five. "Okay, I need to finish getting ready. I'll text you the details of my hotel. Just let me know when you're getting in."

"Um, quick question," Nate says, suddenly looking sheepish and unsure.

"Yeah?" I have a feeling I know what's coming.

"Shall I book myself a room or …?" He leaves the question hanging in the air.

He's beyond cute. Most guys would just show up, no room booked, so we'd have no choice but to share. Nate's good Midwestern values just forbid him from being so presumptuous. He really is a gentleman at heart.

"I'd try and book one if you can," I say kindly. "Not like you can't afford it."

Nate flattens his lips into a tight line and nods his head. "Sure thing, princess. Whatever you say. See you tomorrow." He leans forward, kisses my cheek, enveloping me in his clean linen smell, and heads out.

As I watch him leave, I let out a deep breath, nagging guilt gnawing at my gut. I sounded like a bitch when he asked me about sharing a room. There's nothing I'd like more than to spend a few nights wrapped up in his raw sexuality, but I just can't allow myself this luxury. I need to focus on this meeting, and Nate Halsted is too much of a sexy distraction.

Once I hear the lock snick closed, I pull my phone out of the pocket of my kimono and bring up my business partner's contact.

"Andre, you will not *believe* what I just did," I purr when he picks up.

Nate

"Did Landon get everything sorted?" I ask Bugs as we sit in the meeting room waiting for Coach Casey to arrive for the team debrief. We need to go over the game last night, which won't be pretty because we played like shit, and I'm expecting Coach to give us a roasting.

"Yeah, he has a flight to New Orleans later today, but Mila's still not picking up her phone." Bugs stretches his long legs under the table.

"Ah man, that sucks. I hope she listens to him. They're meant to be together. You can tell," I mumble.

Bugs' head whips round, and he gapes at me. "Dude. You're an old romantic at heart, aren't you?" He pulls me into a head lock and gives me a noogie. I guess I'm not keeping my feelings about Beth as close to my chest as I thought I was. I must be as transparent as my visor.

"Fuck off." I laugh struggling out of his grip and shove him back into his chair as Coach Casey comes in, followed by the assistant coaches.

"Listen up, ladies," he shouts as he reaches the podium. "This won't be pretty, so hold onto your butts."

Ah shit.

"What're y'all doing for Bye Week?" Ford asks in his lazy Tennessee drawl as he loads his plate with pasta.

My line is standing at the buffet table, grabbing a bite in the players' lounge before we all head our separate ways for some much-needed vacation time.

"Heading back to Edmonton for a few days, catch up with my dad, play with my dog, go fishing," Bugs replies, spearing a huge salmon fillet with his fork.

"I'm off to Tijuana with some buddies. Drink me some tequila." Brett laughs. "Maybe hook up with some hot chicas."

"Jesus, man." Bugs chuckles, shaking his head. "Chicas? Seriously."

"What about you, kid?" Ford asks. "Are you going back to Kansas or whatever?"

"Oklahoma," I correct, the mention of my home causing my stomach to spasm in an uncomfortable cramp. There's nothing for me in Oklahoma except violence and disappointment.

"So? Are you heading home?" Ford presses, grabbing two cartons of milk from the bucket of ice.

I swallow dryly. "No, no plans to go home. I might just book a flight somewhere and see what happens."

"Come to Mexico. Be my wingman," Brett offers as we take our seats at the table and dig into our mountains of food.

"No thanks, man. Not my scene," I mumble.

"Seriously? Cheap tequila and drunk college chicks from San Diego aren't your scene? You're a twenty-one-year-old NHL player. What the fuck is wrong with you?" Brett teases through a mouthful of chicken.

"Just not my thing. Sorry." I don't feel like explaining to this table full of goons that I've had a much more attractive offer.

"Your loss," Brett sniggers before he entertains the table with tales of his many trips across the border to Mexico and the shenanigans that inevitably followed.

2

Beth

"**I** can't believe you convinced Nate to give up his vacation time to come here and do this for you," Andre coos as we sit in the bar at The Standard Hotel sipping martinis—mine dirty with olives, his with those weird little onions.

"I know, right?" I gloat, giving my platinum bob a triumphant shake. "I very much doubt any of our competition will be bringing a hot NHL player to the benefit."

Andre runs his hand over his perfectly shaved head which shimmers like polished mahogany and fixes me with an annoyed glare. Today, his eyes are emerald green thanks to the contacts he has in.

"This means I'm gonna have to find my own date now," he huffs, scanning the bar.

"Oh, come on, like you need an excuse to go trawling for hot guys." I smirk, sipping the last of my drink and sliding the olives off the cocktail stick with my teeth.

"Speaking of trawling, are you coming to that club with me tonight? I'm meeting a few friends. It'll be fun. It's been too long since we got silly and danced the night away."

Andre and I have been business partners for three years and friends for even longer. We bonded in high school over our insane devotion to '90s boy bands and Lady Gaga and began hanging out, messing around with makeup, and making our own clothes. When I think back to some of our creations, I laugh at how clueless we were and what a weird couple we made. I'm five feet nothing, popping curves all over with sleek, pale blonde hair and icy blue eyes whereas Andre is almost seven feet tall and lean with wiry muscles and rich brown skin. His features are delicate and ethereal, and his head is shaved bald, but he does have a fondness for extravagant wigs.

After high school, we reluctantly went our separate ways; I headed to Boston to study business with a minor in cosmetology and movie makeup, and Andre went to Beauty College in Illinois. The summer between our junior and senior years, we got totally hammered on tequila and made a pact to set up our own business after graduation. With some seed money from my parents and a lot of hard work, we set out into the adult world of work.

We started out doing hair and makeup for local kids going to prom and a few weddings, we set up a website and an Instagram account, and things just grew and grew. Now we barely have a weekend between May and October when we don't have a wedding, then we get busy again around the holidays. The New Year is our quietest time which is why we decided to pursue the opportunity to do a movie following a tip from a bride we worked on in Seattle over the summer. Her father-in-law is the movie director Hector Riley, and she kept talking about the stress he was having with the pre-production for his new romantic comedy. I remember the look Andre and I shared, both of us having the exact same idea at the exact same time.

And so here we are in L.A. preparing to attend Hector's Clean Up Our Oceans benefit and hopefully land a lucrative and career changing job on his new movie.

"C'mon, Bee! Come dancing with us," Andre whines, draining his martini.

"Listen, honey, I need to go over the business plan again. You know what I'm like. Until this meeting's over, I'm not really going to relax." I stand and pull Andre down to kiss his lips. "You go and have fun. I'm gonna check through the business plan, read up on the charity, and go to bed."

"Ugh, you're so diligent and professional. Now I feel bad," Andre pouts.

"No, you should go and visit with your friends and try to find a date for tomorrow night." I grab my purse and gently push him away. "Now, go and find hot boys. Be careful, and we'll go out for brunch at the Roosevelt tomorrow."

"Okay, baby girl." Andre drops down to kiss me again and swishes out of the bar.

I would love to go and dance the night away with him, but to be honest, I'm exhausted. All the drama with Matt and Mila really took it out of me. I don't understand why people crave being in a relationship. Yes, I love men, and I do have sexy, fleeting flings, but as soon as they start wanting to do everything together and monopolize all my time, I cut them loose. I'm young, and I want to have fun. Is that so wrong? I look at my parents who got married right out of college, and even though they are the happiest, most solid couple ever, it makes me sad they didn't give each other time to explore other options.

At this point, thirty years married with two adult children, they're more like best friends than a married couple. I can't remember the last time I saw them have a heated argument or a passionate exchange of any kind. And I was appalled when I found out my mom goes to the bathroom with the door open. That's the death of romance right there. I want no part of that. Give me first kisses, butterflies, and hot sex all the way.

And once that goes away, it's my cue to cut ties.

Speaking of hot sex, when I get back to my room, I check my messages and see one from Nate.

[NATE: flight gets into L.A. at 4. I have a room at the hotel. Meet you in the lobby at 8. Got my tux. N]

Yikes, Nate in a tux. That image makes my breath hitch in my chest, and my lady parts throb with need. Damn, that man can wear the hell out of a game day suit. God knows how good he'll look in a tux. I was going to be strong and not have sex with him on this trip, but that might well be shot to shit once I get a peek at that little treat.

And to be fair, I haven't had sex since the last time we were together, and that was back in the fall.

What the fuck have I been doing with my time?

With the mental image of Nate in a tux, I know exactly what I want to do now. I grab my trusty waterproof vibrator from my suitcase and decide to have a little me time in the shower with my memories.

As I strip off my wrap dress, I think about the night Nate and I met at O'Connell's.

I'm in hockey man heaven after agreeing to go out with my roommate Mila and the guys from the Seattle Whalers to celebrate winning their first exhibition game against the Dallas Diamonds.

Most of the guys in the team are loud and rowdy, drinking and chirping on each other. It's a great atmosphere, and they seem like a fun group. I can already tell that Mila's totally smitten with her guy, and I must admit he seems nice enough.

As I talk to them, I notice the kid, Nate, standing quietly on his own staring into his pint. I'm immediately taken with his size—I love a big bear of a man, the bigger the better which is why I guess I'm drawn to professional athletes. And Nate's a big guy, tall and muscular; his dark dress pants hug his thighs perfectly, and his white shirt stretches dangerously across this chest and biceps. But he's not all raw masculinity. He has a sweet, thoughtful expression which is only marred by the black eye he's sporting. He seems like such a mix of contradictions, and that intrigues me.

I slink across the room, doing my best sexy hip sway. As our eyes meet, I make up my mind that we're going home together tonight. He's a little shy as we talk, but he joins in with the flirty banter, and I feel my heart begin to pound at the possibility of what's to come.

Just when I think I'll have to take the lead, Nate surprises me when he pulls away and gives me a look that almost melts my panties right off. Damn! He takes my drink out of my hand, puts it on the nearby table, and leads me right out of the bar and into his truck.

Once we get to my apartment, all bets are off. We fall through the door, mouths fused together and grabbing at each other's clothes, breathy gasps and moans filling the dark corridor. Nate picks me up, making me yelp, and I wrap my legs around his waist. My skirt rides up around my middle, but I don't care. As we kiss, I give him mumbled directions to my bedroom where he kicks my door shut with his foot and spins us around, so I'm pressed against it.

"What do you want?" he asks me while I ravage his thick muscular neck with wet open-mouthed sucking kisses.

God, he even tastes amazing.

I lock my eyes on his. I've never been embarrassed talking about sex or telling my lovers what I want, and the fact Nate has just come straight out and asked me makes my blood run hot in my veins.

"I want you to eat my pussy," I gasp, letting my legs fall from around his waist, and I slide down his body, feeling his thick hard length against me.

Nate smiles so broadly it feels like I'm momentarily blinded, then he's gone. Kneeling in front of me. Sliding his big hands up the outside of my bare thighs. Under my skirt. As his fingers travel toward my center, I feel myself become slick with desire.

BETH

Nate slowly pushes my skirt farther up around my waist, so my panties are exposed, and it feels so dirty, doing all this while we're both still fully dressed. And then this wholesome farm boy just about kills me.

"Lift up your shirt. I want to see you play with your tits while I eat you out," he growls, gazing up at me with his gorgeous blue eyes that darken with lust.

I huff out an excited breath and do as I'm told, loving the way he's taking charge of me and my body. It's not what I expected, and it's so hot. I lift my camisole with slightly shaky fingers as Nate slides my soaking panties down my thighs, holding me steady as I step out of them. I gasp when he holds the scrap of lace to his nose and takes a deep huff of my arousal.

"God, your pussy smells amazing. I can't wait to get a taste."

I laugh throatily. "Damn, Nate, where did this dirty talking guy come from?"

"I guess you draw him out. Now let me see your tits, princess," he demands, slowly drawing circles with his fingertips over the sensitive skin of my inner thighs which are quivering with need.

I flip the catch on my bra and pull the cups to the side, seeing my deep need reflected in his eyes as they crinkle with his sexy smile. He licks his lips and leans forward to plant soft, wet kisses across my bare mound, holding my glistening folds apart with his thick thumbs.

As Nate's tongue slides down across my throbbing clit, I feel him tense up and pull away.

"What the …?" He studies me quizzically, his eyebrows drawn together in confusion.

"Oh, yeah," I giggle breathlessly. "I have a clitoral hood piercing. It's fine. Keep going."

Bless him. Nate looks like he'd just seen a unicorn or a three-headed dog. I guess he hasn't come across many of those out on the prairies.

"Does it hurt?" he asks quietly, his head cocked to the side in adorable curiosity.

"Kind of at the moment because I really need you to make me come, so have at it, man." I'm getting impatient to feel his tongue on me, and all the stalling is ruining the mood.

He gives me one more heart racing grin and presses his face between my thighs, holding my folds open and flicking his tongue over the small silver ring. This sends shockwaves of pleasure through me, and I moan loudly, tilting my hips forward to gain more friction.

"Work those tits, princess," Nate grunts, looking up through his thick lashes. I stare down to see his lips glistening with my arousal, and I can't help but moan, cupping my breasts and rolling my nipples as he goes back to work…

"Oh god!" I gasp, slapping my free hand against the wet tile as I work myself over with my vibrator, drawing it back and forth over my swollen clit, then sliding it inside as my orgasm throbs through me. I let go and allow the ripples of pleasure to continuously roll until it almost hurts.

Damn, that memory gets me every time. And it helps me make up my mind. I'm going to have sex with Nate tomorrow night.

I need some fresh material for my spank bank.

Nate

Flying coach when you're as big as I am is not a pleasant experience. It was the only ticket I could buy that got me to L.A. in time for Beth's benefit. To make it worse, the guy next to me happened to be a rabid Whalers fan, and he proceeded to talk my ear off the whole flight. The first hour was fine, but then I had to fake tiredness, put my earbuds in, and pull my ball cap down over my eyes. It gave me some time to think about Beth and what might happen on this trip.

We've been skating around each other since we hooked up after the Diamonds game and then again at Matt's game night. After she ran out on me at the Halloween party, I thought that was it for us. When I messaged her a few days later, she replied, chewing me out for getting in her business about her commitment stuff. But we agreed to stay friends and have exchanged a few flirty texts since then. She's a very interesting woman, not to mention sexy as hell, and I need to find out more about her beside the obvious physical attraction.

This weighs heavy on my mind as I get dressed in my hotel room, preparing to take Beth to her fancy benefit. I know it's all part of repaying her for helping Matt get back with Mila, but I feel like this is my opportunity to really connect with her on more than just a physical level and try to break down some of those walls she's built up around her heart.

When we were fighting at the Halloween party, she kept yelling at me about relationships being the death of romance and becoming too comfortable with each other and all sorts of other crazy shit. I didn't understand it and got frustrated. I ended up calling her emotionally unavailable, and she got so pissed she stormed out crying. I felt like complete shit for making her upset, so I'm glad we're back on solid ground with each other.

At five minutes to eight, I double check my bow tie in the mirror and smooth down the jacket of my Hugo Boss tuxedo. I had to have the damn thing custom made for a wedding I was in which cost me a fortune, but fits like a glove, and if I'm being honest, I look pretty damn good. I've given my hair an effortless messy style, and there's just enough scruff on my face to appear stylish and not too much like a goon. I adjust the Omega on my wrist and grab my wallet, phone, and key card. I thought meeting Beth in the lobby made this a little less like a date, so she won't get all freaked out.

As I leave the elevator and stride across the marble lobby, I feel several pairs of female eyes flash over me. I've been well over six feet tall since I hit puberty and started filling out with muscle thanks to hours of hockey and baseball.

But that's not what I should be thinking about right now. What I should be thinking about is the fabulous, stunning creature slinking toward me.

Beth is a vision in a pale gown covered in embroidered gems that literally make her sparkle. The plunging neckline shows off her magnificent cleavage, and the split in the skirt exposes a toned leg.

"Well, don't you look handsome," she purrs in her sexy voice.

"Right back at you, princess," I reply as her exotic jasmine scent envelops me. "You look sensational."

"Thank you, Nate." Beth smiles and blushes a little, tucking a loose strand of hair behind her ear. She's wearing her signature red lipstick, and all I can think about is how it'll look smeared all over my cock.

Stop it, man! Get a fucking grip.

She steps into me for a hug, and with her hair up in some fancy twist, I hold the back of her neck and run my hand down her bare back. Shit, the dress is open almost all the way down to her butt.

Fuck, she's so hot I feel my cock thickening in my dress pants, and I pull out of the hug to avoid embarrassing us both. But from the cheeky smirk on her face, I can tell she felt it.

"Is Andre joining us?" I croak, fiddling with my watch and pulling down the cuffs of my jacket.

"No, he's meeting us there," she smiles. "He got lucky last night, so he's picking up his date."

"Wow, good for him." I hold out my arm for her to take. She's wearing ridiculously high strappy sandals, and my momma taught me well. Manners maketh man. "What's this benefit for anyway? I bought my check book." I pat my breast pocket.

"Hector started a fund to help clean up the beaches and ocean along the West coast," Beth explains as we walk out of the lobby to catch a cab. "He supports innovation in technology to help clean microplastics from the ocean. He sponsors beach clean ups and other events. It's a great charity."

"Sounds amazing."

Growing up in landlocked Oklahoma, I didn't even see the ocean until I was a teenager and went to hockey camp near Vancouver. It's vast and wild and beautiful, so I promised myself at some point in my life, I'd live on the coast.

As we travel to the venue, we talk easily about our evening to come. Although the conversation is light and friendly, there's an undeniable sexual tension between us. I can't help my gaze drifting to her cleavage or the split in her dress. And I feel her eyes roaming over my large thighs that are stretching my dress pants to the max. I have a feeling this night will end with one or both of us making a move.

3

Beth

Wow! When I see Nate come out of that elevator looking like James freaking Bond, I almost lose my stride. I live in high heels, so I never stumble, but he's magnificent, and it totally throws me off. I've never seen a tuxedo fit a man of his size so perfectly. The jacket stretches over his broad shoulders and tapers to his trim waist, and his pants hug his amazing hockey player thighs and butt.

As I walk toward him, I almost say to hell with the benefit and drag him up to my room to fuck him sense-less, but Andre would never forgive me, so instead we have some flirty back and forth on the cab ride. Just sitting in such proximity has me on a sexual contact high.

I'm kind of nervous. This is a huge deal for our business, and I hope that bringing Nate won't seem like a desperate attempt to sway Hector Riley toward choosing us, even though that's exactly what I'm doing.

"What's our play tonight?" Nate asks in his deep Midwest drawl, and I realize I'm staring at his thighs.

"Huh?" I gaze up into his denim blue eyes and see he's smirking at me. Damn, he caught me totally checking him out.

"What are we telling people tonight about why I'm there? Am I your boyfriend? Your date? A friend?" he asks.

"Um, a friend, I guess. Maybe if we get to speak to Hector, you can say I told you about the charity, and you wanted to come and support it," I suggest and even as I say the word friend, I see Nate's face fall a little.

Shit, maybe this isn't a good idea. I know Nate has feelings for me, and I suddenly feel like a bitch for dragging him all this way on his vacation.

"As long as you're okay with that," I quickly add.

"Whatever works for you, princess. I'm here to serve and repay a debt. That's all." Nate smiles and bows his head slightly.

When we arrive, there's a long line of cars and limos dropping off, so we sit for a while until the cab can get close enough for us to get out. Ever the gentleman, Nate pays the driver and hops out to open my door, stretching his large, calloused hand out to help me. I noticed earlier that his knuckles are a bit raw and scraped up; I guess he got into it during his last game.

As I think about him on the ice, throwing his gloves off and squaring up to his opponent, I get ridiculously turned on. It's stupid to find two grown men fighting over a little rubber disc arousing, but I just can't help it.

"You still with me, Beth?" he asks, jolting me out of my inappropriate fantasies.

"Yeah, let's go. We're in the Grand Ballroom, I think," I reply, taking Nate's arm. As we walk up the red carpet to the main entrance, he lets out a grunted laugh. "What's so funny?"

He chuckles again. "Ballroom."

"Seriously, dude?" I laugh. "You really are twenty-one, aren't you?" I shake my head, and we stop to pose for some photographers who suddenly realize they have a celebrity in front of them and start yelling Nate's name. He gives them a few shy smiles, then literally drags me into the hotel.

"Jesus, hold up," I yelp, trotting behind him in my heels.

"Sorry. I hate that shit," Nate says once we're inside the safety of the lobby. He turns to me and runs his hands up my arms, causing me to shiver at the contact. "I'm sorry. Did I tell you how beautiful you look?"

I smile brightly, and we just stand there for what feels like forever, so close I must tip my head way back to stare into his hooded eyes. The heat between us crackles, and I notice his big chest rising and falling quickly.

"Well, look at you two." Andre's voice breaks the spell, and I take a step back from Nate, sucking in a huge gasp of air as I realize I've been holding my breath.

Nate and I both turn to see Andre and his date approaching, both impeccable in their tuxedos. Andre's in a classic black tux, but instead of a shirt and tie, he's bare-chested and wears a majestic statement necklace of purple gems with matching contacts in his eyes. His date looks like a frat boy with dirty blonde hair slicked back and deep brown eyes.

"Hey baby," I say, stretching up as tall as I can to kiss Andre on both cheeks.

"Beth, Nate, this is Carlton," Andre purrs, acting like the cat who got the cream. It makes me laugh that he always goes for these hot jock types.

"Hey," Carlton shakes my hand, and when he goes to shake with Nate, his face lights up. "Holy shit. You're Nate Halsted."

"Babe, I said there'd be famous people here. Be cool," Andre growls at his date.

Nate laughs good-naturedly and shakes Carlton's hand. "Nice to meet you, man. Are you a hockey fan?" They start to walk away together, chatting about hockey, but Nate glances over his shoulder, his gaze falling to mine before he turns back around.

"That boy is all kinds of hot for you," Andre whispers as he takes my arm, and we follow them into the ballroom.

"Shut up," I hiss, elbowing him in the side. However, inside I get a little jolt of excitement. I don't want a relationship with Nate or anyone, but the thought that this gorgeous, athletic hockey god has eyes for me gives me a thrill.

The ballroom, which is decorated in accents of blue with huge sculptures made from plastics found in the oceans, is already swarming with guests drinking champagne and eating canapes.

Our little group grabs some drinks and snacks and makes a few circuits of the room, checking out the items in the silent auction and listening to people from the charity talk about their program.

Nate manages to detach himself from Carlton when Andre takes him over to choose an item from the silent auction to bid on.

"He's a funny guy," Nate whispers as we walk over to the table selling cute bracelets made from recycled plastics. His lips brush the shell of my ear, and a ripple of pleasure rolls down my spine.

"He seems nice," I manage to say in a steady voice. "We should go bid in the auction before dinner." I look up at Nate, and he's smiling, like he knows exactly what he does to me.

"Sure thing, princess." His big hand goes to the bare skin at the small of my back, and he leads me over to the table where the auction items are laid out: everything from meals at fancy L.A. restaurants and paddleboard yoga taster sessions to a helicopter flight to Catalina Island and an all-expenses paid trip to Hawaii. As we scan the items, I see Nate pick up one of the bidding cards and scribble something on it, stuffing it in the sealed box before I can see what it says.

"What did you bid on?" I ask, nudging him with my shoulder.

Nate smirks and taps the side of his nose. "That's for me to know…" He takes my hand in his and leads me away. "Come on. Let's go find our table. They're getting ready to serve dinner."

Nate

I attend quite a lot of charity fundraisers as part of my job, and I always enjoy them. It feels great to give back to a good cause, and as I grow into my position in the team and the NHL as an organization, I want to set up my own fund. I was talking to Matt at the gym a few weeks ago, and he was telling me about the scholarship fund he set up to help disadvantaged kids afford hockey gear. It sounds like an awesome idea, and I offered up my help without a moment's hesitation.

Sitting here with Beth listening to the keynote speaker from the Clean up our Oceans charity, I'm inspired to lend my support. They organize beach clean ups along the Pacific coast; if I have time, I want to do one near Seattle. It might be a fun thing to get some of the other guys involved as well.

Thinking about Beth makes me instinctively reach out and cover her delicate hand with mine. The silver rings she wears on her first and ring fingers press into my skin, and I gently rub my thumb over the pulse point on her wrist. It's such a small gesture, but I feel her body tense and then relax slightly next to me, her eyes flicking momentarily to our joined hands, then she's back listening to the speaker as he informs us about the dangers of microplastics in the food chain.

I'm trying my hardest not to push her too much, but I've made up my mind. We're spending the night together. Judging by Beth's body language, I have a feeling she'll be on board with that. I keep up the gentle circling pressure of my thumb on her pulse point and enjoy the way it thrums, much like her clit when I perform the same action between her legs.

"I need to hit the ladies' room," Beth suddenly whispers and pulls her hand free, excusing herself from our table and disappearing.

4

Beth

I hold my wrist under the cold water and stare at my reflection in the ornate mirror. I'm trying to cool off, and it's not working. My pupils are dilated so wide only a halo of ice surrounds them, my cheeks and neck are flushed, and my breasts are heaving.

Jesus, the way Nate was caressing my wrist mainlined straight to my clit, and I think I had a teeny tiny orgasm. I can't keep letting him affect me like this. I know I promised myself I'd sleep with him tonight, but I don't know if I can let that happen.

He's too tempting.

Too dangerous.

If I'm being one hundred percent honest with myself, I could easily fall for him, let him in all the way and have every part of me. But that's not what I want at the age of twenty-six, maybe even ever. And it sure as shit shouldn't be what he wants at his age.

The laughter of two women entering the ladies' room startles me, and I quickly turn off the faucet and dry my hands, smiling at them in the mirror as they pass behind me and disappear into the stalls.

Right, I need to get my head in the game. I haven't even made contact with Hector Riley yet, and that was the purpose of this whole excursion—not getting into Nate Halsted's sexy, tight pants.

As I enter the ballroom, I see the seat next to Nate has been taken by none other than Hector Riley himself, and they're talking animatedly while Andre attempts to look interested. Well, it seems bringing my hockey star is about to pay off.

I approach Nate from behind and rest my hands on his broad shoulders, feeling him jump a little under my touch. As he turns around, I lean forward, pressing my breasts against his back, stretching my hand out toward Hector to introduce myself.

"Mr. Riley, I'm Beth Aston. It's great to see you again."

"Ah Beth, I was hoping to see you tonight." He shakes my hand, enveloping it in his and smiling broadly, showing off his crooked teeth almost hidden under his russet beard. He seems more like a lumber-jack or deep-sea fisherman than a movie director, but with a back catalogue of some of the highest grossing romantic comedies in history, that's certainly what he is.

"Well, I wouldn't miss supporting such an amazing cause," I reply, walking around Nate who quickly vacates his seat so I can sit down, pulling up another chair.

"And I had no idea you knew this guy." He slaps Nate on the arm in a friendly manner and Nate smiles broadly. "I've been a Whalers fan since I was a kid, and you, my man, are killing it this season. That dust up you had during the Vancouver game was one for my permanent collection." He laughs and goes on to explain what he loved so much about Nate beating the shit out of some other player.

I sit and listen to them talk back and forth until I notice Andre making his "we need to talk face" at me, so I excuse myself and meet him over at the bar.

"What's up?" I ask as Andre orders another round of drinks from the free bar.

"He's so enamored with Nate, I can't get a word in edgeways about the movie," he whines, sticking out his pouty bottom lip.

I huff loudly. "Andre, that was the point of bringing Nate. I didn't want to start harassing Hector about the movie at his charity benefit, but I thought if we can give him an exciting memory he'll link to us, it'll give us the edge tomorrow."

Understanding dawns on Andre's face, and he smiles broadly. "You scheming little tramp," he hisses. "I love it! Come on. Let's get back to the table."

The rest of the evening flies by in a flurry of martinis and good conversation. Nate is amazing, and Hector barely leaves him alone except when he must go to the stage to announce the winners of the silent auction. Andre manages to win the couples massage at a fancy spa in Palm Springs, then it comes to the big-ticket item—the all-expenses paid trip to Hawaii.

Hector stands on the stage and opens the gold envelope, and I can see people all around the ballroom talking excitedly about whether their bid has won.

"This is amazing!" Hector exclaims as he pulls the card from the envelope, a huge grin on his face. "This is so generous. Our winning bid for the trip for two to Hawaii is a whopping fifty thousand dollars."

There are gasps, and a round of applause fills the room as people try to see who made such a massive donation. I look around myself, expecting to see someone stand up to take their moment in the limelight. But no one moves.

"I wish I could tell you who made this very generous donation, but they've asked to remain anonymous, so please join me in giving our new benefactor a round of applause." Hector claps loudly and smiles like he's just won the lottery.

"Wow, I wonder who that was," Carlton asks.

"Probably some tech billionaire or an actor with a movie to promote," Andre replies, sipping his martini.

"Then surely they'd want credit for the donation. It's great PR," I say, suddenly noticing that Nate has gone quiet and doesn't seem to be looking around the room like the rest of us. I give him the side-eye, and he just concentrates on his bottle of beer. "Was it you?" I whisper.

"Huh?" He takes a sip of his beer, but I see the smile forming on his lips as they wrap around the bottle.

"Did you bid fifty thousand dollars for the Hawaii trip?" I whisper again, getting right up in his ear so I can smell the clean scent of his shampoo.

"Maybe," he whispers back, turning his face so our lips are almost touching. "Why? Would you like to go to Hawaii?"

I let out a small breath. Being this close to him makes my heart gallop in my chest. "Nate, you could buy a trip to Hawaii for a fraction of the cost of that bid."

"That wasn't the point, princess. I wanted to do something good, but I didn't want my status as a hockey player stealing the limelight away from the cause. They get the money either way."

Jesus, does he have to be such a good person as well as so sexy?

"Maybe we should dance," I say in a husky voice, desperate to break this intense moment but still intent on staying close to him.

Nate smiles and drops a soft kiss on my cheek. "As you wish," he whispers and stands, taking my hand and leading me to the dance floor.

As he takes me in his arms, the melodic tones of Ed Sheeran's "Perfect" start to echo around the ballroom. Nate puts his big hands around my waist, drawing me close. He rests them on the small of my back, and I stretch my arms around his neck, pressing my cheek against the lapel of his tuxedo. The feeling of his strong arms around me as we sway is so amazing, and the words of the song hit me right in the feels. I can feel Nate's breath in my hair and the press of his pillowy lips to my temple, those magic fingers of his making that circular pattern on my bare back. I take a large breath, inhaling his special scent, and my chest tightens as the couples swaying around us disappear into the background.

The emotion inside me builds with the song. I feel compelled to look up, and when I do, I see Nate's beautiful blue eyes gazing down at me. He holds me with his stare, and as the song reaches its crescendo, he bends his head down and presses his lips to mine in the most perfect kiss of my entire life. Our mouths move slowly together, and I open beneath him, his strong tongue sliding against mine as his hands pull me against his hard body. I tilt my head and crush my breasts to his chest, standing up on my tiptoes to get as close to this beautiful man as I can.

As the final notes of the song play out, our kiss breaks, and I gaze up at him, both of us breathless and desperate.

"Let's go," he growls, taking my hand and leading me back to the table, where I collect my purse and shoot off a hurried goodbye to Andre and Carlton. He whisks me through the hotel lobby and outside to find us a cab, and I wonder why the hell I hadn't booked a room at this fucking hotel.

Damn my stupid plans.

When the doorman finally hails us a cab, we're in the back seat and making out before I can even catch my breath. Nate's tongue is back in my mouth, but with much more urgency this time, his hand cupping the back of my head to hold me in place. I fist the lapels of his tux and drape my legs over his lap, feeling his free hand slide up my thigh as my panties cling to my wet pussy. All I want is for Nate's fingers to explore how wet I am for him, but before he can go that far, the cab pulls up at our hotel, and the driver coughs loudly to get our attention.

I drag my lips away from Nate's and laugh quietly, sliding my legs off his lap but not before nudging the sizable bulge that lay beneath.

"I guess we're here," I sigh, running my finger along my bottom lip that's swollen from our frenzied kissing.

"That's good because I was about to fuck you in the back of this cab," he chuckles huskily, adjusting his hard-on and reaching for his wallet.

Oh, I am in so much trouble!

Nate

Trying to keep my hands off Beth as we walk across the lobby is the hardest thing I've ever had to do in my entire life. Forget skating when I was thirteen with tonsillitis, forget skating at fifteen with bruised ribs and broken fingers, and forget getting over my secret high school girlfriend after my father forced me to break her heart.

No, walking across what feels like the biggest hotel lobby in the world without pushing Beth onto one of the couches and fucking her brains out—that's the hardest thing I've ever done.

"Your room or mine?" I ask once the elevator doors slide shut behind us. I crowd Beth into the corner of the elevator, bracing my hands on the metal bar behind her, caging her in.

"Mine," she breathes, reaching out and pressing the button for her floor. She's so close to me, her hips are pressing against mine, and there's no hiding my straining erection as I kiss the satin-soft skin of her shoulder. "Is this a good idea?"

I see a little flicker of doubt in her eyes, but mostly there's just lusty arousal. It gives me pause to stop in my tracks even though my cock is so hard it'll have the imprint of my zipper on it for a week.

"If you don't want to do this…" I say, taking a step back to give her some space.

"No!" She holds onto my biceps to stop me moving too far away. "I want this. I want you so much. But I know how you feel…"

"Hey," I cup her face in my hand, and she nuzzles into it, taking me in with her gorgeous crystal blue eyes. "Don't you worry about that; I've got that locked down. This isn't about my feelings; it's about two people having the most incredible sex of their lives and who make each other feel great." I push my hips against her, and she makes a mewling, needy sound.

Beth squints at me to double check I'm being serious. "You're sure?"

"One hundred percent." The ping of the elevator makes us startle, and I smile at Beth, taking her hand and leading her out into the lobby where she directs me to her room.

"Before we get into this," she says as she slides the key card into the lock, "I want to say thank you for tonight. You were a massive hit with Hector, and I think it totally helped us…"

I press my lips to Beth's, sliding my hand up her arm and behind her neck, pushing her against the door. My need for her is reaching fever pitch, and if she keeps babbling away, I'm going to lose my shit and undress her in this fucking hallway.

When I pull away, Beth lets out a huff of laughter. "Okay, then. I guess no thanks are necessary." She turns and opens the door, and we move inside, the room partly illuminated by the lamp and the lights from the city. "Would you like a drink?"

I stalk toward her like a predator, but she stands her ground. "No," I whisper, reaching up and taking the jewelled clip from her hair, allowing it to fall in a blonde curtain around her shoulders.

Beth swallows loudly and holds my gaze, her pretty pink tongue sweeps across her bottom lip, and she reaches up to push my tuxedo jacket off my shoulders. It's all so painfully slow, but part of me loves the anticipation of getting naked with her. I remember clearly what an incredible body she has, all luscious curves and soft skin.

"Go over to the bed," I growl. Something about Beth makes me want to take charge of her, take her in hand, and dominate her.

With a cheeky smirk, she does as I command, turning around so I get a clear view of her swaying, heart-shaped ass and that cascade of tattooed stars falling down her bare back. When she reaches the bed, she turns around and cocks her eyebrow as if challenging me to make my next move.

In four long strides, I'm in front of her, my fingers hooking under the thin straps of her dress. I know that if I slide them down off her shoulders, the whole dress will puddle at her feet, so I lift them up and out, lowering them to slowly reveal her firm breasts topped with already pebbled pink nipples. My mouth is literally watering at the prospect of taking one in my mouth, but I keep my cool despite the fact I'm so hard it's painful.

I continue to lower the dress, uncovering her firm stomach, the glittering jewel in her belly button piercing, the flare of her hips, and her tiny white lace thong. By now I'm kneeling in front of her, and as I remove the dress from round her ankles, Beth leans on my shoulders for support, her chest rising and falling quickly, her pupils totally blown out with desire.

"My shoes," she whispers, wiggling her foot encased in the strappy sandal.

"Leave them on," I reply, gazing up at her with a wicked smile, running my hands up the back of her legs to cup her ass.

"Kinky," Beth giggles, running her fingers through my hair as I plant wet kisses across her stomach from hip to hip along her panty line.

"What do you want?" I ask because I know Beth likes to direct her pleasure, and I want to please her.

"It seems a shame to waste these heels. I want you to fuck me from behind against the window," she replies in her throaty sex voice. Her demand makes my cock kick inside my pants, and I get to work.

I quickly strip her of the tiny lace thong and push her down onto the bed, standing in front of her, gently pulling off my bow tie and unbuttoning my shirt. Beth rises on her elbows and watches me with hooded eyes, bringing her hand up to her breast where she lazily rolls the hard bud of her nipple between her fingers.

"Fuck, princess. That's so hot, watching you touch yourself," I moan, stripping my shirt off and throwing it on the floor.

Beth grins at me and slides her hand from her breast, down her smooth body and across her bare mound, bringing one foot up onto the edge of the bed so she can spread herself for me. I feel like I'm going to stroke out when her fingers slip between her wet petals, and I see the glint of her clitoral piercing before she covers it with her eager fingers. Her head falls back as she works herself with the pad of her middle finger, her eyes closing as she loses herself in pleasure.

I must touch her right now, so I quickly unbuckle my belt and rip my pants and boxers off in one go. There's no finesse; it's pure carnal desperation on my part, and once my shoes and socks are gone, I fall onto Beth and cover her with my body, kissing her deeply.

Beth moans and arches her body up to meet mine, spreading her legs wide so my throbbing cock can slide against her wet center. My mouth seeks out the nipple I coveted earlier, and as I take the puckered nub into my mouth, Beth grabs a handful of my hair and thrusts her hips up to grind on me.

"Please Nate, the window. Fuck me against the window," she gasps as I work my way over to her other nipple, my fingers sliding across her pussy which is now drenched with desire.

"Yeah, let me get a rubber. Go over and wait for me." I roll off Beth as she scrambles to her feet, slightly wobbly on the high heels while I grab my pants and pull out my wallet.

Once I'm suited up, I make my way over to the floor to ceiling picture windows and find Beth facing the glittering lights of L.A., her hands pressed to the glass, her butt pushed back, and her legs spread. My eager cock bobs as I stride toward her. I want this to be great, but I'm not sure how much staying power I'm going to have.

"Jesus, I need to take a picture of that," I choke out, feeling the tingle at the base of my spine.

Beth whips her head around and scowls. "I'm pretty liberated Nate, but don't you fucking dare."

That makes me laugh loudly and takes the edge off, thank god. I feel like I can carry on without busting a nut in ten seconds like it's my first time. I stalk toward Beth, and when I reach her, I drop to my knees, grasp her butt cheeks in my big hands, spread them and bury my face between her legs, causing her to jump and squeal in surprise.

As my tongue and lips get to work, those squeals turn to groans and needy little breaths, her butt pushing back against my face. I stretch my tongue out to circle her wet entrance, and I bring one hand round to massage her throbbing clit.

"Nate, that feels so good," she gasps, her hips rolling in time with my tongue and fingers as her orgasm rips through her, moisture flooding my mouth. I love how responsive Beth's body is. There's no shame or embarrassment about how she reacts to me, and that's such a fucking turn on.

But I've reached my limit; I have to get inside her before I combust. I stand up and grip Beth's hips, pushing my muscular thigh between her legs to spread her wider to accommodate me. With one hand on her shoulder and the other gripping the base of my cock, I push the head into her wet entrance, watching as she accepts me inch by delicious inch. We both grunt and sigh as I slide home, Beth pushes against me, and I'm buried to the hilt.

"I hope you're ready for this, baby," I growl into her ear. "You made me so fucking hard. I just need to pound you."

"Oh God, Nate. Do it. Fuck me hard," she moans, adjusting herself so her breasts and cheek are pressed against the window. I can't even think about what it must look like from the outside, but we're thirty floors up, so it's doubtful anyone can see us.

With a swift slap to her gorgeous ass that earns me a satisfying squeal, I set a brutal pace. I thrust my hips back and forth, digging my fingers into her shoulder and hip. We both pant and grunt as we rut against each other in an animalistic frenzy. The sound of our sweaty skin slapping together is the only other sound in the room.

"Touch your clit, Beth. I need you to come on my cock," I pant, never breaking my rhythm as she shifts to put one hand between her legs.

"That's it, Nate. Oh god, I'm coming!" she cries as I feel her pussy ripple and throb around my cock, becoming impossibly tight, so tight it triggers my own climax. I groan and grab her leg, lifting it up and out to the side, holding her open while she milks me of everything I've got, holding my breath so I see stars.

As we come down from our sex high, I hold the base of my cock so I can withdraw and Beth slumps back against my body. I wrap my arms around her chest and waist to hold her steady while her breathing regulates.

"Damn it, Nate. Why are you so good at that?" she asks in a breathy whisper.

"It's all you, princess." I tie off the condom and throw it in the trash can. Then I pick up her bone-less body and carry her over to the bed. Her head lolls around, and I gently place her on top of the comforter, her eyes heavy with sleep. Clumsily, I unbuckle her sandals and put them on the floor, grabbing a bottle of water from the mini bar so she has a drink if she wakes in the night.

I know Beth isn't really one for a sleepover, so I pull the comforter over her naked body and gather my clothes.

"Where're you going?" she asks in a cute, sleepy voice.

"Back to my room, baby. I know you like your space." I pull my pants on and make a grab for my shirt.

"No. Stay. I wanna snuggle," she whines, stretching her arms up to me, making grabby movements with her fingers.

Well, this is interesting. I was all set to leave her to sleep, but obviously she has other ideas. And to be fair, I'm totally on board. Quickly, I whip off my pants and slide into bed next to her, wrapping my body around hers so I'm the big spoon. With my nose buried in her hair, the smell of her jasmine scent and our lovemaking is an intoxicating combination.

5

Beth

W*hat is that noise?*

Deep, rumbling, and it seems to be vibrating through my entire body. I crack open one eye, the many martinis I drank last night rush back to me, and my head throbs sharply. I need to hydrate desperately, so I reach out to grab the bottle of water on the nightstand, but I can't seem to move.

What is going on?

Then, it comes back to me. The deep, rumbling noise and the reason I can't seem to move is because I have two hundred and twenty pounds of hockey player draped over me, snoring contentedly. I peek over my shoulder, and sure enough, I see Nate's sleep messy, sandy hair on the pillow next to me and his thick, muscular arm holding me hostage against his hot body.

Ugh, I need that water urgently, so I hold Nate's wrist and lift his heavy arm, scooting out from under it, so I can grab the bottle on the nightstand. Just as I open it and take a much-needed swig, I'm pulled back into bed.

"Where you goin'?" Nate mumbles in his sleepy, husky voice.

"I need a drink. I lost a hell of a lot of fluids last night," I deadpan, taking another swig before screwing the lid on and settling back against Nate's body.

Oh, it feels like all parts of him have woken up. There's a definite prodding of morning wood against my butt, and I wiggle teasingly, eliciting a moan and grind from Nate.

"Don't do that, princess," he growls, sliding his hand up my body to cup my breast, my nipples hardening under his touch.

"What?" I ask innocently, wiggling my butt again.

"You know that if I wake up properly, I'm gonna fuck you again." Promises, promises.

Nate's words make me wet with blossoming desire, so I take the hand that's fondling my breast and guide it between my thighs. I push his fingers into my slippery pussy, and he grunts his approval, humping his hips against my ass to get some friction. I feel his lips explore the back of my neck, so I reach back between us and grasp his thick, hard cock, running my thumb over the crown so I can spread the pearls of pre-cum down his shaft.

Both of us are panting hard as we masturbate each other slowly. Nate's thick fingers explore me, slipping one then two inside, and touching that spot inside that jolts pleasure through my core.

But, just as I'm about to climax, Nate's fingers are gone, and so is his cock from my fist. I roll over and come face to face with his broad, muscular back, completely unblemished by marks or tattoos. I can't remember the last time I slept with a guy who didn't have ink of some kind, and it just adds to his wholesome persona.

"What happened?" I ask, running my fingers down his spine.

"Just getting a condom," he says, holding up the gold foil packet before tearing it open and rolling it on.

Oh goody. I thought he decided against a little hot morning sex. I lie on my back and kick my legs excitedly as he rolls back over and climbs on top of me, sweeping my messy hair away from my face and kissing my lips softly.

Suddenly, a deep rumbling hum starts up under the pillow next to my head, and both Nate and I look over with quizzical expressions.

"Is that your phone?" he asks, reaching under the pillow. However, what he comes back with certainly isn't my phone. In his hand, he holds my favorite purple vibrator that must have clicked on when he rolled over it.

"Um, I hope this is yours," Nate smirks, examining the silicone, cock-shaped device in his hand. "Otherwise, you might want to complain to the hotel."

I try to snatch it out of his hand, but he holds it out of my reach. "Yes, of course it's mine. Now put it down and get back to fucking me," I whine.

"Oh no, this is too good." A devilish grin spreads across his handsome face, and I feel like I'm in for a massive treat. "I'm making use of this bad boy."

An hour later, Nate's ordering us room service, and I'm showering in preparation for the meeting at Hector Riley's office. As I soap my tired, well-used body, I think about the last hour I spent in bed with Nate. Jesus, the things he did with my vibrator while he fucked me make my toes curl and my pussy spasm. He's become like a drug to me; I just can't get enough of his body and his sweet attentive nature. When he takes charge of me, taking what he wants and dominating me in bed–Fuck! It's so hot.

"That smells incredible," I moan as the scent of bacon and coffee hits me square in the nose as I open the bathroom door. I smooth down my freshly blown out hair, taking a seat opposite Nate at the small table.

"I ordered most of the breakfast menu because I wasn't sure what you'd want," Nate mumbles through a mouthful of pancakes and bacon. His eyes drag up and down my body as he chews slowly. "Aren't you getting dressed?"

I cock my eyebrow and look down at myself–I'm wearing a pair of pink lace boy shorts and a matching bra. "Am I naked again?" I ask sarcastically.

He can hardly talk; he's sat opposite me in just his boxer briefs.

Nate snorts out a chuckle and shovels another forkful of food into his mouth, shaking his head. I love that he gets my weird sense of humor, just like I get his. The breakfast smells incredible, and my stomach growls loudly, so I serve myself some scrambled eggs, wheat toast and a few crispy strips of bacon. Nate pours me a coffee, and I fix it up with some half and half.

As we eat quietly, I think about how completely relaxed and happy I am in this domestic situation. This is normally the stage of a relationship that I hate: the comfortable silences, going about everyday tasks like cooking and eating together. I'd normally be running for the next hot hook up by now. However, with Nate it just feels natural. He's given me some mind-blowing orgasms, we've snuggled, and now he's asking me questions about the upcoming interview with Hector Riley.

Why aren't I feeding him some bullshit lines and making a quick exit?

"What's going on in that head of yours?" Nate asks, sitting back in his chair and sipping his coffee, his abs twitching as he relaxes.

"Just thinking about this," I reply, waving my fork between the two of us. "It feels nice sitting here with you."

"And that's got you making the frowny face because...?" he questions, his lips quirking up into a little smile.

"I've told you about my commitment issues, and you've called me out on them more than once," I say, remembering Halloween when he called me "emotionally unavailable."

Nate peers guiltily into his cup. I guess he's remembering that night too.

"I was just thinking that this feels ... nice, and it's not terrifying, which is an odd sensation to me. That's all," I mutter, staring intently at my eggs, afraid to meet Nate's gaze.

Suddenly, his large hand covers mine, and he squeezes it gently. "Beth, look at me."

I meet his intense gaze, his denim blue eyes a shade darker than normal.

"I have no expectations of you," he states firmly. "I like spending time with you. I really like fucking you, but if that's all you can give, I'd rather have that than not have you in my life."

Wow! I feel a weird sting in my nose, and I realize it might be the start of tears. I'm definitely not a crier, so this feels totally alien to me. I don't trust myself to speak, so I just nod in acceptance of what he's said and go back to picking at my breakfast.

"I'm gonna hit the shower," Nate says, giving my hand one final squeeze before standing and walking his cute butt into the bathroom.

When the door shuts, I let out a wobbly breath and sit back in my chair, my breakfast forgotten. Did I just make things weird with us? Shit, I don't need this today. I grab my phone and send Andre a text to confirm what time we need to meet in the lobby, and I get a hasty reply saying he's having brunch with Carlton, and he'll meet me at noon.

I decide I don't want any more awkward conversations with Nate, so I quickly apply light makeup, dress in my favorite business appropriate wrap dress and heels, and pack my bag with our business iPad and a hard copy of our proposal.

I'm about to slip out of the room when the bathroom door opens, and Nate comes out in a billow of steam, looking so fucking sexy I swear I get wet instantly. He has a towel wrapped around his trim waist, and his defined chest is still glistening with droplets of water that fall from his wet hair. I stand there with my mouth open like a goddamn moron for a moment too long, and when Nate notices, he smirks at me and runs his hand through his hair just to finish the drool-worthy spectacle.

"What time's your meeting?" he asks, sitting on the edge of the bed.

"One, but Andre and I have a few things to do first, so I'm gonna head out." I try to make my voice as steady as possible. "Are you going back to Seattle today?"

"I've booked a flight for tomorrow afternoon," he replies, that shy unsure expression crossing his face. "I thought if things went well, we could go out and celebrate."

"Yeah, that sounds good." I sling my bag over my shoulder and grab my phone. "Will you be alright on your own today? I'll text you when we're done."

"Yeah, I'll be fine. I'm used to my own company." I notice sadness flit across Nate's face, but as quickly as it's there it's gone again. "I thought I might go down to Venice or Santa Monica."

"Good. Have a great time. I'll call you later." I lean over and kiss his cheek, but as I pull away, Nate holds the back of my neck and turns my head to press his lips to mine. Our mouths move gently against each other, and when I move back, Nate holds my bottom lip between his teeth.

"Good luck, princess," he growls, and my eyes drop to see the beginning of his erection straining against the towel.

"Thank you," I whisper, standing up straight and praying he can't see my rock-hard nipples pressing against the cups of my bra. "Um, see you later."

I stumble out of the room, and once I'm at the elevators, I stop and lean against the wall, gasping for air.

This is why I don't get involved; this shit is way too complicated.

Nate

The Uber drops me off on Ocean Avenue in Santa Monica. The sun feels great on my skin as I step out of the car. Although it's not hot enough for shorts, I'm comfortable in jeans, a polo shirt and sneakers. Plus I've got my favorite University of Nebraska Mavericks ball cap pulled down low for shade and anonymity.

I walk along Ocean Front Walk with my iced coffee and drift into a few shops, browsing with very little interest. The street is busy, and the farther I walk, the more I realize I'm anonymous here, which is great.

I finally start to relax and enjoy my day, and I find myself at the site of the original Muscle Beach. The outdoor gym is pretty busy, full of huge pumped-up guys in tiny shorts and tank tops, straining and grunting as they lift weights and do pull ups. Now, I'm a big strong guy, but these men are on a whole other level, and to be honest, I feel a bit puny compared to them.

"Failure isn't an option, Doug. You hear me!" The sudden barking voice makes me physically flinch, and I almost spill my remaining coffee down my light blue polo. My head whips around toward the voice that sounds so much like my father's I could've sworn I was a kid again.

However, what I find is an oily African American man who must be three hundred pounds of solid muscle. He's yelling commands at another large man doing pull ups on a high metal bar, but for that moment, he's my father and the guy hanging from the bar is me: skating sprints, running laps, doing crunches and weights until I puke.

Suddenly, I'm sweating bullets, and my heart's racing at the memories–I need to put some distance between me and this grunting, sweaty scene that's taking me to places I'd rather not revisit just now.

I set off down the street at a quick pace, and before I know it I'm virtually sprinting blindly toward the pier, trying to outrun the demons of my past …

"What the hell was that?" my father barks in his best Drill Sergeant voice as we stand in the cold garage. "We worked for hours on that wrist shot, and you had the perfect opportunity to use it tonight, and you choked."

The slap lands on the side of my head before I even see it coming, and I'm ashamed at how my head rocks to the side from the impact. With my ears ringing, my eyes shift back down to meet the cold blue ones glaring up at me. I wonder why I let my father, who is barely six feet and a good fifty pounds lighter than me, rough me up like this. If I wanted to, I could pummel him into a bloody stain on the concrete. But instead, I nod and accept his words and my failure, hanging my head.

We've just lost the State Championship by one goal, and I had the opportunity to score the equalizer that would've forced overtime. But as my father reminds me with his rough words and sharp slaps, I fucked it up. All the hours on the ice, in the gym, pounding the streets on cold frigid mornings were for shit.

"I'm sorry, Sir. I thought I had the shot, but the goalie was too quick..." I mutter pathetically. God, I hate myself right now. Stop being such as pussy and tell him to go fuck himself.

"That's bullshit and you know it!" he barks again, poking me in the chest. "Tomorrow we'll sit and watch the game and make a list of all the things you're gonna work on this summer at camp. I'm not letting you slack off with that little girlfriend of yours. You can forget about that. It's your senior year next year. You stand to make captain, and I won't have you risk it all for some piece of ass!"

The mention of Jenna both makes me hopeful and terrified all at once. She's my happy place, the one person who tells me it's going to be okay, even when I do fuck up. The fact my father called her a "piece of ass" makes my blood boil, but as usual, I pussy out of saying anything to defend her. I just go about storing my hockey gear on the shelves in the garage while my father continues to bitch and moan at me about my shortcomings and failures as a son, a hockey player, and a human being.

Once he's had his say, virtually breathless from the tirade of poison he's just spewed on me, I'm allowed into the house where I find my mom sitting at the kitchen table with a cup of tea waiting for me. She smiles sadly, and I know what she's thinking. She wishes she could say something to my father as well, stand up for me, but she's as powerless as I am.

I've only seen my parents kiss and embrace once, and that was when my little brother Max was born. I was eight and thrilled to be a big brother. I had such plans to teach him to skate, build a treehouse in the yard, take him fishing to my special spot.

But all those dreams came crashing down when he died of Sudden Infant Death Syndrome aged seven months. My mom shut down completely. She fell into a depression so deep and bottomless I thought I'd never see her again. So my father took over my upbringing, pushing me harder into hockey to give us both a distraction from our grief. It worked to a certain extent, but it just made my tough Army Sergeant father even harder and more emotionally distant. The physical element to our interactions really developed when I hit puberty and grew bigger and stronger—it never went further than a few clips round the ear or a shove, and the first time it happened, I was so shocked I couldn't even react. The second time it happened, I told my mom, but she quietly informed me it was "his way" and to just try harder next time. The third time it happened, I tried to shove him back, and that earned me a hard slap to the face and a warning that if I tried that again I could expect much worse.

I never tried it again, but I vowed to be the best player I could be so he'd have no cause to show me how bad it could get. And when I skated well and we won, I got muted approval but also a list of improvements to make. When I messed up or we lost, I wanted to hide in the locker room and disappear. I often sat there after a bad game in my gear, the sweat coating my skin in a cold sheen and thought about quitting. I loved hockey more than anything, but if I gave it up, my father would have no cause to get on my back about it. Then I thought about Max and how when he died, I was left as an only child, so I should just do my duty as a good son and suck it up.

The night we lost the State Championships, I had arranged to sneak out and meet Jenna at our spot. So once my father finishes his third beer and heads up to bed, I slip on my sneakers, climb out the window of my ground floor bedroom, and jog a few blocks to the park. As I approach, I see Jenna sitting at the bottom of the slide, her knees drawn up under her chin and her arms wrapped around her legs. Her pale blonde hair hangs in a thick rope over her shoulder and her glasses reflect the moonlight. Jenna usually wears contacts during the day, but I always want her to wear her glasses more. They make her look so cute and nerdy.

"Hey peanut," I say once I'm in earshot. It's the nickname I've used for her since we were little kids. Ironically, she's allergic to peanuts, so it always makes her a little bit mad that I make light of something that could legitimately kill her.

"Hey." She stands up and climbs onto the end of the slide to add a few precious inches to her tiny frame. Once I'm in front of her, she puts her arms around my neck and presses her lips to mine, her kiss washing away the last few uncomfortable hours and making me feel whole again. Her sweet, pink tongue slides against mine, and I'm so hard I could bust a nut right here, especially when she presses her perfect tits against my chest.

When I pull away, Jenna's lips are swollen, and her eyes are dark with longing. "I'm sorry about the game. Are you really disappointed?" she asks as I sit on the end of the slide, and she plops herself on my lap, squashing my hard dick. I wince.

"*Yeah, it sucks for the team, especially the seniors,*" I grumble, *playing with the end of her braid.*

"*And your dad?*" *she says quietly, stroking the back of my neck.*

"*Usual shit. He's gonna make me go to hockey camp in Canada again this summer, so I'm really sorry, but our plans aren't gonna work out.*" *The words stick in my throat as I feel Jenna's tiny body stiffen in my arms.*

We have plans to spend time at her family's cabin this summer. Her parents are always really welcoming to me, and I think her mom has an idea of what I have to deal with at home, so they offered to have me spend a few weeks with them this summer. I guess my father has other ideas.

"*I'm sorry, peanut. I know it was meant to be our summer.*" *I lean down and kiss her lips softly, sliding my hand up the back of her sweater so I can feel her warm skin against mine.*

As we make out in the moonlight, I feel like the happiest man alive. All the bullshit that comes with hockey and my father disappears with each sweet kiss and gentle sigh.

However, that feeling evaporates like an ice shower when my father's sharp shout echoes across the night, and I realize I'm in deep shit.

The memories of Jenna make me feel particularly melancholy as I sit on a bench on the Santa Monica pier and stare out at the ocean. On those balmy summer nights when we talked about our future life together, we fantasized about living on the beach somewhere. We'd walk in the sand with the dog we both desperately wanted, I'd play hockey, and she'd teach first grade. It was our perfect teenage dream, and it all seemed so simple.

The bitter taste on my tongue reminds me of the way that summer panned out, and the pulsing hatred I have for my father that lives deep in my gut rears its ugly head. I clench my fists and take deep breaths. This rage inside is what makes me such a strong D-man. I only let it out on the ice where it's allowed to fight and punch and destroy.

I close my eyes and clear my mind, letting the salty sea breeze cleanse the poisonous memories. It's been a really long time since thoughts of my past have hit me so hard. I wonder if it's to do with the feelings I'm developing for Beth. The only other time I've felt deeply for someone was with Jenna, and that ended so badly I'm worried I won't be able to let myself take the risk with Beth.

"Excuse me. Are you Nate Halsted?"

I snap my head up and see a young boy in a Whalers cap standing in front of me with what must be his dad. My face splits into my automatic public smile, and I stand up, towering over them.

"I sure am. And who are you, big man?" I ask, thankful for the distraction. At least now I have something to keep my mind busy while I wait for Beth to finish her meeting.

Beth

Andre and I are silent as we step into the elevator at Hector Riley's office. As the doors slide shut, we take a moment to look at each other, massive smiles splitting our faces in half.

"Oh my GOD!" I squeal, grabbing Andre's hands as we jump around in the elevator car, making it shake on the descent to the lobby.

"We did it," Andre sings, picking me up and squeezing me tight. "We are Hollywood bitches!" I laugh joyously as he spins us in the tight space, then the doors slide open revealing us to a lobby full of people.

We snigger as Andre drops me to my feet, and we scurry out of the elevator, through the lobby, and out onto the street where we resume our happy victory dance.

The meeting couldn't have gone any better. Hector and his creative director loved our portfolio of work and our mockups for the main characters; he complimented our work on his daughter's wedding and seemed more than happy with our quote.

He explained they plan to film on location in Seattle and the surrounding area for the most part. However, there would be some studio work in L.A. after that, probably for about a month.

Andre and I both confirmed that would work, and we shook on the deal, my heart racing at this amazing opportunity. We talked for a while longer about the extra stylists we'd need to bring on, the budget, and the timeline.

"Baby girl, you know this is gonna change our lives," Andre gushes as we wait for an Uber to pick us up. "How are we celebrating? I can make some calls." He takes out his phone.

"Do it. Our flight isn't early, so we can let our hair down a little." I'm just contemplating a night of drinks and dancing with my business partner and bestie when I remember I have a very large hockey player waiting for my call. I have a momentary flicker of annoyance followed by guilt. He came all this way to do me a favor; I can't just ditch him.

"What's with the frown? It'll give you wrinkles." Andre's voice jolts me back.

I tut and slap his arm. "Nate's still here."

"So? If you don't want to party with the hockey hottie, I'm sure there'll be plenty of girls out there who will," he replies giving me a knowing wink. "Just call the boy and either put him out of his misery or invite him along."

I hate that Andre knows me so well and refuses to let my bullshit take hold. Also, I feel a stab of jealousy at the thought of Nate hooking up with anyone else.

"Fine," I grumble as the car pulls up. "I'll bring him along. Are you bringing Carlton?" I decide Andre could use a little pressure of his own.

He tuts as we slide into the back seat of the town car and tell the driver the name of our hotel. "Carlton and I have run our course."

I laugh and shake my head. "You're such a hypocrite."

"No!" He holds his finger up at me. "Carlton and I are a one-time thing; we have an understanding."

"One time?" I cock my eyebrow at him.

"Fine, a seven time thing, but whatever. You and Nate are different. Any idiot could see that by the way you two danced at the benefit."

I whip my head around and stare, my cheeks blushing at the memory of that incredible dance. Andre cups my face and strokes it with his thumb.

"That boy is all sorts of crazy about you. Would it be so terrible to see where it goes?" he asks quietly.

I don't know. Would it?

Andre's set up a celebratory dinner in West Hollywood with a group of his friends, and I'm just putting the finishing touches to my makeup when there's a knock on the door. I messaged Nate earlier with the plans, telling him to swing by my room at eight to pick me up.

Checking my phone, I see he's right on time, so I put my lipstick down and rush over to answer the door, my heart pounding a little harder than I want it to. Why does the thought of seeing Nate tonight do that to me? We had sex just this morning. It's not like its prom night or something.

However, when I open the door and see Nate standing there, all tall and handsome, I feel just like a girl on her first date. He's wearing a simple light blue Ralph Lauren shirt, light jeans, and Timberland boots. His sandy hair is effortlessly styled, and his blue eyes twinkle as he hands me a single purple gerbera daisy. He's every bit the wholesome Midwestern boy, and the prospect of going out with him tonight makes my palms sweaty.

"Congratulations, princess," he says, stepping in and kissing me sweetly on the cheek. God, he smells incredible. I close my eyes briefly and quietly huff him in.

"Thank you." I pull away and take the flower, placing it on the table. "I just have to finish getting ready." I smooth my hands down over my yellow bardot style jumpsuit. It's one of my favorite outfits because it shows off my tanned shoulders, and the wide pants make my legs appear longer because they hang down over my towering high heels.

As I fuss around applying my signature red lipstick and stuffing things into my best Gucci clutch, I notice Nate's eyes eating up my movements. He has that hungry look on his face, his eyes hooded and lustful, and it makes me hot and twitchy.

"Take a photo. It'll last longer," I sass, smirking at him over my shoulder, proud that I manage to make his cheeks flush with embarrassment.

"I tried that last night, remember?" Nate growls. Now it's my turn to blush. I look over at the window that still bears the smears from when I was pressed against it while Nate took me from behind. The memory floods my core with desire.

"Come on," I croak. "We're meeting Andre at the restaurant." I grab my clutch and swish past Nate, trying to ignore his cocky smile and intoxicatingly clean scent.

Nate

Now, I'm a pretty enlightened guy. I may be from Oklahoma, brought up Baptist and an Army brat, but I'm not a clueless yokel who has no idea what goes on in the big wide world. However, I must admit that when we enter the non-descript looking bar, I have no idea it's a drag cabaret with dinner and compulsory karaoke.

Andre and his group are already seated when we arrive, and I try to appear as relaxed as possible as I shake hands with the three men and two women. They're polite and smile, but none of them have a clue who I am, so immediately relax. I can just be Nate—no pressure to talk hockey, stats, or Stanley Cup prospects.

"I hope you're ready to sing, big man," Andre coos as I squeeze my large frame into the circular booth next to Beth. I hate this kind of seating; the table is fixed, and I'm not exactly the smallest person in the world.

"Am I ready to do what now?" I enquire, staring at Beth who's trying to hide her smile behind the cocktail menu.

"It's drag karaoke, baby," he laughs kindly. "The girls get up and sing as their favorite diva, and then it's our turn. It's an absolute riot."

"Oh no. I don't sing," I chuckle nervously, wagging my finger at him just as our waitress arrives. She's clearly dressed as '80s Madonna, snapping her gum in bored impatience.

"Are you okay?" Beth whispers, leaning in close so her breath skims over the shell of my ear. When I turn my head, she's got an enormous smile on her face, and I have the distinct feeling she's mocking me.

"Yep, all good here," I reply, taking a big gulp of my water.

After we order a round of drinks and make our choices of entrée, Andre continues to enlighten me on how the evening will work. As he explains that the karaoke is mandatory for all, I feel my palms sweat and my throat close. There's no way in hell I'm getting up to sing in front of all these people.

"Did you know about this?" I hiss at Beth when the conversation around the table switches to another subject.

She giggles and adjusts her top. The way it exposes her smooth tanned shoulders is very distracting. "Maybe."

I reach under the table and squeeze her thigh with my large hand, brushing my finger across her center, making her gasp. "Don't think I won't get you back for this," I growl just as our appetizer platters arrive and the first act takes to the stage—a very convincing Shania Twain tribute.

After a few more beers and plenty of coconut shrimp and jalapeno poppers, I feel a bit more relaxed. Andre's friends are really fun, and once I let it slip that I'm a pro-athlete, they all seem interested but not in a creepy stalker fan way. It's nice to share my enthusiasm for my sport with people who have no preconceptions or alliances.

I glance over at Beth several times during the evening, and when she's not sharing secretive whispers with Andre, she smiles and laughs openly. She's one of the most carefree people I've ever met, and I feel great when I'm around her, even when I'm freaking out about the prospect of imminent public humiliation.

Once we've eaten our entrées, I excuse myself to use the bathroom and wonder if I can squeeze out of the tiny window above the urinals. Jesus, get a fucking grip. It's just three minutes of your life. It's doubtful anyone in here will recognize me, but I really don't want to come off like a douchebag in front of Beth and her friends.

Come on! I can face off against massive, toothless hockey players. I can do this!

As I steam out of the bathroom with a renewed sense of purpose following my pep talk, I collide with Beth, almost knocking her across the corridor.

"Shit, sorry princess," I gasp, grabbing hold of her arms to stop her bouncing off the wall.

"Making a run for it?" she smirks. "They've just brought the song book round."

Suddenly, I've got sweaty palms again. I look down at Beth with pleading eyes. "Do I have to do it?"

Beth laughs. "You're unbelievable! You perform in front of thousands of screaming hockey fans, and you're scared of this?"

"It's totally different. I'm good at hockey. It's what I do. This is certainly *not* what I do. I've never sung in public. Fuck, I don't even sing in the shower." I realize I'm rambling like an idiot, and I must seem like a total pussy.

But I see an expression of understanding cross Beth's beautiful face, and she takes pity on me. "How about we do a duet? There's no rule against that."

A sense of relief washes over me. I can do that. With Beth by my side, I feel like I could pretty much do anything. My mouth is so dry with nerves I can't even speak, so I just nod my agreement.

"Cool. And I have the perfect song."

An hour and three beers later, I'm on stage with the spotlight blinding me and Beth by my side. The opening notes to our song are playing, and the mic feels like a lead weight in my sweaty hand. I'm thankful I can only see the amused faces of a few people sitting at the very front tables. Everyone else is hidden by the spotlight.

This is it—abject humiliation or immortality. "Now I've … had … the time of my life…" My deep baritone voice echoes out around the room, and the chatter falls silent. Is that my voice? Holy shit, it's fucking terrible! But I've started now, so what's the worst that can happen?

Beth begins to sing her part, and oh my god–she sings like an angel. Okay, that's the worst that can happen. I'm butchering a song while Beth sings her parts like a pro! I gaze over at her, and she's never looked more beautiful. The spotlight makes her hair glow like a halo around her face, and her self-assured smile is breath taking.

That is until she scowls at me because I'm gawking at her, and it's my turn to sing. We progress through the song, and I loosen up a bit. As the audience reacts and sings along to the classic tune, I even start to enjoy myself, shaking my butt in time with the song and grabbing Beth's hand and spinning her around. When the song reaches its climax, I drop my mic to the stage, grab Beth around her waist, and lift her clear over my head like she weighs nothing. She squeals with joy and flings her arms and head back, and the audience goes completely wild! I feel incredible, the cheers and claps ringing in my ears as I lower Beth down, her small body sliding over mine, making my dick thicken in my jeans.

Once she's back on her feet, we stand there for what feels like forever, staring into each other's eyes. All I want to do is dip her back and kiss the hell out of her, so I man up and do exactly that. Beth lets out a squeak of surprise as I press my mouth to hers, my hands holding her body against me, my tongue probing to gain entry. She holds my biceps as we kiss deeply on stage in front of a room full of strangers, and I couldn't give a fuck.

Despite my nerves and reluctance, this has been one of the best experiences of my life so far.

7

Beth

It's so nice to be home. Sunday dinner at my parent's house is one of the highlights of my week, and as I walk in the back door of their modest waterfront property, I feel at ease immediately. A pile of my younger sister's sneakers and boots clutter up the mud room, my dad's fishing gear is propped up in the corner, and the smell of mom's special spaghetti sauce drifts invitingly from the kitchen.

Despite the fact both my parents come from money and could easily live off their inheritances, we've never lived an extravagant lifestyle. Yes, we take a couple of nice vacations every year and we have a house in St. Barts, but they don't live like people with a lot of money. They've both worked all their lives–my dad, Bryan, as a lecturer in economics at the University of Washington and mom, Maria, as a therapist. She used to see patients in the apartment over the garage which my dad tricked out into a sleek office and consultation room for her. It worked out well when my sister and I were young because she could schedule patients around school runs and play dates and still be there to meet us from the bus and take us to our extra-curricular activities.

As I kick off my sneakers and hang up my coat, I hear my mom calling me from the kitchen.

"Beth, is that you?"

"Yeah mom, I'm here. Sorry I'm late. The flight was delayed so I crashed last night," I explain as I walk into the kitchen. My mom is standing at the stove tasting her sauce which I'm sure has been simmering away since yesterday. The whole room is full of the sweet smell of tomatoes and garlic, and my stomach gives off a loud, embarrassing grumble.

When I kiss my mom on the cheek, she feeds me a spoonful of sauce, and I smack my lips and kiss her again.

"Always spectacular, momma," I sigh, taking a seat at the counter. I watch her move about the kitchen like a pro. I guess I shouldn't expect anything else. Her Italian roots are strong, from her dark hair and eyes to her short, round figure. I've seen pictures of her in her teens, and to say she was an hourglass knockout is an understatement. Now in her mid-fifties, she's soft and comfortable, her dark hair peppered with streaks of white, and her face lined with years of laughter and love.

"So how was L.A? I got your message, but I need all the details. Will you have to move there for filming?" she asks, balancing her favorite wooden spoon on the edge of the pot.

"No. In fact, it works out really well. It'll mostly be filmed on location here, but there will be some studio work in L.A., so we'll probably have to move there for about a month," I explain.

"Move where?"

I turn my head and see my dad wander into the kitchen with a huge pile of Sunday papers under his arm. I constantly tell him he can read them all online and save a few thousand trees, but he just grumbles about the smell of newsprint and how he recycles.

"Hey daddy." I greet him with a hug and a kiss, going up on my tip toes so I can reach his cheek.

"Hey, pumpkin. So where are you moving?" he asks, sitting next to me at the counter.

"L.A. For the movie Andre and I are going to work on." I see the look on his face and add, "But only for about a month to do the studio stuff. Mostly we'll be filming on location here."

The deep crinkles in his forehead smooth out, and he seems a little more at ease. I'm definitely a daddy's girl, and we've always been really close. When I moved clear across the country to go to college, he wasn't happy, but he dealt with it.

I continue to fill them in on my new business venture and explain that after this job I should be able to pay them back all the seed money they loaned me. They've never once asked for a payment plan or a date when I'll get it back to them, but I want to show them that I'm not taking their charity. It was a business loan, and I'll be much happier when it's paid back so Andre and I can own the business fifty/fifty.

"I'm going to serve dinner soon. Will you go and dig your sister out of her pit? I swear she spends more time sleeping than ever." Mom moans as she begins to drain the noodles.

"With pleasure." I chuckle, taking every opportunity to get on my sister's nerves.

I hit the stairs at a run, taking them two at a time and burst into her room. As expected, the room is dark, smelly, and all I can see of my eighteen-year-old sister is a lump under the blankets.

"Rise and shine, lazy girl," I sing in a loud, obnoxious voice, dragging open the drapes to let the January sun fill the room.

"Go fuck yourself" is all that's mumbled from under the pile of blankets.

"Come on. Get up. It's Spaghetti Sunday!" I decide she needs the Tigger treatment, so I climb onto the bed and stand with my feet straddling her and bounce like her favorite childhood cartoon character.

Eventually, the covers are flung aside, and I stare down at my little sister Katie. She's all huge brown eyes and bed messy dark curls. She definitely got the Italian genes whereas I'm fair and blue eyed like my dad.

"What the fuck, dude? Get off me," she grumbles, popping her ear buds out and rubbing her eyes, smearing yesterday's eyeliner and mascara everywhere.

"Mom told me to get you up. Dinner's almost ready." I plop down onto the bed and lie next to my sister. "You know you shouldn't sleep in your makeup. You won't have eighteen-year-old skin forever."

Katie grunts at me and rolls her eyes. "Whatever."

She throws the blankets off and over me and slides out of bed, unselfconsciously hooking her sleep shorts out of her butt. She's a typical angry, rebellious teen who gets pissed off at everything, but I love her so much. Being seven years older meant I was always her protector, but now she towers over me and sometimes *I* feel like the little sister. "Privacy please!" she snarls as she picks through the pile of black clothes thrown over the back of her chair.

I untangle myself from her questionably smelling blankets and head for the door. "Alright, Miss Sassy Pants. Don't be long. The noodles won't wait." As I leave her room and close the door, I hear something that sounds like a book or a shoe hit the other side, and I smirk at how moody she is.

Dinner is the usual mix of deep conversation, news, and laughter. I love hearing about my dad's work at the University. Obviously, most of what mom does has to remain confidential, but she still regales us with funny little stories, disguising them by saying "This happened to a colleague of mine…"

Katie generally just grunts and mutters when we ask her about school. She's in her senior year and has already been accepted for early admittance to Stanford to study literature and creative writing. She only really comes alive when I ask her how her volleyball team is doing. Katie is athletic, and she not only plays for her high school volleyball team, but she runs track as well. It's such a strange juxtaposition—on the one hand she's this emo, sulky goth, but on the other, she happily takes part in such a conventional high school experience.

"So, what's up with this movie?" she asks, ripping into a chunk of cheesy garlic bread. God, I wish I could eat carbs like a teenager again. "Is it some bull-shit chick flick?"

I hear my dad grunt back a laugh. He's always given us free reign to speak our minds, and I think it amuses him to have such opinionated, snarky daughters.

"I guess you could call it a chick flick, but I think romantic comedy is more accurate," I reply.

Katie snorts and rolls her eyes. "Whatever." She loves to rip apart my choice of career, moaning about me perpetuating the misogynistic ideal that all women should be beautiful, blah, blah.

Mom quickly changes the subject to more Katie-friendly territory and asks her about her upcoming game against her high school's biggest rivals, and thankfully Sunday dinner continues without her busting my balls any further.

"How are things going with your hockey player?" Dad asks me as we load the dishwasher after dinner. Katie has retreated to her room, pleading homework, and mom is having a well-deserved glass of merlot in the den while she watches *Antiques Roadshow*.

The mention of Nate makes my pulse pick up a notch, and I look up at my dad, trying to keep things nonchalant. "Fine, I guess. It's just casual. Nothing serious."

Suddenly, my dad's large hand covers mine as I load a plate into the dishwasher. "Beth, you say this all the time. You're twenty-six, and you've never even brought a boyfriend home. Your mom and I worry."

"Seriously dad, we're doing this again?" I snap, pulling my hand away and busying myself by wiping down the countertops. "I thought mom was the shrink."

"We just worry that you go from fling to fling and never form any deep connections. We don't want you to be left behind when all your friends go off and start their lives with their partners." The expression on my dad's face breaks my heart, but I stand firm.

"What's wrong with wanting the excitement of first kisses and new adventures?" I ask through gritted teeth. We've been having this debate since I was in high school. I was so anti-commitment that I even went to my high school prom with Andre as my date. The thought of some bumbling teenage suitor arriving on my doorstep with expectations of a prom night love story made me feel icky.

"Nothing pumpkin, but I'd hate for you to miss out on something wonderful just because you're scared…"

"I'm not scared!" I yell, finally losing my cool. "I don't want to end up in a marriage with no passion, no za za zoo! For fuck's sake, you and mom live like roommates at this point in your marriage, and I want no part of that."

At that moment, my mom walks into the kitchen, obviously drawn by the raised voices, and the look of hurt on her face makes me lower my eyes in shame. Jesus, I didn't mean to just blurt that out. I've never expressed these feelings to my parents before, and now I feel like a massive asshole.

"Beth, you have no idea what it takes to make a marriage work in the long term," she says in her quiet, therapist voice. "And with an attitude like that, I fear you never will. You have no right to comment on what your dad and I have."

"I'm sorry. I just think I'm too young to settle down," I say quietly, feeling completely ashamed of myself. "I didn't mean to hurt your feelings."

Thankfully, I feel my dad's arm snake round my shoulders as he pulls me close to him. "We know that, sweetie." He kisses the top of my head, and I look at my mom. She manages a tight smile and disappears back into the den.

God, I'm an asshole.

Perfect! After the awkward as fuck dinner at my parent's house, I walk back into the apartment I share with my college roommate and best girlfriend Mila to the sounds of her and her boyfriend, Matt, fucking enthusiastically in her room.

I guess they've just got back from New Orleans. And his quest to win her back went well. Jesus, it sounds like they're tearing each other apart in there.

As I creep into my room and close the door, my mind drifts to my last night in L.A. with Nate. After our karaoke triumph, we were so hot for each other that we virtually ran off stage, jumped in an Uber, and fucked our brains out all night. Nate was so commanding and alpha, I was panting for him to take me every which way.

When we'd finally worn each other out, we lay in bed and talked about all sorts. We speculated on what might be happening with Matt and Mila in New Orleans. Other than the text she sent to say she'd arrived, I hadn't heard anything.

I spoke a bit about my family, but when I asked Nate about his, he kind of shut down. His normally open face clouded with something akin to anger, and instead of answering me, he kissed my mouth and dove under the sheets and ate me out until I was gasping for breath and begging him to stop. Once he was done, he made his excuses about an early flight and almost ran back to his own room. It was so weird; I was usually the one that made the excuses and fled. I think I hit a nerve, and part of me is desperate to find out more.

The memory of that night and the sounds coming from Mila's room make me feel incredibly horny, so I decide to take a walk to the local coffee house to try and cool off. I leave my cell in my room because if I don't, I'm likely to call Nate and ask him to come over so we can make some noise of our own.

However, as I walk through my neighborhood in the early evening, I can't help my mind drifting to him. Why was he so caged and angry when I asked him about his family? He seems too well-adjusted to have had a terrible upbringing. But then what the fuck do I know? I had an amazing childhood, and I'm still messed up about a lot of stuff.

My dad's words about my issues with relationships still sting, and I feel terrible all over again for yelling at him. He's only watching out for me. Of course he doesn't want me left on the shelf after all my friends pair off.

Ugh, this day sucks. Only a huge, creamy, frothy, mocha monstrosity from the coffee shop will make me feel better. I just hope Matt and Mila have finished their fuckfest by the time I get home. I'm feeling way too needy right now.

Nate

The treadmill bounces under my feet as I pound my way through a gruelling workout post Bye Week. Foo Fighters blast my ear drums and fill the team gym, only slightly drowning out the grunts and groans of my teammates being put through their paces. Matt and Thor are working the ropes, their huge arms whipping the heavy, thick twists into rippling waves. Bugs is doing pull ups like a fucking machine, and Brett is spotting Ford on the bench press.

I felt the need to run today, so I ignored our trainer's request to work the weights and hit the treadmill. Running helps to clear my mind and work through my problems. Today's problem is a five foot nothing platinum bombshell that makes me crave her pussy like a fucking drug addict.

The time we spent together over Bye Week was incredible but, on some level, deeply unsatisfying. Sexually, we fit together perfectly, the feel of her tucked into my side as she sleeps, snuffling sweetly, is comparable to nothing else in my life. The fire in her eyes when she comes is burned into my mind. She never turns away; she never closes her eyes. She looks into my soul and takes me all the way.

But on our last night when we had one of those great post-orgasm talks, she asked me about my family, and the deep shame of everything I went through completely shut the conversation down. The only way I could think to distract her from more questions was to make her come until she passed out.

I'm not proud of the way I fled from her room and then L.A. without making contact with her again, but I didn't count on Beth delving into my past just yet. I suppose I could've just made something up or omitted certain uncomfortable facts although that feels almost as bad as telling her the horrible truth.

For fuck's sake, I want her in the worst way. I pump my arms and legs as I speed up the rate of the treadmill. I want to obliterate this feeling with physical exhaustion, so I run until my lungs burn and my heart pumps, lactic acid flooding my muscles. Suddenly, I see Bugs standing in front of me slapping manically at the controls to slow me down.

"What the fuck, man?" he yells as I bend over gasping for breath, sweat stinging my eyes. "You're gonna kill yourself or cause an injury running like that."

I lift my head and shake it, wiping sweat from my face. "Sorry, Cap. Just needed to blow off steam." I pant, rubbing the stitch that twists in my side.

"Fine, but that little show was fucking stupid," he mutters. "Now hit the shower. I don't wanna see you back until morning skate tomorrow."

"Yes, Cap." I drag my sorry ass to the showers to wash away the sweat and confusion. Everything becomes clear under the harsh fluorescent lights. I've made my decision: I want Beth, and if I must share my most shameful secrets with her, then so be it.

We're playing our first home game after Bye Week against the Detroit Devils, and we're tied at two with three minutes on the clock. Our third line is coming to the end of their shift, and I've got my leg flung over the boards, ready to hit the ice. My heart is pounding in my chest, and my hair is sticking to the back of my sweaty neck as I listen to Bugs explain our play.

Coach Casey yells for us to hit the Devils hard in the final minutes, and as the shifts change, I leap over the boards and hear the home fans go wild. Matt and Ford power into the Devils third, and Bugs and I skate backward toward Thor in our goal.

The Devils' center holds the puck behind their net as the seconds tick by, then he makes his move, shooting the biscuit to his left along the boards to his teammate's waiting blade. He takes off up the rink on a breakaway, outmaneuvering Ford, but Matt's hot on his tail. Just as Matt makes his move to steal the puck, one of the Devils hooks his skates, and he slides across the ice, smashing headfirst into the boards.

There's a huge gasp from the fans, and out of the corner of my eye, I see Mila leap up and hang the top half of her body over the boards to get a look at what's happening. But Matt's made of tough stuff, so he gets up and shakes it off as play is called to a stop and the officials discuss the penalty. I glance up at the clock–2:54 left of the period. If we can get a two-minute minor for hooking and a final power play, we can take this game.

And to my immense relief, the officials call exactly that. Bugs gathers us for a huddle as we stop for a TV break, and he explains the play. I love and hate this part of the game. Everything we do in these final minutes and seconds count. Before we know it, we're back from the TV break, and Bugs positions himself for the face off. The fans are surprisingly quiet until the puck drops, then they go off like a nuclear bomb.

Bugs wins the puck, and after a quick look my way, I bang my stick on the ice to show him I'm open, and he flicks it to me and I'm off. I sprint toward the Detroit goalie, my quads and glutes burning after my stupid run yesterday. Flicking my eyes to the right, I see Matt, so I pass to him and position myself ready to receive the puck back for the shot. As it hits my blade, I control it, laser in on the gap I've spotted between the goalie's leg pads, draw my stick back, and slap the puck with everything I have.

Motherfucker! The goalie's quick as a cat and closes his knees, and my five-hole evaporates. But he doesn't get his glove on the puck, so as it bounces off his pads, it falls perfectly for a deflection, and instinct takes over. I use my best wrist flick to chip the puck into the impossibly small gap between his body and arm, and the red light glows.

Holy shit! I scored. I sail around the back of the net and into a massive bundle of pads, sticks, and sweat. I get slapped on the ass, back, and helmet and the sound of the home fans is deafening.

"The fucking kid did it!" Ford yells in my face, showering me in spit, but I don't care. The adrenaline spikes through my system, and all I can think about is Beth and how much I want to see her tonight. I know we'll be heading to O'Connell's after the game, so I make it

my mission to get her there too. We just have to sur-
vive the final seconds of the game.

8

Beth

I don't usually watch hockey religiously, but since I've started hanging out with the team, I try to watch the games when I'm home. And let's be honest, getting to see Nate Halsted look hot as fuck in his hockey gear, skating like a demon and, fuck me, scoring a goal in the final minutes is totally worth it.

When the puck hits the back of the net, I manage a hearty fist pump without dislodging the heated bean bag draped across my stomach. Fucking cramps are the worst, and I feel like shit, but seeing Nate get the goal that wins the game makes me feel a little better.

As the game comes to an end, I breathe a sigh of relief. That was intense, and the last thing I need is more tension right now. I adjust the bean bag and decide it needs to go back in the microwave to warm up, so I drag my ass off the couch and zap it for a minute to warm it through. When my cramps are bad, this is the only thing that helps: a warm bean bag, my fuzzy bunny slippers, and copious amounts of peanut M&Ms.

While the bean bag is warming, I dig around in the candy cupboard and search for the comforting yellow bag of goodness. However, my search comes back empty-handed, and I stomp my foot petulantly on the floor, causing my cramps to spasm.

"Goddamn it!" I curse as the microwave pings at the exact same time as my phone. Slamming the microwave door shut, I hobble back to the couch and flop down, pressing the warming bag to my stomach, reaching for my phone.

[MILA: Did you see Matt hit the boards? He has to stay for concussion protocol, so I'll probably stay at his place. How's shark week?]

That was a gnarly slam, so I totally don't blame her.

[BETH: I understand. Shark week is as shit as ever. BTW did you finish the M&Ms? (angry face emoji)]
[MILA: Oops, sorry. Matt had a craving.]

As that message pings in, another drops in behind it.

[NATE: Did you watch? We're going to O'Connell's. I have a lot of excess adrenaline I need to work off ;) (eggplant and peach emojis)]

Shit. There's no way I'm going anywhere near Nate tonight. My hair is greasy, and I'm breaking out in zits on my chin. Plus, it's like a crime scene in my panties, there's no way he's getting a look in, so I need to blow him off.

[MILA: Do you want us to get you some M&Ms and swing by on our way home?]

Well, it's the least they can do.

[NATE: Come on, princess. I need you here for my celly.]

My fingers fly over the screen as another cramp hits, and I drop the phone, groaning and clutching my stomach, waiting for it to pass. Fuck this shit! If men had to go through this every month, they'd invent much more effective pain relief.

[BETH: Yes, I want the Jumbo peanut M&Ms and another box of super tampons. You used those as well biatch :(]

I wait for Mila's apology and wonder how I'm going to get out of seeing Nate without telling him the horrible truth about my period situation. I see the three typing bubbles appear and disappear several times and wonder what the fuck Mila is typing.

When the reply comes through, I have a moment of confusion, then my stomach drops out of my butt and I squeal.

[NATE: I'm happy to bring you M&Ms, but I assure you I didn't use your tampons ;)]

OH, MY FUCKING GOD! I sent the period plea to Nate not Mila, and now I want to actually die. How do I get out of this? I ignore Nate's message and frantically message Mila, begging her to head Nate off and stop him from coming here.

[MILA: Sorry B. I'm in with Matt getting his checks. At least you'll get your M&Ms quicker this way (laughing crying emoji)]

I growl out my frustration at my soon to be *ex*-best friend and try to get my hormone-muddled brain to function above a second-grade level.

[BETH: Thanks for nothing Mils :(]

And to Nate I send

[BETH: Forget that message. It wasn't for you. Can't come out. Speak soon.]

There, that should do it. I fling my phone across the couch, slump down under my comforter, and set up the next episode of Drag Race. Jesus, that was so embarrassing! Guys shouldn't know about things like periods, waxing, douching, or bloating so the fact I exposed that part of me to Nate is just humiliating. Thankfully, the pain relief I took a little while ago begins to kick in, and I drift off to sleep.

Nate

On the drive over to Beth's apartment, I wonder for the millionth time whether I'm overstepping the mark. I must admit when her message came through asking for candy and tampons, I was very confused. Were we suddenly in that type of relationship? That sounds distinctly like a "boyfriend" errand. But then I read the message again and realized she must've sent me a message meant for Mila, so I chuckled as I typed out my reply.

Now I'm armed with a jumbo-sized bag of candy, tampons, and the door code to Beth's building. That came courtesy of Mila who felt terrible that she couldn't run the errand herself because she had to hang out with Matt while he went through concussion protocol.

The guys were also pissed I was blowing off drinks at O'Connell's, especially as I had the game winning puck which automatically meant I had to buy the team their first round. So as I hefted my duffel over my shoulder, I threw my credit card at Bugs and told him the first round was on me. It was probably a dumbass move. Knowing this bunch of idiots, I'll have a massive bill next month.

When I pull up to Beth's building, I have to drive around to find a space. I manage to find one on the next block which means I have to stomp through the drizzle with candy and tampons hidden under my coat to keep them dry. Thankfully, the code to the door works, and I shake myself off in the lobby before taking the stairs two at a time. As I reach Beth's apartment door, I'm suddenly filled with self-doubt. Her text message was clear–she doesn't want me to come over, so will my presence piss her off and ruin this delicate thing we have going on?

Fuck it.

I knock confidently on the door and brace myself. But after a minute or two with no answer, I knock again, harder this time, and pull out my phone to check the time. It's only ten thirty. Could she be in bed already?

"What?" The door flies open so suddenly it scares the crap out of me, and I juggle my phone, trying not to drop it and the other items I'm balancing. Once I've got shit under control, I take in the sight before me. I've only ever seen Beth totally put together or freshly fucked, so the woman in front of me is surprising to say the least. She's wearing pink and purple plaid pajama pants, a huge grey Boston University sweatshirt, pink bunny slippers, and a scowl. Her normally perfect hair is in a loose ponytail, her eyes are sleepy, her skin is shiny and slightly blemished, and she's clutching some kind of beanbag to her belly. She's never looked more adorable, and I feel my heart thump against my sternum.

"What the fuck, Nate? I told you not to come," she barks, trying to shut the door on me, but I jam my foot in the way. Her hand comes up to her pimply chin, trying to hide it.

"I brought you your things," I offer, waving the candy in front of her, but keeping the tampons discreetly tucked in my jacket. No sense in enraging her more.

Beth's eyes widen at the temptation in front of her, and she makes a grab for them, but my reflexes are professionally honed, so I manage to whip them out of reach.

"Nate, give me the candy," Beth whines, stomping her little bunny foot, making me smirk which makes her hiss like an angry kitten.

"Only if you let me in," I tease, waving the bag just out of her reach.

"We can't fuck. I'm on my period, so why do you want to come in?"

Ouch!

I've got to admit, her words sting a little. Is that the only reason she thinks I've come over?

"That's not why I'm here. I just thought I'd help you out since Mila has to stay with Matt." I hold out the candy and tampons, and she takes them, her eyes dropping in what appears to be embarrassment at her outburst.

"I'm sorry," she says quietly stepping back and opening the door for me. As I move over the threshold, I hide my triumphant smile and move down the corridor to the living room.

Beth takes a quick detour into the bathroom, and while she's busy there, I put the kettle on the stove and dig around in her cupboard for some of her stinky herbal tea bags.

"You don't need to do that." Beth's voice startles me, and I drop the box of tea bags on the counter.

"It's fine. You like the peppermint ones, right?" I ask, picking up the box and waving it at her.

"Yes, please," she replies, settling back on the couch, snuggling under the comforter I recognize from her bed. "I watched the game; your goal was epic."

"Ah thanks, princess. It felt great to get on the score sheet after such a long dry spell," I say as I fix her tea and carry it over to the couch.

Beth giggles and sips her tea, shaking her head.

"What?" I ask, wondering what I've said that's so funny.

"Nothing. Sorry. I just got an image in my head of you at the drug store buying the tampons," Beth chuckles. And as the idea of it takes hold, she begins to laugh uncontrollably, holding her stomach and rolling onto her side.

"Yeah, yeah. Let's all laugh at the hockey player with the feminine products," I grumble, but this only makes her laugh harder, letting out little snorts as tears fill her eyes.

"Thank you so much," Beth gasps, slapping my hard thigh. "You really helped me feel better."

"Glad my embarrassment helped you out," I scoff, pulling her across the couch and tucking her into my side. I feel her body resist at first, but then she relaxes and snuggles in, resting her cheek against my dress shirt.

"Sorry I was a bitch," she murmurs into my chest, her arm snaking around my waist.

"You weren't. Don't worry. Just relax and eat your candy."

But judging by the soft snoring sounds coming from her and the way her breathing has evened out, she's already fallen asleep.

I have pins and needles in my arm, and I'm desperate for a piss, but the thought of moving and waking Beth doesn't feel right. She's been asleep on me for the last two hours, and I've watched more *Drag Race* than I care to admit to anyone. It's actually been nice to sit with her and watch her sleep—she has the cutest little snore—and every now and again her nose wrinkles up and she sighs.

I can't help but laugh to myself. I'm a twenty-one-year-old NHL player who scored the game winning goal, and instead of hitting the town with my team-mates, I'm comforting my "not girlfriend" because she has cramps. A little snorty laugh bursts out of me, and Beth moans and wriggles against my side.

"Nate?" Beth's sleepy voice causes me to turn my head away from the screen where a drag queen in a feathery costume has just performed something called a Death Drop. I look down at her and smile.

"I'm here, princess. You passed out hard." I reach over and tuck a strand of slightly greasy blonde hair behind her ear and stroke her cheek.

"Oh god, I'm so embarrassed that you've seen me like this," she moans, trying to bury herself into my side. "I'm a greasy, bloated mess."

I laugh kindly and shift my body so she can't hide behind it anymore, and I take hold of her wrists, moving her hands away from her face.

"You're always beautiful to me," I tell her sincerely, my voice deep and gravelly.

Beth gawps at me like I'm either blind or insane, nibbling on her plump bottom lip, but I can tell she appreciates the compliment even if she doesn't really believe me.

"Can I get you anything?" I ask. "More tea? Heat up that bean bag thing? Hand feed you M&Ms?"

Beth giggles and shakes her head. "I'm okay. Thanks." Suddenly she looks shy and uncertain. "Would you stay with me?" Her cool blue eyes blink up at me through her naturally long, thick lashes, and I'm a complete goner.

"Sure," I croak, clicking off the TV, rising off the couch and holding my hand out for her. Beth takes it and grabs her comforter, flicking off the lamp as she leads me down the corridor to her bedroom. I take a small detour and quickly use the bathroom because I'm beyond bursting.

When I enter her room, it's dark, but I can hear the bed springs squeak as Beth moves around. I'm not as used to her room as she is, so when I move farther in and shut the door, I bang my shin on something hard and curse loudly.

Thankfully, the room is quickly filled with a soft yellow light as Beth puts on the lamp by her bed. I glare down and see that I've walked into the chair by her dressing table. I give it a swift kick and rub my shin.

"Are you alright?" Beth asks, pulling her sweatshirt over her head to reveal a white lacy tank top. I immediately notice she's not wearing a bra, and I try to keep my eyes off her as I move closer to the bed and toe off my dress shoes. It would be completely inappropriate to pitch a tent right now.

"Yeah, I'm a big, tough hockey player." I pretend to flex my muscles and Beth laughs, sliding under the covers, pulling them up modestly over her breasts.

Shit, what do I do now? If I strip off, she might get pissed thinking I'm expecting sex. But I really don't want to sleep in my suit.

As if reading my mind Beth says, "You're not planning on sleeping in that monkey suit, are you?"

I laugh and shake my head, beginning to unbutton my shirt. "I didn't want to be presumptuous."

"I think we're past that, Nate," Beth replies, arching her perfect eyebrow at me. "Now hurry up and get into bed. I'm cold."

I release a relieved breath and quickly shuck off my clothes, leaving my black boxer briefs firmly in place, climbing into bed beside her. Beth leans over and flicks off the lamp, and I feel her slide into the crook of my arm, pressing her body against me and laying her palm on my hard abs. It feels comfortable and safe laying in her arms, but there's a part of me that worries she'll start asking those awkward questions about my past again.

9

Beth

I've had a shit few days between upsetting my parents and getting my period, but now I'm laying in the dark snuggled up to the hottest man I've ever been with. I guess things can turn on a dime. He smells fresh and woodsy from the body wash he must have used after the game, and his skin is so warm and comforting, I'm struggling to keep my eyes open. But I can feel the tension in Nate's body, and I want to know what that's all about.

"Are you okay doing this?" I ask into the dark room.

"What?" he replies.

I shift self-consciously. What *do* I mean? "Just lying here, with no prospect of sex."

Ugh, why did I start this conversation?

I feel Nate's arm tighten around my back and he gently squeezes my butt. "I'm perfectly capable of controlling myself, princess. I like spending time with you. It doesn't always have to be about sex."

His words give me a gooey feeling deep in my belly that feels nice, if not a little alien. This is not something

I've had before; all my flings have been purely sexual. Even when we'd do something like go out to dinner or a movie, sex was always the end game. With Nate, I want sex—of course I do. I mean, he's built like a Greek god, and he's got crazy amounts of stamina. But it's not just that. When we hang out, we have fun. He's sweet, funny, and attentive, and he makes me feel like I'm the most precious thing in the world.

I ponder on all this a little too long, and I think it freaks him out because he asks, "Do you want me to go?"

"No, no. I was just thinking that I've never wanted a guy to hang around when there wasn't sex involved," I say quietly.

I feel Nate move, my eyes adjusting to the dark so I can make out his shadowy features. He looks intense and serious as he reaches out, cupping my face and leaning down to gently kiss me. His lips are plump and soft; the graze of his stubble feels comforting and familiar.

"I want more than just sex with you," he confesses. "I've been thinking of nothing else since L.A. But I know how you feel about all that, and I don't want to push you."

I take a deep breath and decide to tell Nate about the confrontation I had with my parents at dinner the other day. He listens quietly, I feel him nodding, and he holds me tighter when I confess to yelling at my mom.

"They're just worried about you," he says. "It must be nice to have people look out for you like that."

Suddenly, I feel like I might be able to get Nate to open up. He seemed to shut down completely when

I asked about his family, but now he's given me an in, so I take it.

"Don't you have that?" I ask carefully, not wanting to push too hard. But even as the words come out, I feel him tense up. "You can tell me, you know."

Nate takes a deep breath and kisses my hair. "My father ..." His words falter, and I move so I'm propped up on my elbow.

"It's fine," I say quietly. "You can tell me anything." I press my palm to his chest, and I can feel his heart thrumming under my fingers.

Kissing my nose, he says, "My father's an Army Drill Sergeant, and he's not a warm, kind man. He chose to raise me like one of his recruits, and let's just say when I didn't live up to his expectations, he didn't shy away from showing me how displeased he was."

I draw in a breath at his words, and I run my fingers over his chest. "I'm sorry."

"Nah, it's fine." He shakes his head dismissively. "He'd always been a disciplinarian, but when my little brother died..."

"What?" I gasp, jerking a little at the shock of his confession.

"Yeah, I was eight, and he died at seven months. Sudden Infant Death Syndrome is what they called it. My mom had a total breakdown, and my dad became obsessed with pushing me into hockey to try to keep my mind off everything. I guess to keep himself busy as well." His voice has taken on a raspy quality that tells me he's getting choked up, and my heart just breaks for him.

"He was critical and pushy, but things became physical once I hit puberty and had a massive growth spurt. I grew seven inches and gained a hundred pounds of muscle over one summer. He started to knock me around when I backtalked or messed up in a game or practice."

I can hear the shame and anger in his voice, and my eyes sting with tears. "Oh Nate, I had no idea."

"No one did, except my mom and my best friend. Jenna and I had been friends since first grade, and as we grew up, we became close and eventually started dating. Of course, my father hated that, and we kept it secret until he finally caught on. He tolerated it for a while, but at the end of my junior year, I made a mistake that cost us the State Championship. That night he tore me a new one, so I snuck out to meet Jenna, and he found out." I feel Nate shrug. "He forbade me from seeing her again, saying that if I'd not been so focused on getting in her pants, I wouldn't have fucked up the game. That summer he sent me to hockey camp in Canada, and even though Jenna and I called and texted, she ended up meeting someone while she was staying at her parent's cabin, and we were over."

"Shit, Nate. That's not right." Now I'm pissed that a sweet, sensitive guy like him had to endure such a brutal childhood at the hands of an abusive asshole.

"It was just his way. I guess he was hurting too. Losing Max hit us all differently. He could've just checked out like my mom did…"

"That did not give him the right to abuse you!" I growl, grabbing his scruffy chin and turning his face toward mine so he can hopefully see how pissed I am.

"No. It wasn't abuse. He was tough, that's all."

Jesus, how is he still defending his father? I feel like if I keep going along this path, he's going to shut down again, so I take a different route.

"How did you feel about losing Jenna?" I feel weird asking Nate about a girl that was quite obviously his first love.

Nate sucks in a massive breath and lets out a groan. "It fucking blew. We managed to see each other a few times before I went off to camp. I was supposed to go away with her that summer, and we'd promised to ... you know ... lose our virginities to each other. So instead of it being romantic, we ended up doing it in the back seat of her car." I can hear the regret in his voice, and it kills me.

Instead of talking more, I lean over and press my lips gently to his, stroking his cheek, allowing his arms to hold me tight, crushing my breasts to his chest. Even though the kiss could turn into more, we keep it strictly PG-13, holding each other for comfort until we drift off to sleep.

Nate

The jasmine scent of Beth's neck, the soft press of her ass against my aching cock, and the dawn light filtering through the drapes coax me from sleep. Beth is snuggled into the front of my body in the fetal position, my arm draped over her hip. It feels amazing to wake up with her even after the awkwardness of my confession about my father.

I've never admitted that to anyone before, and I feel a bit lighter for it. My father and I hardly have a relationship these days. Once I headed off to college in Omaha with a full scholarship, he had very little say in my life and career. I made sure of that. Of course, he and my mom were there for my draft pick, and they came to several games, but everything is very strained and awkward with my mom working her butt off as a go between. I feel like shit a lot of the time for not seeing her as often as I should, and I'm in two minds whether to take her away somewhere in the off season. While I'm deep in thought about this, I feel Beth stir in my arms, rolling over to face me.

"Morning," she croaks in her sleepy voice, bringing her hand up to her mouth. "Sorry, I've got M&M morning breath."

I smile and reach out to move her hand, leaning forward to kiss her gently. "You taste great." I'm pleased to see a pink blush stain her cheeks as she snuggles into her pillow.

"I doubt that. I'm gonna brush my teeth," she giggles, moving to get up, but I reach out and hold her wrist. There are a few things I need to say, and I need to say them while I still have the courage.

"Beth. What I told you last night … I've never told that to anyone. No one on the team knows, and I want it to stay that way."

Beth looks at me and smiles kindly. "I promise. Anything you've told me stays between us."

Again, I feel that lightness wash over me. It's the same feeling I get when I take my hockey gear off. I almost get used to the weight of it pressing down on my body, and it becomes the norm. That is until I take it off and realize how heavy it is. It's the same with the feelings I have about my father. I didn't realize how heavy they've been weighing on me until I confessed them out loud.

"Can I take you out to lunch today?" Beth asks quietly. "To thank you for rescuing me last night?"

I release the breath I've been holding and squeeze her tightly. "That sounds great. I've got a free day, and I'd love to spend it with you."

Several hours, a shower, and a change of clothes later, Beth and I are sitting in a small family run Italian restaurant drinking Chianti and eating delicious homemade pasta. It's a really traditional place with red-checked tablecloths, melted white candles stuck in wine bottles, and hundreds of sepia-toned photos all over the walls apparently chronicling the history of the family's journey from Naples to America.

I'm thrilled to learn that Beth's mom has Italian roots and even more so when she speaks to the owner in flawless Italian. It's also sexy as hell to hear her speak another language, gesticulating wildly.

Once we're seated in a quiet booth in the back, I can't hide the goofy grin on my face.

"What?" she asks, checking out the menu.

"That was fucking sexy," I growl, leaning toward her. Beth snorts out a laugh and shakes her head.

"Don't be a dork." She pushes me in the chest. "The veal ragu is really good here."

I can tell I've embarrassed her with my compliment, so I squeeze her thigh and get back to looking at the menu.

Conversation is easy and flirty as we work our way through a big portion of pasta served family style. We share more little details about our childhoods, like the fact I wanted to be a ninja when I was six, and she was obsessed with The Backstreet Boys. Beth tells me more about her family, talking about her little sister Katie and her sporting achievements, her parents, and the fight they had when she got back from L.A.

"I still feel like such an asshole for what I said," she sighs, pushing her half-eaten meal away, completely beaten by it. To be fair, I'm struggling myself.

"I'm sure they knew you didn't mean to offend them," I reply, although I feel like a fraud trying to give her advice about how to handle disgruntled parents.

"I mean I wasn't dissing their marriage so to speak. It's more the whole institution of long-term relationships I can't get my head around."

I put my fork down and take a long drink of wine. I need to get to the bottom of this. I'm beginning to realize I'm developing some really deep feelings for this beautiful woman, and I need to know if I'm wasting my time.

"What's your bottom line?" I ask, locking eyes with her. "Do you plan to fuck your way through your twenties and thirties and then settle down when you've had enough, or do you plan to never settle down?"

Beth physically flinches at my words and reaches for her glass which is empty. I refill it and let her take a long drink, her eyebrows knotting in thought.

"I have no idea," she confesses quietly. "To be honest, I don't even think I know how to date."

Interesting.

I must admit I don't have a multitude of experiences myself. Jenna and I were only teens when we dated, so it mostly consisted of going to the movies, school dances, and messy fumbling, but I did organize a few romantic dates for us. After our relationship ended, I didn't date anyone until college, and even then, I spent so much time training and studying it never lasted. Other than a couple of deeply unsatisfying one-night stands, that was the extent of my experience.

But being with Beth feels completely different from anything I've ever had before, and I really want to explore it further. I need to find a way to do that without scaring her off. With the seed of an idea germinating in my brain, I decide to jump in with both feet.

"How about we make a little arrangement?" I ask, leaning my elbows on the table, trying to appear confident even though my heart is thundering as if I've skated two hundred feet at full speed.

Beth sips her wine and cocks a questioning eyebrow. "What kind of arrangement? Like a Pretty Woman deal?"

I laugh loudly and shake my head. "That's a random old movie reference, Grandma."

"Hey! It's a classic. I can't help that you're such a baby," she sasses. "So c'mon, what's this arrangement you want to discuss?"

Here goes.

"I want to prove to you that dating can be fun and sexy and not dull and scary," I say. "And in return, I want you to teach me more about … being intimate."

Suddenly it feels like all the air has been sucked out of the room as Beth gives me a squinty, quizzical look, her teeth worrying her plump lower lip.

"Let me get this straight," she finally replies. "You want to take me out on dates to prove that it's not the death of hot sex and romance, and in return," she lowers her voice to a throaty whisper, "you want me to teach you about fucking?"

Hearing her say it like that, it sounds ridiculous and desperate. "I guess."

Beth lets out a breathy laugh. "Baby, I don't need to teach you anything about fucking."

Jesus, those words coming from her soft, red lips make my dick swell, but I need to focus and keep blood pumping through my brain, not other places.

"That's kind of you, but I've done more with you in the few times we've slept together than I've done with anyone else, and I want more," I state firmly, holding her gaze, satisfied when I see her breath quicken and her chest rise and fall more rapidly.

"Oh," she says quietly. I watch her swallow and disappear into thought for a while. It's like the worst kind of torture waiting for her to speak, but I know I have to wait. If I speak first, I'll retract the offer, and I'm pretty sure that'll be it for us.

"Let me be clear." Thank fuck she spoke first. "You want to take me out on dates to help me get over my commitment stuff, and in return, we get to have hot, experimental sex."

I bark out a nervous laugh when an elderly couple sat at the next table look over at us.

"That's pretty much the size of it, princess."

"Explain to me how this is different from us just dating?" She asks me the question I knew she would.

"We'll put an expiration date on it." This is how I'll hook her in. "You give me five dates, and if by the end of it, you still don't agree that it can be romantic and sexy, then we can part as friends. No hard feelings."

She's working that lip again, and god help me I want to chew it so badly. "And the fucking part?" We draw the attention of the elderly couple again.

I cough and lean in to keep my words private. "We can do as much of that as you like between the first and fifth date," I growl into her ear, satisfied when I feel her shiver and see her squeeze her thighs together.

Beth pulls away and turns on the bench seat to face me, a determined expression on her angelic face. For a horrible moment, I think she's going to blow me off, but instead she sticks out her tiny hand for me to shake. "Let's do it."

I envelop her hand in mine and we shake. "Bring it on, princess. I'm gonna prove to you that dating can be just as hot as a fling."

"And I'm gonna ruin you," Beth grins wickedly, and I can't help but feel my dick punch against my zipper.

10

Beth

It's been a week, and I haven't seen Nate since our lunch date (although he made it very clear that it didn't count as one of the five, so I could forget that). The Whalers have had a manic week, travelling to the Midwest for a series of three games back-to-back, so I haven't seen Mila either.

Andre and I have been busy as well, thank goodness, because I've needed the distraction. We had several video conferences with Hector and his team about the movie, and we spent a very frustrating day reviewing resumes for makeup and hair assistants. All the candidates were either too wet behind the ears or too experienced for the money we have to offer. Maybe tomorrow will be better.

After an exhausting few days, Mila and I decide to have a roommate date to catch up; it seems like we haven't connected properly since she came back from New Orleans, and I have a feeling she's itching to talk about her new relationship.

"Do we need more parmesan?" Mila asks as we wheel our shopping cart through the dairy section of our favorite grocery store.

I laugh at the ridiculous question. "We always need more parmesan." I pick up a large wedge of delicious cheese and drop it in the cart while Mila grabs a tub of low-fat cream cheese.

"I thought I'd make my chicken parm for Matt tonight," she says, quietly perusing the yogurts.

"Reeeeally?" I smirk, cocking a brow. If I know my bestie like I think I do, she only breaks out the chicken parm for guys she's serious about. She didn't even cook it for me until our sophomore year at college.

"Yes. What's with the eyebrow?" Mila asks, her cheeks blushing red to match her hair.

"I know what the chicken parm means. You loooooooovvvvvve him," I tease, tickling her ribs so she squirms away from me and slaps at my hands. But then I see the expression on her face, and all the teasing stops.

Shit, she really does love him.

"Seriously though Mils, we haven't talked about what happened. I assume from all the sex you've having that you made up. But what about that chick from Chicago and the baby? How did he explain that?" I ask. I need to be sure my girl isn't putting her heart at risk again.

"It's not what I thought," Mila reassures me as we wander down the aisle. "It was a scam, and when he blew her off, she hooked up with one of his ex-team-mates. She decided to contact him while she was in town with the Rush, and apparently thought I was his assistant who had a crush on him. It was a whole, big, fucked up mess, but I believe him. Bugs told me Matt confessed the whole pretend baby scam to him earlier in the season."

"And you're happy?" I ask quietly, examining a cantaloupe way too carefully.

Mila reaches over and takes the melon out of my hands, placing it back on the pile, looking deeply into my eyes, and I can see everything I need to know. "I love him so much, Bee. I really do. And we're happy, so please be happy for us."

I lean over and kiss her cheek hard. "I am, honey. I really am."

We continue to wander around the grocery store, getting the ingredients for the chicken parm along with other things we need for the apartment.

As we stand at the checkout, my phone buzzes in my back pocket. It's Nate, and I can't help but feel my stomach flip a little when his picture fills my screen. It's a snap I took in L.A. while we were in bed–he's lying on his back with his arm behind his head, his biceps bulging, that sexy smile and ruffled hair on full display. If I remember rightly, I was straddling his stomach at the time, and shortly after this picture was taken, I impaled myself on his hard cock and rode us both to an amazing, sweaty climax.

"You gonna answer that?" the surly woman at the checkout asks me as I feel my cheeks redden at the memory.

"Yeah. Sorry." I move away from the checkout while Mila pays for the groceries.

"Hey, princess." God, even his voice makes my stomach flip. "What're you doing today?"

"I'm out with Mila. We're having a roommate date."

"That explains why Matt's wandering around the gym like a lost puppy," he laughs, and I hear a loud, grumbling voice in the background I can only assume is Matt's denial.

"What can I do for you, Nate?" I ask as Mila walks toward me, pushing the shopping cart.

"I want to discuss our first date," he growls in his sexy, deep voice which I feel everywhere.

"What did you have in mind?" I reply, pressing my key fob so Mila can load the groceries into the trunk. I feel like a douche not helping, but this is a particularly important call.

"Hopefully, when you get home, there'll be a little something waiting for you. That should explain everything."

Oh, very mysterious.

"You don't have plans for tomorrow night, do you?" he asks, and I can hear the smile in his voice.

I think for a moment. "No, but I'm assuming you do. Don't you have a game?"

"Yes, but you're free?"

I smile at the thought of seeing Nate. "Yes, I'm free," I reply in a throaty voice, already feeling turned on at the prospect of being with him.

"Great, see you tomorrow, princess. I can't wait." With that, I hear some yelling in the background. "Alright man, I'm coming!" And he's gone.

I get into the car beside Mila, and when I look over, she's got a massive mischievous grin on her face, her eyes twinkling.

"Who was that?" she asks, giving me her best innocent face.

"Nate," I say, eyeing her suspiciously. "He wanted to set up a date for tomorrow."

"Really? So is this the first 'date,'" Mila giggles, using air quotes. I told her about our little arrangement.

"Yes, but I'm slightly confused because he said it's tomorrow, and the team has a game, right?" I start the car and pull out onto the street.

"We do," Mila says, smirking.

I snap my head quickly in her direction. "Why are you being so cagey? You know what he's got planned, don't you?"

Mila laughs and holds up her hands. "I'm just acting as a delivery person. You'll see when we get home."

"You brat," I curse. Hating myself slightly, I press my foot down harder on the accelerator, and my sky-blue VW bug lurches forward as Mila laughs loudly next to me.

Mila makes me wait until we unpack and put away the groceries before she disappears into her room and returns with a large flat box wrapped in a navy and gold ribbon. She lays it on the table with a flourish and a "ta daaaaaa!"

I eye the box suspiciously and turn to Mila for answers. "Just open the box, Bee. Nate said everything you need for tomorrow night is in there." She smirks and turns toward her room. "He also said there are a few personal items in there, so I'll give you some privacy."

When I hear Mila's door close, I approach the box as if it's a bomb and reach out to flick the big loopy bow on top. Those are the Whalers team colors, so I have a horrible feeling he's going to want me to go ice skating or something.

Fuck it. Bring it on Nate. Do your worst.

Quickly, I pull off the ribbons and slide the lid off the box. When I get a peek at the contents, my stomach rolls, and I begin to sweat.

That bastard!

I run my fingers over the Halsted and the 17 on the back of the jersey, my pulse thrumming in my neck. He can't expect me to wear this. I remember when Mila lost a bet with Matt and he made her wear his jersey for the entire season. Of course, now that they're an item she's totally down with it.

Huffing out an exasperated breath, I pull the jersey out of the box and hold it up against me—it's fucking massive and will totally drown me, but I can't help but feel a tiny thrill. It's like Nate's marking me as his, and I don't hate the thought.

Underneath the jersey are a few more items—an envelope with my name on it and a small black velvet bag with a drawstring and a gold tassel. I leave the envelope because the bag intrigues me more. When I pick it up, it has some weight to it, so I pull the tassel and peek inside.

Oh boy! I feel everything south of my belly button clench as I reach inside and remove the smooth glass object. I hold it in the palm of my hand, knowing exactly what it is. Who knew innocent Nate Halsted would send me a butt plug! And not even a beginner level one.

Holy shit.

My entire center is on fire at the thought of him using this on me. I feel something else in the bag, so I reach in again a little cautiously and pull out a small bottle of lube. That makes me laugh loudly. At least he's properly prepared.

I guess I should open the envelope and find out what this date will include besides jerseys, butt plugs, and lube. Inside I find a ticket for tomorrow's game, an All-Access pass on a Whalers lanyard, and a hand-written note in Nate's scruffy script.

Beth,

Our first date will be on my turf. I want you in the stands when I play. And better yet, I need you marked with my name and number—one great thing about a relationship is the feeling of belonging to someone. I hope you'll feel that when you wear the jersey.

The other stuff is for after the game—consider it a little bonus.

I'll be looking for you tomorrow night.

N x

Oh wow. The fluttery feeling in my chest is out of control, and I have the urge to rub between my breasts to ease it. What the hell is that? Is it excitement? Nerves? I guess I'll find out tomorrow night.

Nate

I usually feel a nervous churning in my gut before a game, but tonight it seems magnified. I go about my game day rituals like normal—work out, morning skate, team lunch, home for a nap then back to the arena for the team briefing and warmups. I put some time in on the bike and kick a soccer ball around with my line.

I sit in front of my cubby lacing up my skates while the rest of the team dick about and get pumped up for the game. It's the home leg against the Tampa Tiger Sharks, and if we win this, it'll pretty much guarantee our playoff spot, so there's a lot riding on tonight.

"You're quiet, kid." Matt sits next to me and slaps my shoulder. "Everything alright?"

I huff out a breath and nod. "Yeah, all good. Just in my head a bit tonight. It's a big game."

"No shit," he laughs, pulling his jersey over his pads. "Listen, Mila filled me in on what she helped you with, and I think it's great."

I turn to him. "Sounds like there's a 'but' coming."

"Just keep your head in the game. I know what it's like to have the object of your desire sitting at center ice. It can be distracting if you let it," he advises.

"How do you deal with Mila being there for every game?" I ask.

"I know she's there to support me, so I take power from it. It makes me do everything harder, faster, and better because she loves me." Matt gets a stupid soppy expression on his face and I can see how much he loves her.

"I won't let her distract me," I state firmly, pulling extra hard on my laces.

"Good man!" He slaps me on the back again and returns to his side of the locker room to discuss something with Bugs.

I love the smell of the ice and the noise that pulses above us—feet stomping, hands clapping as the MC announces the teams. I make my way along the tunnel toward Bugs and Matt who gives each of us a body check and a high five as we pass and skate out onto the ice.

As usual, I hit the ice at full speed and zoom around our end for the warmup. The lights are flashing blue and yellow, and the music is pumping as we all get in a few laps before we stop for the anthems and the rest of the pre-game stuff.

I know exactly where Beth will be sitting—in the team family seating just to the right of the penalty box at center ice. Every player has a pair of tickets for each home game, and I never use mine, usually giving them away to Will Call or other players who have family visiting. But tonight, I know that Beth will be sitting in the front row, wearing my jersey.

I make my approach to where she'll be and slow down, my eyes scanning the front row, searching for the platinum blonde hair and blue eyes. When I spot her, I plow to a stop, and her eyes open impossibly wide as I tower in front of her. The people around her bang on the glass as our eyes lock, and I pop out my mouth guard so I can give her my best smile.

She smiles back at me and turns around so I can see the back of her jersey, and I swear to god if I could get a boner in the cup I'm wearing, I would. When she turns back, she's got a massive cheeky grin on her face, and there's something in her hand.

Holy fuck, it's the black velvet bag from the high-end sex shop. She brought the fucking butt plug to the game! I feel my cheeks heat, and I push my mouth guard back in, winking and skating away, shaking my head. When I glance back over my shoulder, I see Beth laughing and waving the bag at me provocatively.

This is going to be a long game.

And hopefully an even longer night.

11

Beth

I leap out of my seat as the red light behind the goal illuminates, and the Whalers crowd screams at the officials for some sort of infraction. The Tampa players are trying to celebrate, but there's a scuffle in the goal mouth between Thor and a few members of the other team, there's lots of pushing and shoving, and I'm not sure what's going on.

I see Nate powering up the ice toward the fray, and just before he slams into the first Tampa player he encounters, he throws his gloves off and grabs a handful of his white and teal jersey. I gasp and press myself against the glass trying to see what's happening.

But it's absolute chaos on the ice; everyone's fighting, the fans are screaming and hammering on the glass, and I'm trying my best to keep an eye on Nate. My adrenaline spikes as I see him wrestling with the Tampa player. His fist draws back repeatedly as he punches the guy in the side of the head, his chest, anywhere he can land a hit. The Tampa player manages to get one or two shots to Nate's face before they fall to the ice, and an official skates over to break it up.

Across the ice, I see the Coaches yelling at each other as well, and once the fighting on the ice is under control, the officials retire to watch video footage of the goal to decide if it's good or not. I spot Nate skating over to the bench where he gets treatment for a cut above his eye, and the blood gets cleaned off the ice.

Jesus, I know this happens, and I've watched enough games on TV, but being here and seeing it live, especially when someone you care about is involved, it's totally different. I don't know how Mila does it time after time. I'm a huge ball of anxiety and adrenaline.

Finally, the officials come back and announce that there was goaltender interference so the goal is no good. Thank fuck for that! The home fans go nuts, and I randomly hug the woman standing next to me in celebration. The Whalers have held onto their one goal lead, for now.

I get a text from Mila during the last TV break telling me to use the pass that came with my ticket to come back to the family room and wait for Nate there. The team manages to hold onto their one goal lead, and as the horn sounds to signal the end of the game, the players converge at center ice to celebrate the win and the likelihood this will lead them to the playoffs. It's amazing to see the dynamic they have as a team, and Nate is a big part of that. Perhaps that's what he meant when he said it felt great to belong to someone. He knows for a fact these guys have his back; he can count on them completely. He might be onto something.

With this thought in my mind, I make my way through the crowds to the family area, showing my pass to various burly security guards and clutching my purse. I've suddenly got a horrible feeling I'll be searched, and they'll find the butt plug and lube, but once I've shown my pass, they let me through.

The family room is already busy with wives, girl-friends, and kids running around. There's a bar and a buffet table set up with mountains of food, but I feel like a total imposter, so I just hide in a corner until I spot Mila looking for me.

"Oh, thank god," I breathe, grasping her hands. "I thought for sure someone was gonna throw me out of here."

Mila laughs and squeezes my hands. "Nate's been chosen to do press tonight, so he's gonna be another hour or so. He asked me to give you his address and his door code so you can go and wait for him there." She reaches for her phone and mine pings with an incoming text which contains the information I need.

"Okay, no problem," I reply, fidgeting in my jersey. It feels weird that Nate trusts me to go to his house when I've never been there before. "I guess I'll go then."

"He's really gutted he can't come straight out, Bee. I promise he'll only be about an hour." She leans over and kisses my cheek before disappearing back out the door to finish up her duties as the Head Coach's assistant.

The drive to Nate's apartment doesn't take me long, and once I type in the code to get into his underground garage, I park in the space he specified and head to the elevator. I use another code to get it to move and another to get into his apartment on the twentieth floor.

I'm nervous as I enter his private space, but once I turn on the light, I'm more at ease. The apartment is like an embodiment of Nate—it's warm, comfortable, and seems more like a college dorm than the home of a guy who earns millions of dollars a year. It's all open plan with a kitchen area directly to the left and to the right the living area with a huge brown leather sectional couch, a massive TV on the wall, and a tangle of games consoles and controllers underneath it. In the far corner, there's a bench press and a treadmill and a corridor which I guess leads toward the bedrooms.

It's tidy and clean, but I can tell immediately that a young guy lives here. There's a pile of sports and car magazines on the coffee table, dirty plates and cups in the sink, and a selection of hoodies and workout gear draped over the back of the couch.

Nervously, I have a bit of a snoop. His fridge is full of pre-made meals which Mila tells me a lot of the guys have. There are a couple of bottles of light beer and a few bottles of water, but no other food. I suddenly wish I'd taken advantage of the buffet in the family room as my stomach grumbles. The dirty dishes in the sink agitate me, so I quickly put them in the dishwasher and move into the rest of the apartment. As I suspected, there are no family photos scattered around which immediately makes me sad, but I completely understand why. I smirk to myself when I find a girlie mag under the pile of sports magazines on the coffee table. I have no problem with porn if it's not too weird, extreme, or illegal. Perhaps we can look at it together later.

Next, I make my way down the corridor toward the bedrooms. The first door I try opens into a room full of boxes, so I shut it and move on. Further along, I find a large family bathroom that doesn't seem to have ever been used, but it houses an enormous whirlpool tub which I might make use of later. Finally, I open the door at the end of the corridor and find Nate's bedroom which has the same dorm feel as the rest of the apartment. He has a few framed game jerseys on the wall and another massive TV with more game consoles attached. It's decorated in soft greys and whites with a gigantic California king-sized bed. I guess when you're as big as Nate you need a bed that size. I suddenly feel guilty for the times he's squeezed himself into my normal queen-sized bed.

I wander into his bathroom and poke about, smelling his body wash and cologne, folding up the towel he's left lying on the floor. I giggle to myself for tidying up. If Nate's trying to prove to me that dating isn't boring and domestic, then so far he's failing.

"I didn't take you for a snoop."

I yelp in surprise as Nate's deep voice interrupts my thoughts. I spin around and drop the towel, finding him leaning against the bathroom door frame in his game day suit minus the jacket, that cute, cocky smirk on his handsome face. It's then I notice the black eye and the steri-strips holding the skin together above his eyebrow.

Fuck me, that's a hot look on him.

"I wasn't snooping. I was tidying," I reply, hanging the damp towel on the heated rail. "And if I'm honest, I didn't expect to have to do that on my first 'romantic' date."

Nate chuckles and shakes his head. "That part of the date is over now. Didn't you find it romantic watching me beat the shit out of that guy?"

I laugh and walk toward him, gently bringing my fingers to his injured face. "It wasn't romantic at all," I whisper.

"Oh," Nate murmurs, leaning his face into my touch. "It wasn't?"

"No. It was hot. It was so hot, I considered going to the bathroom to rub one out during the intermission," I tell him in a breathy voice. I see his eyes go wide, then become hooded and dangerous.

"Fuck," he growls pulling me toward him. "When I saw in you in my jersey, waving that fucking butt plug around, I seriously thought my dick was gonna bust right through my cup."

I press my hips into him and feel how hard he is for me, gazing up into his eyes, trying desperately to keep my cool.

"I guess we've moved on from the 'romantic' portion of the date to the hot, experimental sex part?" I ask, reaching up and loosening his blue silk tie.

"Damn right we are." Before I can say or do anything else, his lips crash down onto mine, and I'm lifted by his strong arms, our tongues sliding together, his huge hands cupping my ass. I wrap my legs around his waist, and he carries me over to the bed where he deposits me. "Where's your purse?"

"On the kitchen counter," I gasp, nibbling my lip.

"I'm gonna get it, and by the time I come back, I want you naked and on your hands and knees," he commands in a throaty growl.

Fuck.

I nod my agreement because there are no words. I watch him leave the room, unbuttoning his shirt cuffs as he goes. More quickly than I've ever moved in my life, I leap off the bed and undress, flinging everything onto a chair. I peer down at myself, and the cute lingerie I chose for tonight, feeling a little sad Nate won't discover it as he slowly undresses me. But hell, this is good too, so I unhook my bra and slide my panties down my legs, taking up the desired position on the bed.

Jesus, in this position, I can feel the cool air on my hot, wet pussy, and I guess I should be embarrassed at how aroused I am. But fuck it, why should I be? I'm about to have very hot sex with a gorgeous man—I dare any woman not to gush like a fountain at the prospect.

"Oh my god," Nate groans as he re-enters the room. I peek over my shoulder and take great joy in the massive tent that's formed at the front of his dress pants. He holds the black velvet bag in one hand, and with the other, he rubs the bulge in his pants.

"Is this what you wanted?" I ask in a sultry voice, cocking my eyebrow.

"Fuck yeah," he breathes, throwing the bag on the bed beside me and quickly ripping his own clothes off, dumping them on top of mine.

"What do you intend to do with the contents of that bag, Mr. Halsted?" I ask quietly as I feel Nate's weight make the bed dip and his hands smooth the skin of my ass.

I hear him chuckle and slide his fingers between my legs to check my arousal. "Oh princess, you were right. You got pretty turned on by that fight, didn't you?" He spreads his thick, calloused fingers through my wetness and moans when he encounters my piercing. "I keep forgetting you've got this."

I groan loudly as he begins to massage my hard clit, bowing my back so my ass pushes higher into the air, uttering moans and curses as my body responds to his touch. I get a little frantic as I feel a climax building, humping against Nate's hand as he slides two fingers deep inside me.

"Oh shit," I gasp as he crooks his fingers against my inner wall, and I come hard all over his hand. My thighs quiver with the release, and I throb deep inside.

"I never get tired of making you come," Nate whispers, giving my butt a slap and reaching for the velvet bag.

Suddenly, my slowing heart rate speeds up again at the prospect of Nate using the contents of that bag on me.

"Do you know what to do with that stuff?" I ask, looking back over my shoulder.

Nate laughs good-naturedly. "I've watched enough porn, baby, so I think I can figure it out."

"Okay, one piece of advice," I say quickly because I have a little experience with ass play, and I've learned a few painful lessons over the years. "If you think you've used enough lube, then always use a bit more!"

"Sure thing, princess," he replies, and I hear the snap of the bottle opening and the cool drizzle of lube between my butt cheeks. Oh boy, this is going to be intense.

As Nate spreads the lube around my pleats, I feel like he's becoming unsure of himself, so I offer him a few more pearls of wisdom. This was our deal after all.

"Slide the tip of your finger around and then gently press inside."

He does as instructed, and I groan loudly when his finger breaches the tight ring of muscle.

"Okay?" he asks in a tight voice.

"Oh god yes!" I sigh as he works his finger in and out of my ass. I let him work me over that way for a while, then talk him through inserting the plug.

The cool feel of the smooth glass replacing Nate's finger feels unbelievable, and I lower myself onto my elbows because my arms are shaking so badly. He continues to push the plug into my ass until it's past the widest point and is seated in place.

"Fuck, Beth. That's the hottest damn thing I've ever seen," Nate groans. "Does it feel good?"

"It feels amazing. Maybe we can try it on you next time?" I giggle, loving the expression of terror on Nate's face. "Relax cowboy, you're not ready for that yet."

"So, do I just fuck you now?" he asks.

"You'd better. I'm about to blow any minute," I moan, desperate for the full feeling I know I'm about to experience.

I hear the foil rip and Nate's deep moan as he suits up. "Will I feel it once I'm inside you?"

"You'll see," I reply, not wanting to give away the surprise.

Nate's hands go to my hips, and he holds me firmly, the pressure of his hard cock pressing into my aching pussy is almost too much. God, I want him inside me so badly. I push myself back, and he slips inside an inch.

"Oh, Jesus!" Nate gasps as he pushes in farther. "It's so tight, baby. I can feel everything."

"Me too. Me too," I gasp as he pushes himself fully inside me and holds still for a moment.

Slowly, I feel Nate move in and out of me, my pussy gripping him tightly as we slide together, his rough hands gripping my hips so tightly I'm sure he'll leave marks.

"I need to see you come, princess," Nate moans, and suddenly I'm being flipped onto my back, his cock plunging back inside me, hitting me so deep my eyes roll back in my head. I wrap my legs tightly around his back and lock my ankles, feeling him pump in and out relentlessly.

My fingers clutch onto his muscular shoulders as we ride the wave to orgasm, Nate grunting loudly into my neck as I feel mine ripple through me.

"I'm coming, Nate! I'm coming!" I cry, every part of my pussy and ass clenching and throbbing around him and the plug, my toes curling so hard I think they might break off.

"Holy shit! That's it," Nate growls, and he thrusts twice more inside me, straining and groaning his release, his eyes on me the entire time. Just this simple act of eye contact causes me to come again, and I cry out in shock.

Wow!

As we come down from our mutual high, I realize five dates might not be enough. I could totally get used to this.

12

Nate

I t's virtually impossible to concentrate at the team debrief. Coach is talking us through the disallowed goal from the Tampa game, but all I can think about is Beth and how she rode me reverse cowgirl this morning.

We made use of the butt plug again, and as she rode me, her curvy hips pumping back and forth, I tapped the plug as per her instructions. I bent my knees so she could rest her chest against them, leaning forward as she came so I could pull the plug out, making her squeal and come in a hot gush all over my balls.

I feel my cock swell in my athletic shorts, and I shift uncomfortably, trying to discreetly adjust myself. I'm sitting next to Matt in the auditorium style seating, and judging by the elbow I get to my ribs, he's seen my maneuver.

"Stop playing with your dick, kid. Coach is talking about our journey to the Cup," he growls in my ear. "Pay attention."

"Sorry," I mumble, trying to focus with every fiber of my being. Now is not the time for sexy flashbacks about Beth or to be thinking about what to do for our next date.

The rest of the meeting has my full attention, and by the end, I'm as pumped as the rest of the guys for our journey to the playoffs. When Coach dismisses us, our line hangs around to review our plays on the big screen, and Bugs points out the wins and the things to tighten up on. It feels good to work on this as a solid, cohesive group, and it's so different from the experiences I had as a teen: my father shaming and berating me but never offering me any constructive steps forward. This is what being part of a team should feel like.

"You seem distracted, man." Matt's voice jolts me out of my daydream.

I notice that the others have already left the auditorium, and it's just the two of us left.

"Sorry, just thinking about the weakness in my saucer pass," I mutter, hauling my large frame from the cramped seating.

"I call bullshit," Matt chuckles. "How'd last night go? I saw Beth in the family area. When I skated past her while you were on your breakaway, she was screaming her fucking head off."

I laugh and shake my head. "She's definitely a pistol." I smile, warming at the thought of her getting all worked up.

"You really like her, huh?"

We walk together down the corridor toward the players' lounge, and I feel comfortable talking to Matt about my feelings for Beth. He's newly in love, so of all the guys on my line, he's the one who'll understand the most.

"Yeah, I really do. I hope I can make her see the benefits of being committed to someone before the end of our arrangement," I reply.

"If anyone can tame that one, it's you." He slaps my shoulder. "Mila's convinced Beth wants nothing more than a happy relationship, but she's got some fucked up ideas. Just keep plugging away. You'll get there."

A loud barking laugh explodes out of me before I can stop it. If he only knew how much Beth and I had "plugged" away last night, he'd understand my sudden outburst.

I shake off the laughter and ignore Matt's quizzical look. "What're your plans for today?"

"Actually, if you're free, do you wanna come and help me with something?" he asks, seeming a little embarrassed to be making this request of me.

"As long as you don't want me to hold your hand at the proctologist, then I'm down," I chuckle.

"Fucking dick!" He punches my arm, and we head into the lounge for lunch.

After a frustrating bumper to bumper hour in Seattle traffic, we're cruising out of the city in Matt's sick Mustang. He recently had all his cars and motorbikes shipped out from Chicago, and Bugs kindly let him keep them at his place. The roar and rumble of the engine is awesome, and when he opens it up, I even feel it rattling through my teeth.

"Do I dare ask where we're going?" I ask as we drive deeper and deeper into the boonies.

"I want a second opinion on something," he replies, slowing down and turning into what appears to be a dirt track. He drives down it for about a half mile, tall fir trees screening my view of anything.

Eventually, we round a curve in the track, and a huge house comes into view. It's made of redwood, stone, and glass with balconies on the ground and first floor, tall stone chimneys and Puget Sound glistening in the background.

"Wow, man. This is amazing," I say as we get out of the car and what I assume is the realtor approaches us. He's a slick, suited douche with dollar signs in his eyes when he sees the pair of NHL players striding toward him.

Once he's simpered and fawned all over us, he leads us up onto the porch and unlocks the large double doors, presenting the foyer with a flourish. As we walk around, he rambles on about architects and the history of the house, the benefits and some of the things that will probably need modernizing.

Matt listens carefully, asking questions about the land and the ability to extend or add outbuildings. It's all a bit scary and grown up for me. Even though I have the funds to buy this place as well, the thought of owning a property at my age is a step too far. I'm happy to rent for now, especially in my position at the club. I could be traded at any point, so I don't feel like investing in a place until I'm more secure.

"So, what do you think?"

I spin around from gazing out of the massive bi-fold glass doors that open out onto the Sound to find Matt behind me. The realtor seems to have disappeared into the chef's kitchen to take a call.

"It's fucking amazing, dude. Seriously, you're thinking of buying it?" I ask.

Matt rubs the back of his neck and shoves his hand into his jeans pocket, seeming a little unsure.

"Is it too much?"

"No, man. You're cramped up in that apartment. You want the space, so I say go for it. It's a killer location." I pick my next words carefully. "Mila'll love it."

Matt looks up at me, and I see something in his face—is he pissed at me for saying that? His blue eyes fix on mine, and I feel like I'm about to get my ass kicked. But instead, he kind of slumps, his broad shoulders sagging in relief.

"You think so?" he asks.

"Yeah, totally." I feel a bit awkward having this conversation with him, so I shove my hands in my pockets and shuffle around. We're guys; this is all a bit deep.

He nods, seeming satisfied with my embarrassed encouragement, and without further conversation, he heads off to find the realtor. I wander around the main room and stand in front of the huge stone fireplace and chimney that soars up into the vaulted ceiling. What must it feel like to be at the stage in your relationship where you're thinking about moving in together? I can barely get Beth to agree to five dates with me, let alone anything as serious as that.

I need to start working on the next date. I have a few ideas, but we're heading to the east coast tomorrow for a three-game series, so I'll use the long flight to do some research.

Beth

I hate fashion shows. It's all rushed and manic—designers screaming, models pouting, and slinking around—and I feel like I can't catch my breath, let alone go to the bathroom or eat something.

Andre and I have been in New York for three days, working for a couple of designers at New York Fashion Week. It was a bit of a last-minute gig for us, but I wasn't about to turn it down because the designer is an ex of Andre's, and even though they broke up years ago, they've remained great friends. The hair and makeup stylists he'd booked fell through, so he called in a favor and flew Andre and me across the country at the last minute to help him out. I didn't even have time to tell my parents, Mila, or Nate what was happening, so I sent them all garbled text messages as we rushed to board our flight to New York.

It was only supposed to be for a day or two, but word got around, and the other designers who'd been let down by the same stylists snapped us up. It felt great to get our names out there and make some important connections, but now it's been three days of little to no sleep, and I'm working my way through this last show like a zombie.

"I hope all the makeup you're using is vegan," the raven-haired skeleton sitting in my chair whines as she sucks coconut water through a paper straw.

I gaze at her reflection in the mirror, my jaw hanging open. She stares back, her sunken cheeks and huge eyes making her look like a comic book character.

"Huh?" I ask, totally exhausted and so not in the mood for her shit.

She rolls her eyes and sucks on her straw one more time. "I hope all your products are vegan and humanely tested," she repeats slowly, as if talking to a small, incompetent child.

I take a deep breath, holding in the burning desire to dump her stupid hipster drink all over her head.

"All my makeup has no animal products and is humanely tested. I promise," I say through gritted teeth, tipping some cleanser onto a cotton pad and sweeping it over her slightly greasy skin.

I can see Andre out of the corner of my eye, looking over at me with a worried expression. He knows the warning signs that I'm getting pissed—the sleep deprivation, my hangriness, and the stupid fucking model with her inane questions are all set to make me blow.

Just as I'm massaging primer into her face, my phone pings in my back pocket, so after wiping my fingers, I open the message and smile broadly.

[NATE: We won! Fuck the Bulldogs! I'm gutted you couldn't make it. Need to see you. We're free tomorrow. Are you?]

The Whalers are in town as well, playing both New York teams back-to-back last night and tonight and the New Jersey Raiders the day after tomorrow. It's been impossible to hook up with him between my crazy schedule and his practices, public appearances, and games.

[BETH: I need to see you too, but I'm stuck here until at least one. Free tomorrow. I'll call you in the morning. We can meet for brunch.]

"Erm, are you gonna make me up or what?" the model snarks, wiggling her stick-like fingers in my face.

I hit send on the text and lock my phone as aggressively as possible, shoving it back in my pocket.

"Sure thing," I say sarcastically, reaching for the foundation and getting to work.

"Please don't ever ask me to do you a favor again," I moan as Andre and I climb into the Uber, totally exhausted. He laughs without humor and just nods his head.

My feet are covered in blisters, my hands are sore, and my fingers keep cramping up. Andre's just as wasted as me. Because he's so tall, his back suffers when he's stooped over all day, and I can only imagine how much pain he's in.

We don't talk as the Uber weaves its way through the late night Manhattan traffic. I love New York, and

I usually thrive on the hustle, but tonight I just want to take a long, hot bath and drink a mojito. I rest my head on Andre's shoulder, and he pats my hand lovingly, making me wince slightly.

Thankfully, our hotel isn't far uptown. Before we can sink into unconsciousness, the car pulls up in front, and we crawl out, getting our rolling cases of equipment from the trunk and trudging up to the revolving doors.

"Oh my!" Andre gasps as we enter the lobby, his hand fluttering at his throat.

"What?" I stare over at him to see his mouth hanging open.

"I'm not sure you'll be getting much sleep tonight," he smirks, cocking his head.

I scan the lobby, and finally my eyes settle on the tall, broad, impossibly handsome hockey player leaning against a pillar. He's in his game day suit, Tom Ford unless I'm mistaken, the navy material hugging his chest, biceps, and thighs in the most delicious way. In his hands, he holds a bunch of gerbera flowers in every color of the rainbow and a massive bag of peanut M&Ms.

Suddenly, my blistered feet and sore fingers are forgotten, and my heart flips in my chest.

"Have fun sweetie. This is my gift to you for helping me out." Andre leans down and kisses my cheek, swatting my butt so I move across the lobby toward Nate. I notice him give Andre a nod and a smile as he passes by toward the elevators, and I realize Nate's recruited another of my friends into his scheme to win me over.

"What's all this?" I ask, slightly breathlessly, looking up into his beautiful blue eyes, the left one slightly marred by another new bruise.

"You sounded super stressed, so I thought I'd come over and help you… relax." He cocks his eyebrow and stares at me with a hungry expression.

"That's so sweet, but right now I want to eat a massive greasy burger and an ice cream sundae, have a bath, and go to sleep." I feel terrible for saying this after he took the time to come to my hotel in the middle of the night to surprise me, but I've got to be real with him.

Instead of disappointment, he smiles warmly and hands me the flowers and candy, taking my rolling case and leading me toward the elevators.

"Did you hear me, Nate? I'm tired," I whine, following him reluctantly.

"I hear you, princess. Just follow me," he instructs, stepping into the awaiting elevator and hitting the button for the floor he wants.

"I'm on eleven," I say wearily, leaning against the mirrored wall, closing my eyes.

"Not anymore," he states with a knowing smile.

I don't even have the strength to argue with him, so I just ride the elevator up and try to stay awake long enough to find out what he's up to.

13

Nate

The expression on Beth's face when she sees me in the lobby of her hotel is priceless, a mixture of confusion, exhaustion, and arousal. It's one of my favorite looks on her.

Ever since she texted me that she had to go to New York unexpectedly for work, I knew that I wanted to set our next date there. It's been a hell of a lot of work and texting back and forth with Andre to get this far, but I'm confident this is going to be incredible.

Armed with all the essential information, I arrived at her hotel and had her things moved to the suite I've booked her for the rest of her stay. When Andre dropped me a text that they were on their way, I had the food and drinks ordered, finished the preparations in the bathroom, and headed down to the lobby.

We ride the elevator up to the suite, Beth leaning against the wall barely able to keep her eyes open. The dark circles under her eyes show through her makeup and her signature red lipstick is long gone, but she's still totally amazing. As I feel the elevator slow on the approach to our floor, I move toward her and scoop her into my arms, the flowers and candy still grasped in her small hand, the other curving round my neck, heating my skin.

It's a bit of a struggle getting Beth and her case out of the elevator before the doors close, but I manage it, carrying her down the corridor to our suite.

"Just putting you down, princess. Can you stand while I unlock the door?" I whisper into her ear.

She mumbles her agreement, so I put her down and lean her against the wall while I put the key card to the lock and prop the door open with her case.

"Up we go, baby." I scoop her up again and carry her over the threshold of the room—images of her in a white dress and me in a tuxedo flash through my mind—but I shake them off.

Pump the brakes, Halsted.

Once Beth and her case are safely in the room, I put her down on the bed and kneel in front of her, her sleepy blue eyes opening and closing heavily. God, she's adorable like this. Don't get me wrong: I love the sassy, strong woman that Beth is most of the time, but I also love her rarely seen vulnerable side.

"Are you ready for your bath?" I ask her gently, cupping her face in my hands and kissing her softly.

"That would be nice," she slurs, sounding almost drunk with tiredness.

"I'm gonna undress you." I stand and take off my jacket and tie, rolling up my shirt sleeves.

Beth just nods and lifts her arms so I can pull her T-shirt over her head, her hair falling out of the loose ponytail, draping over her shoulders. Next, I unhook her bra, trying desperately not to get a boner when her glorious, ripe tits are revealed.

Fuck, her nipples are so pink and delectable I feel my mouth fill with saliva at the thought of taking them between my lips. Trying to keep a handle on my arousal, I get Beth to stand and lean on my shoulders so I can pull her heeled boots and socks off, quickly followed by her leggings and panties.

Kneeling in front of her as she sways sleepily, I'm powerless to stop myself pressing my lips to her mound, covering it in wet, tickling kisses. I hear Beth giggle, and she squirms against my lips, running her fingers into my hair, ruffling it into a mess.

My cock presses painfully against the inside of my zipper, and I know I need to stop kissing her pussy or else she'll never get in the tub. So, I rise and unbutton the first few buttons of my shirt, reaching behind me to pull it over my head. Then I pick Beth up again and carry her into the bathroom, her naked body warm against my chest.

"Oh wow," she whispers as we enter the bathroom that I spent an hour setting up. The room is bathed in the soft glow of dozens of candles, and the scent of jasmine wafts up from the hot water in the tub.

"Thought you could use this, princess," I say, lowering her so she's standing on the thick, fluffy mat. She seems a little more awake now, looking around at the candles, the small table set up next to the bath that holds a bottle of beer, a mojito, and a large silver dome covering our food.

I quickly strip off my remaining clothes and climb into the tub, reaching out to help Beth in, both of us sinking into the hot, scented water. I lean back, and she sits down between my muscular thighs, lying on my chest as the comforting heat cocoons us. She exhales a massive sigh and reaches her arm out toward the table.

"Drink please," she says, sounding more with it. I reach over and grab her cocktail as well as my beer, clinking our glasses together. "I suppose I can thank Andre for this little surprise?"

I laugh quietly, trying not to jiggle her against my chest. "He gave up certain information that I needed."

Beth takes a long draw on her drink and makes a happy noise, setting the glass on the edge of the tub. Carefully, she rolls over so she's laying on top of me, my half hard cock slipping between her thighs. Her eyes lock on mine. They're soft and open, and I have a feeling this is a really important moment for us.

"This is, hands down, the nicest thing anyone has ever done for me," Beth whispers, her eyes glistening with emotion. She presses her palms to the bottom of the tub by my hips so she can lift her body up and brush her lips against my neck, my body breaking out in goosebumps despite the heat of the water. My cock goes from half hard to full mast in a matter of seconds, and I feel Beth shift, scissoring her thighs to massage it against her pussy.

Oh Jesus, I'm going to bust a nut if she keeps this up.

Her soft, pouty lips continue to explore the skin of my neck, nuzzling and licking while my hands hold her ass, helping her rhythmic movement against me. The feeling of her slippery breasts and hot pussy are too much. I have to have her.

"Baby, I need to get a condom," I groan, letting my head fall back against the edge of the tub.

"I'm good if you are," she whispers against my wet skin.

Oh shit, those words are liable to be my undoing. I've always used a rubber, and I trust Beth, so I reply the only way a red-blooded man with a slippery hot woman on top of him does.

"I'm good to go." And with that, I hold her face in my hands, kiss her deeply, and slide her onto my cock.

Beth

After the incredible, bare sex we've just had in the tub, I get my second wind and realize how hungry I am. As we lay in the cooling water, catching our breath, Nate reaches over and removes the silver covers to reveal two massive greasy cheeseburgers and fries. I'm so happy and delirious from the toe curling orgasm that I kiss him deeply, holding his wet face in my hands, tears running down my cheeks.

"Hey, what's with the tears? It's just a burger," he says in a deep soothing voice.

"It's exactly what I want. I don't know how you keep giving me exactly what I want," I sob, feeling a little overwhelmed by everything he's done for me.

"It's easy, baby. When you know someone as well as you know yourself, it's not that difficult to figure out."

God, he's so earnest and wholesome it kills me. *Why can't I get there? Why can't I open my heart up to him as easily as he's opened his to me?* I'm frustrated with myself as I haul my dripping body from the tub, my skin breaking out in goosebumps not just because of the cool air.

When I feel the warmth of the fluffy robe being draped over my shoulders, I turn around and bury my face in Nate's chest, breathing in his special Nate smell and wrapping my arms around his waist.

"What's going on in here?" I hear him ask, his fingers tapping my head.

I swallow hard and decide now is not the time–he's created such a perfect evening. I don't want to dump more of my bullshit over it.

So, I lie.

"Nothing. I'm just desperate to rip into that burger before it gets much colder," I reply, looking up at him and smiling, but I can tell it doesn't reach my eyes.

After devouring the burgers and the ice cream sundaes, we lay on the bed in our robes watching a crappy movie. I snuggle into Nate's chest while he weaves his fingers through my hair, and my eyes slowly grow heavier and heavier.

"It means a lot that you trusted me to go bare." Nate's deep, husky voice makes my eyes flutter open.

I turn my face up to find him gazing down at me, his lips wearing a goofy grin.

"Of course I trust you," I reply smiling genuinely this time.

Nate reaches out and tucks a lock of hair behind my ear. "That's a win for me then."

I cock my head to the side. "Huh?"

"Trust is one of the best things about a committed relationship. Having that absolute certainty that the person you're with is on your side and has your back. If you have that with me, then I'm taking the win."

I see the smug expression on his face, and even that's fucking adorable. I shake my head and dig my fingers into his ribs, causing him to growl, flinch, and shift away.

Oh, the mighty defenseman is ticklish. That's a win for me which I intend to take full advantage of. So, I continue to tickle him while he grunts and tries to get away, slapping playfully at my hands. Finally, when I'm laughing so hard tears are streaming down my cheeks, he rolls on top of me, pulls my robe open, and slips his hard cock inside me. After that, there's no more laughter, just moans and sighs of absolute pleasure.

The next morning, I wake up to find Nate's face buried between my thighs, sliding his talented tongue in tight little circles over my aching clit. I watch him, his eyes drinking in my reaction, getting off on it.

Oh, fuck, he's so good at that.

I come quickly, drawing my knees up to my chest, clutching at Nate's hair as I whimper into the pillow I've pulled over my face. It feels like every muscle in my pussy and butt clench all at once, holding the pleasure on the precipice until I let it go and stars burst behind my eyelids.

"Fuck me," I gasp as Nate slides up to lie next to me, wiping his glistening lips with the back of his hand, a stupid, proud grin on his face.

"No time for that, princess. We've got a day to start. Date number two will begin in an hour." He slaps my ass and rolls out of bed, heading for the bathroom. "I'm showering. Wanna join me?"

Who the hell would say no to that?

Two hours later, Nate and I are drinking coffee in a cute little coffee shop in DUMBO, just across the Brooklyn Bridge.

"That's quite a shiner you've got there," I say, sipping the hot goodness, trying to avoid getting foam on my nose.

Nate self-consciously touches his face which has turned a dark shade of purple overnight. "Yeah, all our games on this road trip have been really physical, especially the Bulldogs."

I reach over and stroke his rough cheek. "I hate to see you hurt like this." I feel a tightening in my chest as I speak the words, realizing they're completely true.

Nate smiles and covers my hand with his, turning his head so he can kiss my palm. "It's just part of my job, princess. I'm the team enforcer, so if shit goes down, I have to step in and drop my gloves."

"Don't you get scared?" I ask, curious that this gentle, kind soul can become a snarling, fighting animal on the ice.

"Nah, it's actually a good outlet for ... certain feelings I let build up. It's like stress relief." He shrugs, and I sense the conversation is over. After his revelations about his father, I understand this is a tough subject for him to open up about. "Are we about done here? I thought we'd walk back across the bridge."

I look down at my almost finished drink and nod. I guess that's the end of the conversation.

Twenty minutes later, my face is absolutely freezing—early February in New York is bitterly cold, and the wind whips my hair and makes my eyes stream. Halfway across the bridge, Nate admits freezing our butts off isn't the most romantic thing to do, so as soon as we're back in Manhattan, he hails a cab which takes us to Serendipity where we warm up with steaming mugs of hot chocolate.

"Don't worry," he says through chattering teeth. "Our next activity is indoors."

"Thank god," I shiver, wrapping my frozen fingers around the hot mug of cocoa. "Despite the near hyper-thermia, I'm having a really lovely time."

Nate peers shyly into his drink, and a happy smile touches his lips. He leans toward me, and we share a kiss over our drinks, the brief sweep of his tongue sweet with chocolate. The slight awkwardness following our conversation in the coffee shop is forgotten, and I must admit Nate has planned a seriously romantic day.

While we talk and laugh, a few people come over to ask Nate for autographs and photos. He's modest and accommodating to all of them, and I just sit back and enjoy the interactions, happy to be ignored for the most part.

Reluctantly, we leave the warmth and comfort of Serendipity and walk west toward the park, catching a cab through it to the Natural History Museum. I'm so excited—I feel like a little kid. *Night at the Museum* is one of my favorite movies, so as we wander around looking at the massive dioramas, I keep referring to parts in the film.

Nate smiles broadly the entire time, holding my hand and following me as I stride from one exhibition to the other, chattering like a monkey. I loved nature as a kid; I was always collecting bugs and trying to rescue birds or chipmunks. My sixth grade ambition was to be a veterinarian, but I never really made the grades in Science, so I made do with volunteering at an animal shelter and walking dogs for my neighbors.

"This has just been the greatest day," I whisper in Nate's ear, snuggling into him as we take a cab to our next destination. We spent hours in the museum, and by the time we walk outside, the sky is dark, and a light dusting of snow is falling.

"I'm so glad you enjoyed it. But I have to admit this last activity is all about me."

My pussy flutters at the thought of some super sexy bedroom fun back in our warm hotel room, and I squeeze my thighs together, nuzzling Nate's neck. He slides his big hand between my crossed thighs, and I feel his fingers tighten possessively, stroking my denim clad center.

"Whatcha doing there, cowboy?" I whisper, enjoying the pressure of his fingers.

"My hand's cold," he growls, kissing the top of my head, making me giggle and snuggle closer.

Somewhere deep in my chest, I feel it happening: the clinking and grinding of the locks I've placed around my heart slowly opening up to this incredible man.

14

Nate

We've had a great day in New York. Now Beth is snuggling up to me in the back of the cab, and I feel like a fucking hero. Apart from the ill-advised walk across the Brooklyn Bridge in sub-zero temperatures, the rest of the day has been a success. I feel a bit shitty for shutting down the conversation in the coffee shop, but I really didn't want my family bullshit to ruin this fantastic day.

Seeing Beth dash around the museum like a little kid made my heart swell. She's always so put together and flawless; watching her run up to the different exhibits, pressing her hands to the glass and taking it all in, jabbering away about her favorite animals and ecosystems only imbeds my feelings deeper.

As the cab pulls up to the bar in Chelsea, I have to shake her gently to wake her up.

"We're here, baby," I whisper, touching my phone to the pay pad and helping Beth out of the cab. The frigid air hits us in the face as we brace against the wind and head inside the crowded bar.

"What is this place?" Beth laughs, unwinding her long chunky knit scarf from around her neck.

The first thing I notice as we enter Barcade is the fact that the bare brick walls are lined with vintage arcade games. There's a large bar at the far end and tables scattered around the central area.

The other thing I notice is that the bank of tables and chairs near the back of the bar are occupied by a rowdy group of hockey players.

Beth gazes around and smiles broadly. "I've heard about places like this. You can get hammered and play video games!"

"Exactly," I laugh, leading her over to my linemates. "I hope you don't mind, but this part of the date is kind of a group thing."

Understanding dawns on Beth's face when she sees the guys from my line. But her expression turns to one of pure joy when Mila and Cameron come charging across the wooden floor squealing and spilling their drinks.

"I'm so glad you're finally here," Mila cries. "Matt's so competitive at Street Fighter I think he and Ford are gonna have an actual fight."

Beth hugs her bestie back, then wraps Cameron with the same warm embrace, the three women immediately breaking away from me, chatting over the top of each other in excited voices. It's great seeing Beth with her friends, and I have no problem with her instantly abandoning me in their favor. I shuck off my coat and beanie and join my teammates at their group of tables.

"Hey, the kid finally shows!" Bugs taunts, wagging his bottle of light beer at me. "You asked us to meet you here over an hour ago."

"Sorry man, Beth was more into the museum than I could've ever imagined," I chuckle, accepting a bottle of beer from Brett.

Suddenly, I hear loud yells coming from a bank of arcade machines, and I see Matt and Ford hunched over the Street Fighter game, shoulder barging each other as their hands furiously maneuver the joysticks.

"For fuck's sake man, stop using that special move on me," Matt growls, his huge body braced against Ford's like they're wrestling at the boards, each man trying to knock the other off balance.

"That's the fucking point, asshole. If you knew how to play the game, you'd use yours too," Ford growls back and the whole crew stands up to gather round our battling linemates. It's a hilarious show of ineptitude, and I'm pretty sure I could kick both their asses. The men are just slapping random buttons and jerking the joystick violently from side to side.

As I watch the pathetic battle, I feel a small hand slip into mine, and Beth stands beside me. She entwines our fingers and smiles up at me, making it impossible to ignore her perfect, kissable lips.

"Are you happy, princess?" I ask quietly, squeezing her hand.

Her smile stretches wider, and she leans up on her tiptoes to gently kiss me. "More than I've ever been." She appears momentarily uncertain, but then her resolve returns. "I'd say this is another win for you, cowboy. Great date."

The pride bursts in my chest like fireworks, and I wrap my arm around her shoulders, feeling like I'm finally on a breakaway and headed for goal. I want to go all the way with Beth, and I hope she feels it too.

We continue to enjoy a few drinks and games, Beth and I jumping into the racing simulator where she basically kicks my ass. I blame it on the fact I can hardly fit into the seat, but she just pats my chest, kisses my lips, and smiles good naturedly.

"Of course that's the reason." She winks at me.

"Hey, don't patronize me," I grumble. "Let's play Donkey Kong. I'll definitely beat you at that."

My man card will surely be torn up in front of my teammates if I let her beat me again, but before I can lead her over to the now vacant machine, my phone pings in my back pocket indicating an incoming text.

"Hang on, baby. Go and hold the machine. I'll be right there," I instruct as I reach for my phone and turn away.

The name and words that fill the banner on my screen make my stomach drop and my throat close.

[SIR: Who's the fucking blonde?]

With a shaky finger, I swipe the message open and along with the words is a screenshot of a hockey gossip blog with a picture of Beth and me in Serendipity, leaning toward each other and kissing over the table. The headline reads "Whalers Enforcer out in the Big Apple with mystery blonde."

Fuck!

As I look at the screen shot, another message pings in.

[SIR: No wonder you played like shit against the Bulldogs if you're chasing pussy all over NYC. Head in the game, Nathaniel.]

"Nate? Are you coming?" Beth's voice jolts me back to the moment, and I realize I'm gripping my phone so tightly I could shatter the screen. I swallow the rising bile down and take a quick swig of my soda to clear the bitter taste from my mouth.

I shove my phone back in my pocket. I refuse to deal with this shit right now, so I plaster a smile on my face and say, "Let's go, princess."

Beth

"We need to make that look more dramatic," I say to Andre as we examine the mock-ups on our iPads. We're sitting at the large pine dining table in his loft on a depressingly wet Tuesday morning. The high from my New York trip has well and truly worn off, and to be honest, I'm feeling a little melancholy.

We're working on makeup and hair design for the upcoming movie we're styling, having spent a day in the studio yesterday with our models. Hector sent us the pictures of the actors he has for the leading roles, so we chose models with similar coloring to get an accurate picture. It was great fun reading the script and designing styles for each important part of the storyline.

"I don't know," Andre sighs, rubbing the short white hair that now covers his head. He's decided to evolve his look, so he's grown his hair for the first time in years but immediately dyed it bright white which is a startling contrast to his dark brown skin.

"It's the moment in the movie when the heroine finds out the truth about her lover. It needs impact," I argue. God, I sound like a whiny bitch today.

"I suppose," he relents, pushing the iPad away and fixing me with an intense look. "We've been back from New York for a week, and you still haven't told me what's up with you and Nate. Quite frankly, it's killing me. So, I'm making us a cocktail, and you're going to spill your guts."

I sit and stare at my best friend and check the clock on the wall.

"It's ten in the morning," I deadpan, pointing at the massive clock that dominates one of his bare brick walls.

"Fine, I'll make us an espresso martini, but I want to hear it, baby, because the suspense is giving me wrinkles." Andre stands and pats my shoulder, sauntering into the kitchen in his silk kimono.

I sigh and try to arrange my thoughts, which are very confused when it comes to a certain six-foot seven hockey player. We haven't seen each other since I flew back from New York because both our schedules have been crazy, but he's been plaguing my thoughts. Our date was so incredible, and it made me start to have all sorts of feelings that are making my head spin.

Honestly, it's scaring the shit out of me, and I don't know what to do. I hope talking to Andre will help. Mila's been worse than useless because she's so loved up with Matt, but I can always rely on Andre to be brutally honest with me.

The smell of espresso draws me back from my thoughts as Andre places a perfect martini in front of me, complete with two coffee beans in the center of the creamy foam. After we clink glasses and take a sip, he leans back in his chair, crosses his incredibly long legs, and waits for me to spill.

"I'm in trouble," I finally admit, setting my glass on the table because my hands are shaking a little.

What the fuck is that about?

"I know you are, baby. Any fool can see that," Andre smiles kindly at me.

"What the fuck am I supposed to do?" I suddenly cry, the frustration at my inability to accept my feelings finally boiling over. "I mean I have this incredible guy making it his full-time job to woo me, and I can't take the next step. Why can't I just let go and do the love thing? I really like him! He's perfect. Maybe that's why it's so scary. Can anyone be that perfect?"

I get up and begin pacing back and forth, feeling the panic rising in my chest like a raging fire. "It's too much, Andre. He's making it too hard to resist."

"Newsflash, baby: he's not perfect and neither are you." He looks at me closely. "Do you want to resist him?"

That stops me in my tracks, and I feel more confused than ever.

"I don't know!" I stomp over to the table and down the rest of my drink, enjoying the caffeine and liquor buzz that hits me. My relationship bullshit is just that ... bullshit! Who ever heard of someone being afraid of commitment because their parents have a happy marriage? I'm being crazy.

"Maybe I should end it," I say quietly. I can't take this out of control feeling any more.

Andre leaps to his feet. "What? No! Are you crazy?" he screeches, putting his hands on my shoulders. "You can't do that."

"I have to! I can't take it any further when I know I'm just gonna end up breaking his heart." I sigh, feeling tears sting my eyes at the thought of hurting Nate.

"See," Andre says waving his finger in my face, "this is why you can't break up with him. You're getting all emotional about hurting his feelings, which shows me *you* have feelings too."

"Of course I have feelings!" I snap, slapping his finger away. "I'm not a total bitch. I just think it's better to end it now. I mean Valentine's Day is coming up, and I'm sure he's going to have planned something amazing."

"How about you ask him for a timeout? That's a hockey thing, right?" Andre looks adorably confused trying to use a sporting term, and it makes my lips quirk into a little smile despite my confused state. "New York was really intense, so perhaps if you have a little distance and don't have the pressure of V-Day, you can get some perspective."

I listen carefully to my friend and decide he's got a good point. I'd be a fool to end things with Nate, but I do need a timeout. It's too much at the moment, and I'm feeling overwhelmed. The last thing I want to do is hurt Nate; he's had enough pain and suffering in his life. I'll be damned if I'll be the cause of more.

[NATE: Practice was good. How's the movie stuff going? Missed you this week.]

I stare at the message as I unlock the door to my apartment. It's sat unread on my lock screen all day because I'm terrified to let him know I've seen it.

After my pre-noon cocktail chat with Andre, I felt like I was strong enough to ask Nate to ease off a bit, but now he's doing the cute texting thing, and I feel my resolve failing. Mila's home when I get back, so I fill her in on what I've decided, and she listens while carefully plucking her eyebrows.

"So, you want to keep seeing him, but you want him to back off a bit?" she asks, turning away from her vanity. I sit cross-legged on her rumpled comforter, and I get a sudden wave of nostalgia for our college days. Life seemed so simple then.

"I guess," I shrug. "I do like him a lot. I mean, he's amazing. It's just too much too soon. New York was incredible, but we can't sustain that level of romance. It's not realistic. Soon enough we'll be sitting at home in our jammies, eating pizza, and bitching about whether to watch *Game of Thrones* or *The Walking Dead*!"

"What's wrong with that?" Mila asks in exasperation.

"Everything!" I throw my hands up in the air and fall back on her bed. I know that's one of her favorite things to do—sit home with her boyfriend and snuggle.

I feel Mila plop herself next to me, and we lay side by side. "I wish you'd allow yourself to accept this wonderful gift," she says quietly, sliding her hand into mine.

I turn to face her, and I see the look of hope and love in her shiny eyes. "What?"

"Love," Mila says simply. "I know you think it's boring and predictable, but I promise you, with the right person there's no feeling like it. I thought I was in love with Greg. I got tingles and we had a good time..."

"Until he put his dick in your work bestie," I sass, squeezing her hand.

"Exactly!" she squeezes my hand back a little too hard to show me she doesn't appreciate my bitchy comment. "I realize now it was always me making the plans and organizing things to keep our relationship going. I thought about him all the time, but I never felt like he considered me in any of his decisions. With Matt though, we're a partnership. I always feel like he considers me. He can be a possessive, growly jerk sometimes, which I really like by the way, but I never feel disregarded by him."

"Is that what love is?" I ask, rolling onto my side so I can face her.

"It is for us. I don't know what love looks like for you, but I can say that when I see you and Nate together, it's pretty close to perfect." Mila tucks a lock of hair behind my ear and smiles kindly. "I know you're scared. Just don't let fear stop you from all love has to offer."

15

Nate

It's been four hours and fifteen minutes since I sent Beth a text, and I'm about to lose my fucking mind. We've been running drills on the ice all afternoon, and for those few hours, I managed to put her out of my mind. But now, standing under the hot, powerful spray of the locker room showers, I'm back to obsessing.

"What are your big plans for Friday?" I hear Bugs ask Matt. They're in the stalls on either side of me, and because the separating walls only go to mid-chest height, we can talk while we shower without getting an eyeful of each other's junk.

"I thought I'd take Mila out to the house. It's empty so I've got the keys from the realtor. I'm gonna make a candlelit picnic and ask her to move in with me," Matt replies, rinsing shampoo out of his hair.

"Fuck, man, that's a big gesture," Bugs chokes, smearing body wash over his chest and under his arms. "Don't you just wanna buy her a necklace or something?"

"No, it's time for this to happen. She stays at my place most of time anyway, and I'm sure Beth'll be pleased to get her apartment back, right kid?"

"Huh?" I realize Matt's addressing me. "Yeah, sure," I mumble, turning off the water and wrapping my towel around my waist, stepping into my sliders.

"You got big plans with Beth for V-Day?" Bugs asks, rinsing his body and following me out of the stalls. We walk into the locker room with Matt following behind, rubbing his hair vigorously with a towel.

I growl to myself and sit down hard on the bench in front of my cubby. "I don't fucking know; she won't reply to my text."

I notice Bugs and Matt exchange a look, and both my linemates sit down on either side of me.

"What's going on, kid?" Matt asks, draping a towel over his shoulders.

"We've both been busy since New York, so I texted her to catch up. That was about five hours ago, and she's not got back to me," I mutter, glaring down at my clenched fists.

The barking laughter that echoes around the locker room makes my head snap up, glaring at my so-called friends.

"What the fuck are you laughing at?" I yell.

Bugs slaps my bare shoulder and shakes his head. "Sometimes I forget how young you are, man."

I'm getting pissed off now. If these douchebags don't start explaining what's so funny soon, I'm liable to kick some ass. I don't care if we are half naked.

"Seriously, what's so funny?" I ask in exasperation, glaring at them.

Matt finally gets control of himself. "Sorry, man. You're freaking out because she hasn't replied to your text after a few hours. The woman has a life, you know. She doesn't sit around waiting for you to text her. Give her a chance. You said she's been working really hard on this movie so perhaps she's busy. You're gonna drive yourself nuts if you carry on like this."

I huff out a breath and put my head in my hands.

My father's been texting me constantly since the pictures of Beth and I appeared all over the hockey blogs. They've steadily been getting more aggressive and derogatory toward Beth, and even though I haven't replied to him, his words are still eating away at me.

Honestly, I can't take the fucking pressure anymore.

I catch Matt and Bugs exchange another look, and suddenly all the chirping and good humor has been sucked out of the room.

I feel Matt's reassuring hand on my shoulder. "What's this really about, kid?"

The words are bubbling up in my throat; these men are my most trusted friends and teammates. Surely, they'll understand if I tell them about my father.

"I'm not sure this is a conversation I wanna have with my dick hanging out, so can we get dressed and go get a beer?" I ask, laughing in a humorless way.

"You got it, man." We dress quickly and head to O'Connell's. It's time I get this weight off my shoulders. Hopefully once I do, I can think more clearly about Beth and whatever the hell is going on with us.

"Fuck," Matt sighs, taking a long draw on his beer, shaking his head, his eyes downcast.

I've just finished my sad, pathetic life story, sparing no humiliating detail. My beer sits in front of me, untouched and warm, and my friends look pissed off and sympathetic all at the same time.

"Ever since those pictures of Beth and me kissing in New York came out, he's been texting me, getting on my case about my performance and calling her all sorts of names." I take a big swig of my warm beer and grimace. "I can't fucking take it anymore."

And that's the truth. He's getting under my skin, and it's driving me crazy.

"What do you wanna do?" Matt asks, waving the waitress over and ordering me a fresh drink.

"I don't know. I can't cut him out of my life because of my mom," I reply, feeling the tug of guilt about how long it's been since I went home.

"Will he listen if you tell him to quit?" Bugs inquires. He's more serious than I've ever seen him, even before a game. He's gone into Papa Bear mode, and I'm really grateful I have such great friends.

"Maybe. I guess I need to man up and call him. Tell him to quit it and hope he listens. I guess if he doesn't, I need to just block his damn number." I run my hands through my hair. Even though I'm exasperated by the whole thing, I feel much better for sharing it. Like after I confessed to Beth, my burden feels lighter.

"That sounds like a plan," Matt says in an encouraging tone. "Now, let's talk about Beth."

I roll my eyes and huff out a deep breath. "Jesus, this is like an episode of Dr. Phil."

The guys laugh and take manly swigs of their beer. I'm thankful that the waitress brings my refreshed drink so I can join in the bro moment.

Seven painful hours later, my phone pings. I throw my game controller onto the floor and reach for my phone, knocking over my soda and flooding the coffee table.

"Fuck!" I bark, rescuing my phone from the swill and safely stashing it on the couch before grabbing some paper towels from the kitchen counter. After I've mopped up the soda and tossed the ruined magazines in the trash, I flop back onto the couch with a fresh drink and read the text.

[BETH: Hi, the movie stuff is good. Thanks for asking.]

Huh? That's a fairly generic, cold text. Not like Beth at all. I compose a reply, but nothing I write seems to get across what I want to say. I want to ask her out for our third date on Valentine's Day, but something in her tone makes me uncertain.

Fuck it, I need to hear her voice. I hit the call symbol and put it on speaker, resting the phone on my chest while I listen to it ring.

"Hi." God, I love her sultry voice. That simple word gives me wood.

"Hey princess. How's it going?" I try to keep it light and sense what kind of mood she's in.

"It's going okay. Been working with Andre and hanging with Mila. Did practice go well today?" she asks in a quiet voice. She definitely doesn't sound her usual sassy, confident self.

"Yeah, it was good."

Jesus, we're talking to each other like strangers. This fucking sucks.

"What's going on, Beth?" I decide to just rip off the Band-Aid and get to the bottom of this weird vibe between us.

I hear her sigh, and I imagine her rolling her eyes as she tries to articulate the thoughts clogging up her brain.

"Nothing. I'm just getting stressed about work."

I make a growly noise in my chest, frustrated and pissed off. "I call bullshit. Come on, what's really going on?" I clench my fist, rising from the couch to pace around.

"Fine, you wanna hear it?" she suddenly blurts. "You're being too intense. It's freaking me out, and I need some time away from you. I need to deal with my feelings, and I can't do that with you up in my face all the time!"

Shit! Suddenly I feel like I've taken a puck to the throat, and I can't get my words out.

"Are you there?" Beth asks. "Now you've got nothing to say?"

All the tension seems to flood from my body, and I sink onto the couch, boneless and defeated. Everything that's been going on with my father and now this stuff with Beth has just overloaded my system, and I need a reboot.

"I'll back off." Those are the only words I can manage as I end the call and launch my phone across the room where it smashes against the treadmill.

Beth

I've never been a fan of commercially-enforced romance, so Valentine's Day is just another day for me. I enjoy chocolate as much as the next girl and if for a few weeks in February I can only buy it in heart shapes, then so be it. But I don't buy into the whole drama and over-exaggerated lovey dovey crap forced upon us by greeting card manufacturers and florists.

However, this year feels different.

Whereas I would usually mock people who are running all over the place planning stupid romantic dates and buying bunches of flowers that will just end up dying, this year I have a feeling that I might be missing out on something. It's that feeling you get when you think you've forgotten to do something really important.

I wake up on Friday morning and plod to the bathroom, the sex noises coming from Mila's room reminding me it's Valentine's Day, and I'm waking up alone. Once I've used the bathroom and brushed my teeth, I decide to hit the gym. There's no way I'm hanging out here while my roommate fucks her hot boyfriend's brain out.

Thankfully, the gym is quiet. Most people are waking up with their lover, having breakfast in bed or doing what Matt and Mila are. I hit the treadmill and plug in my ear buds, cranking up "Jagged Little Pill" by Alanis Morrisette. This album perfectly fits my mood, and soon I'm pounding the treadmill, sweat pouring down my back and between my breasts. It's been a while since I ran like this, and I'm sure I'll be hurting tomorrow. But for now, it feels good to push my body to its limits, numbing my brain.

Once I've exhausted myself on the treadmill, I change into my bikini, head to the steam room, and allow the eucalyptus-scented heat to envelop me, relaxing my overused muscles. Unfortunately, the quiet and solitude allows Nate to sneak in—his ridiculously handsome face, denim blue eyes, sweet smile, and god-like stature. He sounded so hurt and defeated after our strained conversation the other night, and when he hung up on me, my chest tightened, and I immediately regretted being such an asshole.

However, I don't regret asking for space. It's allowed me to sidestep the whole Valentine's Day situation, but at what cost? I guess I'll find out when we finally get around to speaking to each other again.

Whenever that'll be.

"I refuse to allow it!" Andre purrs down the phone. He's on speaker while I paint my toenails a deep purple. It's a free sample from one of my suppliers, and I love it. Once my toes are done, I'll probably give myself a manicure.

"You aren't the fucking boss of me," I whine through gritted teeth. "I'm not going anywhere tonight."

It's late afternoon and thankfully Matt and Mila have gone out somewhere. I'm sure they'll stay at his place tonight, so I intend to eat my body weight in Ben & Jerry's and watch horror movies on Netflix.

"Come on. You usually love Sapphire's Anti-Valentine's Day party. She's hired an actual banqueting room in a Chinese restaurant this year," he coaxes, knowing my weakness for all things Szechuan.

I blow out an exasperated breath and feel my resolve fading. Sapphire is one of Andre's drag artist friends, and she throws fabulous parties. She's most famous for her Anti-Valentine's Day bash, where you can get shit faced with likeminded love cynics or the broken hearted. I usually enjoy the event, and I must admit I've had my fair share of hot hook ups as a result.

I understand why Sapphire's hired a place this time. Last year, some drunk women decided to perform some sort of goddess burning ritual in her apartment, and they had to call 911 when the trash can bonfire got out of control. I did get a cute firefighter's phone number, so it wasn't a total disaster.

But tonight, I just feel sad and pathetic at the prospect of attending. The regret I feel for the way I spoke to Nate has been growing and swelling inside me like a cancer, and I just want to wallow in self-pity. My stubborn streak is stopping me from reaching out to him.

Andre's voice interrupts my pity party. "You *are* going. I'm coming over in an hour to fix up your hair because I'll bet money it's up in some sort of messy knot, and that is unacceptable. So get out your sluttiest dress, your highest heels, and let's go."

"Jesus! Fine! You're so fucking bossy," I huff, feeling the love for my bestie fill my deflated heart. See, I can have love in my life, and that makes me even more confused about my feelings for Nate.

16

Nate

The pizza I've ordered tastes like shit, sitting in my stomach like a heavy, doughy ball. I throw the half-eaten slice back into the box and swig from the bottle of water. I just can't settle on anything to do–I've been to the arena for some conditioning training with the Athletic Coach, had a massage with the physio to help loosen up my tight hamstrings, and I went to get my truck detailed.

However, at every turn I'm assaulted with reminders that it's Valentine's Day, and I'm alone. Whatever Beth and I have going on, it obviously doesn't include being together on this day. She made that clear during the phone call that I can't stop replaying over and over in my head.

It cut me deeply when she complained I was coming on too strong. That's definitely not the impression I got in New York when she came multiple times all over my cock. The confusion and frustration of this is making me crazy, but I've resolved not to make the first move. I need to wait it out and let her come to me.

As I'm clearing away my barely eaten pizza, my phone rings, and my stupid, romantic heart leaps at the prospect it might be Beth. Unfortunately, when I retrieve my phone from my back pocket, I see my mom's number blinking at me. I'm a bit confused because she usually calls me on the last Sunday of the month because that's when my father is out all day with his gun club buddies.

"Hey mom," I say, leaning back against the kitchen counter.

"Nathaniel?" My father's rough voice surprises me so much I immediately stand to attention and release an involuntary grunt.

"Sir? Is mom alright?"

My father coughs. "She's fine. I'm just using her cell because you seem incapable of answering any texts that come from mine."

My mouth is suddenly dry, and cold sweat creeps down my back. "What can I do for you?" I ask in a pathetic, croaky voice.

"I want to know what you're doing about that girl. I've been watching your plays, and I've gotta say you're sluggish. Too much time using your energy else-where—is that the case?" he barks. I involuntarily pull the phone away from my ear as if his hand could come through it and deliver the stinging slap I expect.

I swallow the cotton wool clogging my throat and reply as assertively as I can. "No, sir. Beth is having no effect on my performance on the ice. I've been seeing the physio about my hamstrings and …"

"Bullshit!" my father yells. "No amount of physio or training will make up for the focus you lose when you're chasing pussy. Break it off now before you fuck up your chances of winning the Cup. You know how it feels to be responsible for costing your team the win."

Jesus. Even for him, that's a low blow.

I take a deep breath and decide to shut this conversation down. "Like I said, she's having no effect on my game, so you've no cause to worry about that."

"So why aren't you out with her tonight?" The bitter venom in his hissing voice causes a physical shiver to ripple down my spine. "If this little bitch is so important to you, why aren't you with her on Valentine's Day?"

For once, despite the way he's delivered it, the asshole has a good point. Why the fuck am I letting Beth push me away? Why am I letting her call all the shots?

I feel the anger build inside me. It's the same surge I get on the ice when I charge at an opponent, my gloves hitting the ice. The raging, snarling animal is straining at his leash.

"That's none of your fucking business," I growl. "And neither is my career. You gave up that right the first time you laid your fucking hands on me."

Beth's words about abuse swim through my mind, and I have a startling realization that she's absolutely right. What my father did to me was abuse and unacceptable, and now I'm a grown man—I don't have to stand for it anymore.

I can almost see him at the other end of the line, his face growing red and blotchy, the blue eyes we share bugging out of his head in rage, his hands itching to slap and dominate.

"What the fuck did you say to me?" he seethes.

"You heard me fine. So, unless you want to adjust your attitude and talk to me like a father should talk to his son, there's no need for us to speak again." I feel myself standing taller as the words spill from my mouth, the weight of his disapproval lifting off my shoulders.

"You ungrateful, little shit …"

I end the call and place the phone carefully on the counter. I've already trashed one cell this week, and I need to make a very important call in a few minutes. But first, I need my hands to stop shaking and my heart to slow the fuck down. I can hear a loud, gasping noise, and I realize that it's my breath sawing in and out of my lungs.

Shit, I'm hyperventilating!

I place my hands on the edge of the kitchen counter and bend my head, trying to control my breathing. I close my eyes and pray I don't pass out. This hasn't happened to me since I was a kid, and I desperately try to remember the breathing techniques I was taught.

In for five…out for seven. In for five…out for seven. Don't pass out. Don't pass out.

I repeat the mantra in my head, and slowly I feel the control returning. The tingly feeling in my extremities eases, and I can open my eyes without seeing flashing stars.

When I finally feel capable, I grab my phone and shove it in my pocket, walking gingerly over to the couch where I drop my huge frame into the soft cushions.

Where the hell did that come from? I've never stood up to my father like that, so why now? As I take my phone out and bring up my contacts, I know exactly why.

Beth.

I hit her contact and wait for the connection to be made. All my bullshit about waiting for her to come to me has flown out of the window. I need to tell her what just happened with my father, and I need to lay my feelings out on the table for her. There's going to be no more fucking around, no more dancing around each other. She's either in it all the way, or she's not. No more games.

I groan in frustration when her phone rings out and diverts to voicemail. I'm not leaving a message. I'll bet a year's salary she's with Andre, so I hit his contact next, and thankfully he picks up.

"'Dre, are you with Beth? I need to speak to her now."

Beth

"She told me I spend too much time on the golf course and not enough time choosing fabric patterns with her. Can you believe that?"

I've literally never been so bored in my entire life. The handsome, tall guy in front of me has been droning on about his ex-girlfriend for the last ten minutes, and I just can't find a way to excuse myself. I drained my martini as quickly as possible without looking like a raging alcoholic, but before I could get away for a refill, he grabbed a passing waitress and ordered me another.

Andre and I arrived at the Anti-Valentine's Day party about an hour ago following his "Getting over Nate" make over. This included him barrel rolling my hair into loose, beachy waves, applying a smokey makeup that made my blue eyes pop and my signature red lipstick. While I watched helplessly, Andre trashed my wardrobe, throwing things over his shoulder as he eliminated them from his search. He finally appeared with a silvery sequined dress that I haven't worn since college. It's obscenely short and plunges between my breasts at the front and is open almost to the top of my ass at the back. I literally can't wear any underwear with it.

"No way!" I protest, but Andre just pulls out my favorite silver Jimmy Choos, tosses them on top of the dress, and ignores me.

Now, I'm stuck listening to this guy who can't stop talking about his ex while ogling my tits. Andre walked off somewhere when this douche approached me, and I'm silently cursing him for it. Despite everything I said about Nate, I just can't stop comparing every guy in the room to him—that guy's not as tall as Nate, that guy's not as muscular as Nate, that guy's not as sweet as Nate.

I think what my fucked up, martini-soaked brain is trying to tell me is that none of these guys are Nate.

Finally, I see Andre reappearing from the coat check area with his phone, and he nods at me to come over.

"I'm sorry. My friend needs me. It was nice talking to you," I blurt, interrupting the guy in the middle of another golf story.

Before he can stop me or talk again, I dart around him as quickly as I can in my sky-high shoes, making a beeline for Andre.

"Oh Jesus, there aren't any available men here," I moan. "And the food is terrible. Can we go?"

Andre smirks and immediately I know he's scheming. "Not yet, baby girl. I have a feeling the party will pick up soon."

"What did you do?" I lean up and hiss in his ear, poking him in the belly.

He feigns shock and pats my ass. "Nothing. Just get yourself another drink and talk to Sapphire. She wants to pick your brain about primer." With that, he saunters off to watch a group of women hit a penis shaped piñata with terrifying aggression.

17

Nate

After little persuasion, Andre gave up the address of the Chinese restaurant downtown where he and Beth are attending a party. I thought I'd have to work much harder to get the information, so when Andre drops the pin to my phone, I dash out of the door, barely remembering to grab my wallet and keys.

I drive too quickly through the busy evening traffic, following the droning GPS voice toward the restaurant. As I calm down, I realize I'm just wearing my ratty Green Day T-shirt, faded jeans, and ancient Converse, hardly the clothes I want to wear when I tell Beth … what?

Shit, I'm not even sure what I'm going to say when I get there. I hope the words will come to me because suddenly I'm pulling into the parking lot, swerving my truck into an empty space near the rear of the lot.

Before I leave the cab, I take a few deep breaths and clear my mind. I prioritize the revelations I've come to about my father, my past, and how I feel about Beth.

Right. Let's do this thing!

The restaurant is busy, and I ask one of the bus boys where the party is. He directs me to a large banqueting room at the rear. I can hear female shrieks and loud banging coming from beyond the double doors, and suddenly I wonder what the hell happens at one of these anti-Valentine's parties.

Tentatively, I push open the doors and see a crowd of women battering what I can only describe as a crippled cardboard dick with golf clubs. Fearing a little for my safety, I sneak around the shrieking crowd and search for Beth or Andre.

As I wander through the room, getting curious, lustful looks from some of the women (and men), I keep searching for Beth. I finally spot her talking to a tall woman in a bright blue dress.

Oh my god, she looks incredible in a short, barely-there silver dress and her usual high heels. Her smile is radiant, and I can see her gesticulating wildly which means she is talking about something she's passionate about. As I get closer, I feel my caveman rear his ugly head because I spot several guys loitering close by, waiting for their moment to cut into her conversation. I mean, why the fuck wouldn't they? She's by far the sexiest woman in this room—or any room for that matter.

I stalk toward her, making myself as big and intimidating as possible so I make it clear to the jerks circling her that she's mine, and they should back the fuck off.

Beth is so engrossed in her conversation with the tall woman that she doesn't notice me until I'm almost by her side.

"Nate?" She looks up at me, blinking rapidly as if trying to check her eyesight. "What the hell are you doing here?"

"I have to talk to you," I growl, staring at her plump, red lips. By the end of the night, I want that lipstick smeared all over my cock.

"I'm busy," she sneers, indicating toward her companion.

I quickly check out the woman in the blue dress, double taking when I realize she's actually a very beautiful dude. "I'm sorry to interrupt, but I have to speak to Beth."

"Go right ahead, darling. I can tell you're just bursting for this one." She leans over and kisses Beth's cheek and sashays away.

Suddenly, without the distraction of other people, I'm unsure of how to proceed.

"What do you want, Nate?" Beth asks again, crossing her arms, which causes her breasts to press together.

It's very distracting, but I force my eyes to stay locked on hers.

"I need to tell you …" I begin, but before I can get my words out, one of the circling douches decides it's his moment to pounce.

"Is this guy bothering you, sweet cheeks?" he asks, trying to make his puny body as big as possible.

"For fuck's sake!" I curse, pushing my hand through my hair and tugging it in exasperation.

Beth stares at me, then at her attempted knight in shining armor, her mouth moving as she speaks, but I've stopped listening. It's not the time for words; it's time for action.

With the speed I've honed after years on the ice, I bend and press my shoulder into Beth's stomach, wrapping one strong arm around the back of her thighs, gripping the flimsy material of her dress, lifting her over my shoulder. The squeal of surprise followed by a hiss of anger thickens my cock as I slap her ass and march toward the door.

"Put me down, you fucking asshole," Beth yells, slapping my ass with her purse and flailing her legs. I notice a few guys approaching to intervene, but thankfully Andre blocks them, and before I know it, I'm pushing through the back exit door and out into the dark parking lot.

"I'm serious! Nate, put me down! I'm not your fucking property!" she snarls, but she comes off like an angry kitten, and I chuckle—which just fuels her anger.

Once we get into the parking lot, I finally put Beth down and crowd her up against the side of my truck, caging her in with my body and arms. Her face is a picture of fury, and if I'm not mistaken, lust and arousal too.

"What the fuck, Nate?" she pants, her chest heaving. The material of her dress has shifted so most of her left breast is showing. There's no way I can keep my eyes up this time, and I stare at the plump globe, my tongue sweeping across my lower lip.

Fuck, I need her nipple in my mouth in the worst way.

It feels like we stand there for hours, staring and panting. Neither one of us is willing to speak or make the first move, like two stubborn assholes. The air between us is crackling with the pent-up frustration of days without touching each other. My fingertips itch to rip that dress from her body, and finally I can't stand it any longer.

With one more look to make sure she's on the same page as me, I dart forward and crash my lips to hers, my hand gripping the hair at the nape of her neck, pressing her into the side of my truck. I tilt her head back and press my tongue into her mouth, a moan escaping her which makes my cock impossibly hard. I feel the briefest moment of resistance, then she's sinking into me and pressing her hot, little body against my big, hard one.

I have to feel the needy, wet place I know I'll find between her thighs, so my hand creeps under the short hem of her dress, and now it's my turn to moan. The delicate scrap of lace that covers her pussy is soaked through, and before I can help myself, my fingers tear through it and plunge inside her.

Beth grunts into my mouth, but she keeps grinding against my hand, her fingers gripping my biceps to give herself purchase. I have a vague awareness that we're in a parking lot and someone could pass by at any moment. So, with my free hand I fumble my key fob out of my pocket and hit the button to unlock it.

Without breaking our kiss, I hoist Beth up, so she's wrapped around me like a koala, and I rip open the back door to my truck and bundle us inside. It's not perfect, but at least the back windows are tinted so we have more privacy than out in the open.

In our new location, Beth is straddling my lap, the power dynamic having shifted in her favor. With her in charge, her hot, wet pussy is pressing up against me, making me crazy to be inside her.

"Nate, please," Beth begs, shrugging the thin straps of her dress off her shoulders so it falls and gathers around her waist. Oh man, her tits are just the best. I press my hands to her slim back and bury my face between her smooth globes, making her giggle huskily. My lips search in the darkness until they encounter her turgid peak, sucking it into my mouth, grazing it with my teeth. This elicits a hungry gasp from her as she grinds on me harder, making the rod between my legs almost painful. Beth grabs handfuls of my hair and tugs my head from side to side, so I can treat both nipples to equal attention.

"Let me get my dick out, princess," I growl, pushing my hand between us, so I can flick the button on my jeans and drag the zipper down.

Before I can, Beth thrusts her small hand into my jeans and wraps her greedy fingers around my smooth, hard cock, making me moan. I suck eagerly on the skin of her neck, marking her as she gives my dick a few rough pumps just to make sure I'm ready to take her.

With her head pressed up against the roof of the cab, Beth rises, holding my dick against her slippery entrance. As we stare into each other's eyes, she impales herself on me. The pleasure is so immense I just want to close my eyes and savor it, but Beth holds my gaze, her hips beginning to pump back and forth in my lap.

I move my hands to her round ass and help her along, speeding up her movements, increasing the friction between our bodies to the point of madness. My face finds its way back to her bouncing tits, and I capture her nipple again, sucking on it while she rides my cock.

"Oh Nate, I'm really close! Oh fuck," Beth grunts, her hair flopping across her face, her fingers digging into the muscles of my shoulders, her pussy holding me tightly. I'm right on the precipice, and I need her to fall with me, so I do the one thing I know will tip her over the edge. I quickly thrust my thumb into her mouth, allowing her smeared red lips to suck it eagerly. Once it's good and slick, I reach round and push it into her tight asshole.

"Oooohhhhhhhhh, shit!" she squeals, coming apart and soaking my lap with her orgasm.

With a primal roar, I follow her over, holding her in place with my free hand, as my balls draw up tight and I unload into her in a throbbing, hot gush.

"Damn, princess. I want you mad at me all the fucking time," I gasp, laughing, still feeling the ripples of her pussy around me.

Beth

After Nate carried me out of the party like a fucking caveman, and we screwed in his truck, we've barely come up for air. Once we straightened up our clothes, he drove us back to his apartment with hardly a word exchanged between us.

It feels like there's so much to say, but neither of us is in a place to express it with words yet. Instead, we express it with our bodies. Nate pushes me through his front door, and I sink to my knees, frantically unzipping his jeans so I can get to his cock. As I suck him off, I can taste myself on him. That makes me so wet, I thrust my fingers between my legs to ease the throbbing ache.

Nate holds my head, thrust deeply and unloads down my throat before he picks me up and carries me to his room where he eats me out until I scream my release into a pillow.

After a short power nap where neither of us bother to strip out of our half-discarded clothes, Nate fucks me again. He rips off what's left of my dress, sheds his jeans and T-shirt, and flips me so I'm lying prone on my front, covering my body with his, entering me in one hard thrust.

I guess I should feel a little used and degraded by the way we're rutting like animals, but I'm so not. It's giving us both what we need at this moment; talking and words will come later. And if Nate's going to break off our arrangement, I want as much of him as I can get.

After I come again, his fingertips mark my hips because he's holding me so tightly, he pulls out and flips me onto my back.

Nate rears up, his chest and abs slick with sweat, his biceps bulging as he holds my knees apart, tunnelling his hard cock into me at a punishing rate. The masculinity of his body is enough to set me off like the Fourth of July, but I bite into my lower lip and hold back. His eyes are hooded and fixed on the place where our bodies join, and watching him is so hot, I feel everything tightening in preparation for yet another climax.

"Need your eyes on me when you come again, princess," he growls as he holds my knees apart and plunges into me. Nate fucks me like a champ, our eyes locked, until his eyes drag down to watch himself sliding in and out of my slick pussy.

"Are you close?" I beg, gasping for breath, completely spent but desperate for release. I've never been fucked like this before; it's so raw and primal.

"Rub your clit. Get yourself off," Nate huffs, pulling my already splayed legs even farther apart. I barely get my fingers to work before I'm arching my back and throbbing around Nate's cock. The garbled, nonsensical words that fall from my mouth make me seem crazy, but I couldn't care less. I feel Nate give in to his climax, and the hot rush of liquid unloads deep inside me, his strong fingers bruising the skin around my knees.

"Water," I gasp as we lay in a sweaty, boneless heap. I'm going to be sore tomorrow, but I don't care. I know that my body will be marked by Nate's fingertips, teeth, and mouth; the insides of my thighs will be covered in love bites, and my hips and shoulders will bear small, circular bruises. He's marked me as his, and I hope that means he wants to keep seeing me.

Nate grunts and rolls off me, hauling his huge, sweat-slicked body up, disappearing out of the room. I use his absence to hit the bathroom and clean up, discovering my shredded dress in a pile on the floor. I guess I'll be wearing something belonging to Nate for the walk of shame.

By the time he returns, unashamed by his glorious nakedness, carrying two bottles of water and several bags of chips and dip, I'm back in bed with the sheet pulled demurely over my breasts.

He stares at me and growls, "Drop the sheet, princess."

I smirk and let the sheet fall into my lap, sitting up as straight as I can after the pounding I've just taken, pushing my breasts out. When I look down, I notice small purple marks all over them.

"Jesus Nate, you did a fucking number on me," I moan, giving him a shitty look. There goes any hope of wearing anything but jeans and turtlenecks for the next week or two.

"Just marking what's mine," he replies with a cocky grin, handing me a bottle of water and depositing the snacks between us on the bed.

This is the opening I need. It's time to talk. I couldn't fuck him again even if I wanted to, so now that seems to be out of our system for the time being, it's time to show my hand.

"Am I?" I ask, steadily holding his gaze, challenging him like I always do.

"Are you what?" Nate returns, holding my gaze just as firmly, not giving me an inch, his lips tilting into a small smile.

I roll my eyes in exasperation; the asshole's going to make me say it, just to bust my balls.

"Am I yours? Are we gonna do this? Have a relationship? Because I've got to be honest, these days without you have been torture," I ramble. "I stood at that party comparing every guy to you, and none of them came close. You're fucking perfect, Nate, and even though I know you're probably not, I want this with you."

I'm breathing like I've run three flights of stairs, my bare breasts heaving as I sit there in limbo, totally exposed and vulnerable, waiting for him to respond. Nate's beautiful blue eyes stare at me, and I watch as he processes everything I've just laid on him.

Finally, he speaks. "Do you want guac or salsa with the chips?"

My mouth drops open in astonishment. I've literally just bared my soul to him, laid my cards on the table, told him I want a relationship, and he's asking me about dips? My cheeks burn with indignation and I huff, folding my arms across my breasts.

"Seriously, Nate?" I hiss.

"What?" he smirks. "You seem to be in a decision making mood, that's all."

His adorable grin disappears when I sling a pillow at him and make to get out of bed, but he deflects the missile with cat-like reflexes, sweeps the snacks to the bottom of the bed, and pins me down.

"Where are you going?" he whispers in a raspy voice, holding my wrists above my head in one of his large hands.

I squirm beneath him, struggling to get free, but also feeling hopelessly aroused by his weight on top of me, his hard dick against my stomach.

"You're laughing at me, and I just laid my heart on the line. It's not funny, Nate," I grind out, still struggling against him in vain, trying to control the urge to cry with embarrassment.

"Beth, stop!" Nate commands, cupping my chin with his free hand to stop my head thrashing, locking me in with his serious eyes. "I'm sorry."

I stop squirming and hold still, waiting for the rest of it.

"You are mine, one hundred percent," he says simply. "When I saw you tonight, all those guys staring at you, I realized that if I didn't make you mine, I'd regret it forever. And I have so many regrets in my life, baby. A conversation I had with my father tonight made me understand that. I won't add you to that list."

I feel my heart swelling inside my chest like it's never done before. The fluttering feels like I'm close to panic, but I soon realize my heart is cracking open, and I'm letting Nate all the way in.

"Are we doing this, then? Being together, for real?" I croak, afraid my voice won't be strong enough to ask the question, my eyes stinging with tears.

Nate smiles and releases my wrists, my arms instinctively going around his neck, pulling him down so his forehead rests against mine. I wait with my breath held for his next words.

"Let's do this thing," he whispers. Suddenly, his lips are crashing against mine, and I'm lost in the arms of this incredible man.

18

Nate

Beth's finally agreed to be mine, and I feel fucking fantastic.

We talk late into the night about everything; I tell her about the confrontation with my father and how I've finally come to the realization that what he's been doing isn't right. We share our fears and worries about the road ahead of us, but eventually I hold Beth's face in my hands and press a sweet kiss to her lips.

"You can't know what's gonna happen, princess. We just have to take a deep breath and dive in."

She smiles sweetly at me, her face open to all the possibilities our new relationship can offer.

"Okay." Her simple acceptance of my words makes my chest fill to bursting, and instead of making love to her again, I wrap her in my arms, stroke the tattoo of stars falling on her back, and we fall asleep.

I wake up the next morning in the most pleasurable way possible with Beth's plump lips wrapped around my cock. She proceeds to give me an embarrassingly quick blow job that ends when I push her off, straddle her body, and pump cum all over her fantastic tits.

But it isn't just the mind-blowing orgasm she gives me that makes me smile like a lunatic. She's agreed to be mine.

When I arrive for our pregame morning skate, I get a plethora of quizzical looks from my linemates, and finally Ford breaks the stalemate.

"What's made you so happy, kid?" Ford asks from across the locker room as we gear up for our warmup before the game against the Cincinnati Cobras.

"Just loving life, man. Just loving life," I smirk tightening my skates.

"Seems to me like you got your dick wet," Brett joins in, pulling his jersey over his head.

Catcalls and whistles follow his statement, and I feel my cheeks heat up, so I keep my eyes firmly on my laces.

"Ah shit, and I thought I had the big news today," Matt laughs as he comes around the corner, fully geared up already. "Mila agreed to move in with me."

"That's fantastic!" Bugs lumbers over in half laced up skates and gives him a bro hug, the smile on Matt's face almost as wide as my own.

"Looks like you're gonna get some quality alone time with Beth pretty soon," Matt says, directing his comment at me.

"So that's it!" Ford bellows, throwing his elbow pads at me. "You finally got your girl?"

"Yeah, he did," Matt interrupts. "Went all caveman on her ass and literally carried her out of a party she was at last night."

"Damn, kid. I didn't think you had it in you," Ford laughs, pulling me to my feet for a hard slap on the back.

"How did you know that?" I ask Matt, while I receive more congratulatory hand and shoulder slaps.

"You know Mila and Beth started texting the minute we both left this morning," he chuckles, shaking his head. "You've got a hell of a lot to learn about women, kid."

The chatter in the locker room then turns to the business of hockey and kicking the Cobras' butts, and I'm thankful to have the spotlight off me. When the conversation does turn back to relationships, the guys seem more interested in Matt's impending move with Mila. I'm so happy for them, but I know Beth will be sad to lose her roommate.

It's time to put these things to the back of my mind, and as I step out on the ice, I feel freer and happier than I have in years. The subconscious pressure I usually feel radiating from my father is mostly gone, and all I have left is the tingling joy of having Beth watch me play tonight—in the official capacity as my girl.

Coach Casey works us hard. The Cobras are a tough team, and after the main morning skate, he keeps all the defensemen on for an extra hour of drills and scrimmages.

I've got to admit that after my night with Beth, I'm feeling the pain. My muscles are sore and I'm fucking exhausted. Not that I regret a second of our time together. I just make sure to hit the masseuse and the ice bath before I go home for my pregame nap.

As I dress, I see a text from Beth.

[BETH: Damn you made me sore. But I'm very happy. Can't wait for the game. Mila gave me my ticket and her big news :(See you on the ice, big man. <3]

Goddamn it, even her texts make me hard. I subtly adjust my semi under the towel around my waist and I reply.

[NATE: You're sore? I've just spent that last few hours being pummeled by my teammates. Don't forget to wear your jersey. I wanna fuck you in it later, princess.]

I smirk, hit send, get dressed, and haul ass out of the training facility. Time is ticking, and if I'm going to get the type of long nap I need to be ready for later, I need to get home.

My phone starts to ring just as I put my truck into drive and screech out of my parking space. As I glance down at it resting on the center console, I see my mom's number flashing. I have a moment of anxiety that it's my father trying the same trick again, but I take the risk and answer. I never want my mom to think I'm too busy to pick up.

"Hey mom."

"Hi honey, how are you?" Her voice sounds tight, and I'm immediately on high alert.

"Everything okay, mom?" I stamp my foot on the brake and bring my truck to a stop in the middle of the thankfully empty players' parking garage.

"Oh yeah. Everything's fine," she sighs. "I just wanted to check you're alright. Your father told me what happened when you spoke."

"The less said about that the better," I growl. "I'm finally done with it, mom. He's given up the right to have any say in my life, and if he wants any kind of relationship with me, he needs to adjust his fucking attitude."

"Nate! Language!"

I crack a smile. I love that she still gets offended when I cuss in front of her. It's the kind of interaction we missed out on during her "absent" years when she was too sad about losing Max to even acknowledge I existed, cussing or not.

"Sorry mom. But I've had enough of his BS. I'm happy to be civil for your sake, but he doesn't get to say anything about my career or my love life," I repeat, to make sure my mom knows exactly where our relationship is at.

"Love life?" I hear the sweet smile in her voice and put the truck back into drive and continue out of the garage.

"Yes, I've got a girl. It's new, but I like her a lot, mom. She's feisty and headstrong, and she makes me a little crazy. But she's fun and sexy and really smart." I feel my chest swell with pride as I gush about Beth to my mom; it's something I've never been able to do before.

She knew Jenna, obviously, as we'd been friends forever so there wasn't that excitement of dating someone new and mysterious and introducing them to your family.

"She sounds lovely, honey. Your father did show me the pictures from that blog, and she's very pretty."

The mention of my father and the gossip blog takes the shine off our conversation a little, but I push forward.

"She's beautiful. You'll really like her. In fact, I'd like to fly you out here soon to come see a game and meet her."

Shit, where did that come from?

"Oh, that would be nice," my mom sighs and then, if I'm not mistaken, I hear a little moan of pain.

"Mom? Are you okay?" I ask quickly, feeling a little panic bubbling behind my sternum. Other than her emotional breakdown, my mom has always been physically fit.

"Just a headache, is all. They seem to come on so quickly these days." Another moan and sigh followed by a deep breath. "I'm going to go lay down. A nap and a Tylenol usually get rid of it."

"How long has this been going on?" I ask, quickly noticing I'm about to run a stop sign. Guilt twists my gut; how did I not know about her headaches? Oh yeah, I know. I'm a selfish, self-absorbed asshole.

"Oh, I've had these all my life. I had a doctor check them years ago, and he said they were just migraines. Don't worry, honey. And I'm sure your father will come around eventually, you'll see. He is proud of you."

I huff out a frustrated breath, both at my mom's nonchalance over the headaches and the comment about my father.

"Whatever," I scoff. "But mom, I want you to go back to the doctor. I'll pay whatever it costs. Go and see someone, please."

"I will, honey. Have a good game tonight. Hopefully I'll be watching. I love you."

"Thanks mom. Love you too."

I end the call just as I pull into the parking lot at my condo, and instead of getting out and heading upstairs, I sit in my truck for a few minutes digesting the conversation I've just had. I need to find a way to make my mom go and get checked out. I guess I could call my Aunt Sue, but they aren't especially close, and I think it would just make mom mad. I suppose the obvious option is to reach out to my father and convince him she needs to go to the doctor. But the thought of doing that makes my gut twist and ache.

No, I'm absolutely not ready to talk to him yet. I'll just keep pestering mom until she does as I ask.

Beth

There's a distinct difference between the first time I watched Nate play live and this time. Before, I was excited because it was my first professional hockey game, I was there as a guest of a player, I was wearing his jersey, and I had a butt plug in my purse!

However, this time is on another level. I'm not just Nate's guest—I'm his girl. I travel to the arena with Mila, and she shows me back to the family suite where the player's families hang out before and after the game. She introduces me to a few of the wives and girlfriends who take me under their wings, immediately asking me all about my relationship with Nate. They ply me with champagne and tasty canapes, and soon I'm blabbering like a teenager about her first boyfriend.

And then it hits me like a meteor. Nate *is* my first boyfriend.

Of course, I don't share this little revelation with my new squad, but it gives me a warm, gooey feeling every time one of them calls him by that new moniker. I can't seem to wipe the stupid, goofy grin off my face, and as we move from the suite down to our seats, I can't wait to see *my boyfriend* out on the ice.

"Kick his ass, baby!" I scream, hammering my fists on the glass as I watch Nate and one of the Cobra enforcers wrestle in the goal mouth. The Cobra just charged Thor after the buzzer, so Bugs and Nate have weighed in, all guns blazing. Nate takes a blow to the chin, and his head snaps back just as Bugs grabs the Cobra's jersey and yanks him away. Nate recovers and plows his massive shoulder into the Cobra's belly, and they fall to the ice in a punchy, flailing heap.

I feel the anger boiling over, and all I want to do is jump the boards and go help my man. I'm not deluded enough to think my tiny body would even make a dent in the massive Cobra player, but I have this unstoppable desire to defend what's mine. The only time I've felt like this before was when my little sister would get picked on at school or some bigoted douchewaffle would say something about Andre. I'm passionately protective of those I care about, and I guess now that includes Nate.

While I'm pondering this revelation, the fight is broken up, and Nate skates toward me, gives me a cocky grin, his teeth red with blood from his busted lip. Jesus, even looking like a total meathead, I find him so sexy I squirm in my seat while trying to listen to how long Nate has to serve in the sin bin.

I can't fucking wait to get him home tonight.

19

Beth

It's been a wild night, and after the game, despite the fact I'm extremely ready to take Nate home, the team persuades us to go to O'Connell's for celebratory drinks. The Whalers' win against the Cobras has more or less secured their place in the top three of the Pacific Division—with only Vancouver and L.A standing in their way to finish at the top.

The guys need to have a proper blow out, and no matter how much I want to take my hot, sweaty hockey player home and do filthy things to him, I know how important these occasions are for comradery and morale.

When we all arrive, O'Connell's is full to the rafters. Word has gotten out on social media that the players will be hanging out there, so it seems like the entire arena is packed into the bar. Nate puts his huge arm around my shoulders as we surge our way through the crowd toward the VIP stairs, and once he delivers me safely behind the huge bouncer, he kisses me deeply and heads back out to meet the fans.

Mila, Cam, and I set up pitchers of beer and get the tables loaded with bottles of Grey Goose and Patron. There are countless platters of appetizers and bar snacks, so by the time the guys extract themselves from the fan fest, we're set up at a table with shots and chicken wings.

As my guy comes into view, I feel my stomach flip as he marches straight over to me, lifts me out of my seat, and plants me down on his lap. I feel ridiculously happy as he grabs the chicken wing out my hand and shoves it in his mouth, stripping all the meat off in one impressive motion.

"Damn, cowboy," I'd husk into his ear. "You'd better eat me like that chicken wing later."

I'm pleased to feel his cock harden under my ass, and after that, the night turns into a game of "Who can turn each other on most." I'm pretty sure I win judging by the amount of times Nate pushes his hard-on into my back or ass.

Eventually, the game gets the better of me, and I tell Nate that if he doesn't take me home and fuck me, I'll reconsider this whole relationship thing. With a quick gulp of his soda (he's only had two beers so he can drive us home), he yells a quick goodbye to no one in particular and virtually drags me down the stairs and out to his truck.

We decide to spend the night at my place because Mila has already confirmed she's staying at Matt's, so once I let us into the apartment, I march Nate over to the couch and push him down. I proceed to give him a sexy striptease, removing all my clothes except the

Whalers jersey, throwing my damp, lacy thong into his face.

"Damn, princess," he moans while holding it to his nose, inhaling deeply. I kneel between his muscular thighs and work at undoing his belt and pants. "You gonna suck my dick, baby?"

"You better believe it," I husk, gazing at him through my thick eyelashes, bending my head to lick the entire length of his massive hard-on.

"Babe, you need to move before you suffocate me," Nate gasps in a muffled voice, gently slapping my ass.

I've just finished riding Nate's face, my fingers still gripping my headboard so hard my knuckles are white, my thighs quaking in the aftermath of my powerful orgasm.

"Oh, sorry," I gasp, not realizing I've been catching my breath for so long and am currently smothering my sexy boyfriend with my pussy. I fall to the side and lay next to him, snuggling into the crook of his arm, a place that is quickly becoming one of my favorites.

After a couple of hours of deeply satisfying sex, I think we've finally worn each other out. That's one of the advantages of dating a hockey player—mad amounts of stamina. I lay half sprawled across his chest, and we have one of those great talks you have after sex, where your defenses are down and you start to learn little bits about each other.

I talk about how Andre and I set up our business, about our long-standing friendship, and I express some of the fears I have about starting this movie.

"I kind of feel like a fraud, like an imposter," I sigh, running my fingers over the ridges of Nate's abs.

"What do you mean? You earned that job because you guys are talented. No other reason," he says, shifting so he can lock me with his determined stare.

"I know you're right, but don't you ever get imposter syndrome? Like when you're skating in a really big game, and you suddenly think to yourself that you don't belong there," I ask, suddenly interested in how Nate feels about his career.

"Sure, I did when I first made it to the show. I was a young punk from the Midwest suddenly skating with and against my idols," Nate explains, tracing small circles with his fingertips on the firm skin of my ass. "Every time I step out there, I have to check it's real, but then I say to myself that I deserve to be there, and that belief helps me become a better player. You have to believe that you and Andre deserve this opportunity because of your talent."

The earnest expression in his denim blue eyes fills me with such delight that I lean up and kiss him softly on the lips, cupping his cheek in my hand, stroking the scratchy stubble there.

"Do you wanna come to dinner at my parent's tomorrow?" I suddenly blurt.

What the hell? It just popped out like word vomit. Am I seriously inviting a boy over to my parent's house for dinner?

BETH

Nate keeps staring at me, cocking his eyebrow, his lips spreading into a huge shit-eating grin.

"Are you asking me to meet your parents, princess?" he smirks, giving my ass a playful slap.

I feel my face burn, and I bury myself in the crook of his arm, squirming with the embarrassment that I've done something so "girlfriendy" already. What the hell am I thinking?

"Beth." Nate shifts so I have to look up at him. "I think it's great that you feel comfortable enough to ask me to meet your parents, but if you're at all unsure we can take a rain check. No pressure from me. Although …" He suddenly seems a little sheepish.

"Although what?" I ask, squinting my eyes suspiciously.

Nate swallows loudly. "I did kind of invite my mom to come and stay so she could meet you."

I burst out laughing, pressing my face into Nate's neck, wrapping my arms around his waist. He also starts to chuckle, my body bouncing against his as we crack up.

"We're a pair of hopeless cases, aren't we?" I giggle, kissing his neck. "But seriously, I'd like you to come to dinner. I think it'll be good to keep pushing this new relationship forward before I lose my nerve or fuck it up."

"I'd love to," he whispers, kissing my lips. "But if I'm meeting your folks, I'd better get some sleep."

I let my hand drop to Nate's cock and give it a testing squeeze, feeling it thicken and grow.

"You sure about that, cowboy?" I growl, sliding down his body, intent on getting one more orgasm out of him tonight.

Nate

"This is a nice place," I say as I pull my truck into the drive outside the house belonging to Beth's parents. "Did you live here growing up?"

"Yep, all my life," she replies, fidgeting with the plaid skirt she's chosen to wear. In fact, it was about the tenth outfit she tried on, finally settling on the skirt, heeled ankle boots, and a black sweater that hangs enticingly off her shoulder. The skin there is becoming too much of a temptation, so before we get out of my truck, I lean over and plant a wet open-mouthed kiss on the sensitive place where her shoulder meets her neck. Over the last forty-eight hours, I've memorized the location of all her sensitive places.

Beth huffs out a breath and squirms in her seat. "You need to quit that before we go in there. And full disclosure, you're the first guy I've ever brought home, so don't get weirded out if they look at you like you're a unicorn or something."

I bark out a loud laugh that makes Beth flinch and glare nervously at me.

"Seriously Nate, if they gawp at you, it's not because you're famous; it's because you're my first boyfriend. Why the fuck didn't I do this when I was a teenager?"

I can see Beth beginning to spiral, so I grab her hands and press her palms to my chest, breathing deeply and calmly, hoping to transfer this feeling to her. Slowly, she falls into my steady rhythm and begins to calm.

"It's okay, baby. I don't scare that easy. They're just gonna be happy for you, so let's go in there, eat our body weight in spaghetti, and enjoy it." I lean over and kiss her softly on the lips.

Jumping out of the truck, I rush around the front and get Beth's door open while she gathers the flowers and wine I insisted on picking up on the way. She smiles at me and hops down, handing me the wine.

"Here, you should give this to my mom. It was your idea—you should get the credit," she laughs. "It's her favorite kind, so it'll win you major points."

Suddenly, I have a weird feeling in my gut, and I anxiously adjust the collar of my grey button down and worry that my faded blue jeans are too casual. Even though I've chirped Beth about being uptight about this dinner, I've only just realized that I'm kind of nervous myself. I want it to go well for Beth's sake, but I also want her parents to like me.

We walk a little too slowly up the path, and before my boot even hits the porch, the door flies open, and a tiny woman comes bursting out. She's small like Beth, but that's where the similarity ends. Her mom sports salt and pepper hair in a low ponytail and dark eyes, almost the exact opposite of Beth's lightness.

"Nate! It's so wonderful to meet you," she gushes. "Please come in. I'm Maria, Beth's mom. But then I guess you figured that out."

"Mom!" Beth hisses, glaring at her mom who's rambling as she ushers us into the house. "Will you cool it?"

"Sorry, sorry. We're just so excited to have you here."

Maria takes the wine from me, and Beth and I follow her down the hall into a large family style kitchen diner. Her home is warm and welcoming; the hall walls are lined with family photos and framed kids' artwork. It feels very different from the house I grew up in, which for the most part was utilitarian, cold, and empty, especially after Max died. I feel at ease immediately.

"Hey, daddy." I notice Beth rush past me and into the arms of a large man with greying blonde hair and Beth's blue eyes. He hugs her close and kisses the top of her head.

"Hi, pumpkin," he rumbles in a deep voice. When he releases her, he takes a few large steps toward me with his hand extended for me to shake. "Hi Nate. I'm Bryan. Good to meet you."

"And you, sir." I shake his large hand confidently, although inside I'm full of self-doubt. "Thank you for having me for dinner."

Bryan releases a loud guffaw and shakes his head. "None of that sir crap here, son. Just Bryan is fine. Can I get you a beer or a glass of wine?"

"Just a soda, please. I have a game tomorrow, plus I'm driving," I reply as I watch Beth and her mom chat and fuss in the kitchen.

"Good man," Bryan replies, slapping my back and guiding me over to the large dining table which is covered in various Sunday newspapers. "Take a seat, and I'll get the drinks."

My levels of anxiety begin to ease as I sit and observe the happy family move around their space in complete comfort. It's almost like watching players on the ice; they're totally aware of each other and almost anticipate each other's moves. So, when Bryan reaches up to get a glass from the cabinet, Maria ducks her head out of the way, and when Beth opens the fridge, Bryan spins to avoid being hit by the door. It brings a small, happy smile to my face as I watch the family scene, but there's also the slightly melancholy feeling at what I've missed out on. I guess this is where my need for a committed relationship comes from, the need to have what I've been denied.

"You okay there, cowboy? You seem miles away." Beth perches on my lap and puts my soda on the table, her eyebrows knot together in cute concern.

"I'm great," I reply, leaning over to kiss her chastely on the lips. I'm happy Beth has chilled out and seems a lot less anxious.

Suddenly, there's a loud banging noise from upstairs and the sound of thunderous footsteps. I feel Beth's body tense on my lap as she twists toward the source of the noise.

"Oh shit," she mumbles and tries to bury her face in my neck.

"What?" I ask, bewildered as to what is causing her to react like this.

"When's the hockey guy getting here? I'm fucking starved!"

From the staircase that opens out into the kitchen emerges a tall, gangly girl with a mass of dark hair and huge brown eyes surrounded by perfectly applied black eyeliner. She's wearing yoga pants that have seen better days and a Paramore band T-shirt that swamps her lithe figure. If I didn't know better, there's no way I'd put Beth and her as sisters or even blood relatives. They're such complete opposites, like a photo and its negative.

However, as she skids to a stop at the bottom of the stairs and catches sight of me, she cocks one of her dark eyebrows, and I see the family resemblance immediately. It makes me smile as I remove Beth from my lap and stand up to greet her.

"Hey Katie. I'm Nate." I extend my hand, and as she approaches, I see her eyes scanning me from top to toe.

"Jesus, you're a big'un," she laughs, shaking my hand firmly and flashing her eyes at her sister. "How does he not crush you, sis?"

Beth bursts out laughing, as does Bryan, but Maria tuts and calls for Katie to get her butt into the kitchen to help butter the garlic bread.

"What?" Katie sasses as she stalks past me. "He's massive. He must squash her into the mattress!"

"Katie! Shut it!" Beth hisses, slapping her sister's butt as she passes.

"Ouch. MOM!"

And that's pretty much how the rest of the evening goes.

The bickering continues non-stop between Beth and Katie, and it's like watching a battle of wills that's probably been raging since Katie could talk. But despite the constant biting, sarcastic barbs, family life goes on around them. I guess their parents have learned to zone it out over the years because dinner is served, grace is said, and food is consumed while this craziness continues.

Bryan and I talk about hockey for a while to get a break from the bickering, and I'm happy to discover he's knowledgeable about the game, so we can have a good conversation about the Whalers' chances for a cup win. I must remember to put some tickets aside for him.

At times during dinner, I feel Beth's hand on my thigh, giving me a reassuring squeeze while her mom or dad grill me about different topics. She squeezes particularly hard when Maria asks about my family.

"My folks still live in Oklahoma. My father still works at the base, and my mom volunteers with her church. Nothing too exciting to tell," I reply as lightly as possible, hoping that doesn't draw out any more questions.

"No siblings?" Maria asks before forking spaghetti into her mouth.

"Mom!" Beth hisses, flashing warning eyes in her direction. I see Maria blanche and stop chewing, her eyes go wide as if she's just realized she's said something she shouldn't have. I feel my heart buck in my chest and gaze around the table and see three sad faces looking back at me.

Maria quickly finishes her mouthful and wipes her lips with a napkin. "Nate, I'm sorry. That was insensitive. Beth did tell me about your tragedy. Please forgive me for bringing it up."

I take a breath and smile. "It's really alright. Max died when I was eight. It's been a long time."

Maria smiles kindly at me and reaches over to hold my hand. "I'm still sorry."

"Thank you," I reply, squeezing her hand back.

"I guess that explains why I constantly have my foot in my mouth," Katie chuckles, and the tension breaks as everyone goes back to their dinner. I release a deep breath and smile at Beth when she leans her body against mine in reassurance.

After a gut-busting meal, we have a little break before dessert, and while Katie and her dad load the dishwasher, Beth gives me a tour of the house. I know that Beth's family have money, but they live a modest, normal life. The house is large and comfortable but in no way grand or showy. There are a couple of informal sitting rooms and Bryan's office downstairs and four bedrooms and several bathrooms upstairs.

As we tour upstairs, Beth opens the door to a room, and I immediately know it's hers. From the jasmine scent, the Lady Gaga and Backstreet Boys posters and the huge vanity mirror surrounded by lightbulbs–it's totally Beth.

"So, this was my room," she says quietly, shutting the door. "I've told my parents numerous times to redecorate it, but they insist on keeping it like I left it when I went to college. It's a bit creepy really."

Being in Beth's teenage bedroom gives me a naughty little thrill, and while she talks about her posters, I crowd her up against her vanity table. Slowly, her light blue eyes meet mine, and she stops talking; a cheeky little smirk lifts her plump lips.

"Whatcha doing?" she whispers, putting her hands on the edge of the vanity, leaning back slightly.

"Thinking about fucking you in your teenage bedroom," I growl, nuzzling her neck. "It's making me hard."

I feel Beth's small hand cup my rock-hard dick, and she makes a little mewling sound, sliding her fingers up and down my shaft through my jeans. I see her chest rising and falling as I continue to plant wet, sucking kisses on her neck and shoulder.

"We really shouldn't—my parents are right downstairs," she sighs, but her fingers keep on stroking my dick. It's making me really hot, like we're in high school trying to sneakily make out while we're supposed to be studying. I feel like a little role-play might make it into our bedroom repertoire in the future.

"I can be really quick, I promise," I groan, pushing my hips forward against her insistent digits.

Beth laughs loudly and removes her hand, causing my head to snap up.

"That's not something a girl wants to hear, cowboy," she giggles, scooting around me and heading for the door. "Come on. You don't want to miss mom's tiramisu."

I cough and turn around, my boner pressing obscenely against my jeans. "Uh, I may need a few minutes."

Beth smirks into her hand and opens the door. "Come down when you're ready, but don't you dare jerk off in here." She points a warning finger at me and leaves, her lyrical laugh disappearing down the corridor, and I take several deep cleansing breaths.

20

Beth

Andre and I are attending our first read through for Hector Riley's movie, and we're sitting at a table alongside some of the biggest names in Hollywood rom coms.

"Is it pathetic that I'm so excited I might pee my pants?" Andre whispers into my ear.

"Nope, I'm totally with you," I whisper back, clutching my takeout coffee cup so tightly I fear it might crumple and dowse me in scalding hot Americano.

Today is the first day the lead actors have been present, and I'm fangirling hard. Cleo and Axel Henderson are two of the hottest young actors in Hollywood right now, and Andre and I have been watching all their movies for research. Of course, the fact that they're both insanely beautiful doesn't make that job too difficult. Cleo (one name only, like Madonna) is a tall, Amazonian beauty with smooth jet hair and mocha skin that appears to be completely flawless. I literally can't wait to get my hands on her face.

Axel on the other hand looks like he's just rolled out of bed after fucking an entire women's volleyball team. He's got long, dirty blonde hair that curls over the collar of his leather jacket. His rough, handsome face is covered in a week's worth of scruff, and his sea foam green eyes gaze around sleepily, checking out every woman in the room with bored disinterest. At one point during Hector's welcoming speech, he pulls his aviators down over his eyes, and I'm sure he falls asleep. I like him immediately.

This has been a massive learning process for Andre and me. We've discovered that the point of the read through is to familiarize the cast with each other and their roles, and for the technical crew to discuss locations, costumes, lighting, and, for us, hair and makeup.

We've been at the read through for two days now, holed up in a large loft space near Pier 55. Andre and I have scribbled pages and pages of notes about the way Hector wants each main character styled for each major scene, and I've got some really exciting ideas I want to float past him when it's time for us to have our one on one.

The new assistants we've hired aren't at the read through, but I'm so happy that's now taken care of. The stress of trying to hire the right people to work with us was really getting me down, but Andre called in a few favors from his hairdressing circles, and I scouted the local beauty schools. We finally hired four people to assist us, and it now feels extremely real.

Away from my professional life, my personal life is also in unchartered territory. It's been a month since Nate and I made our relationship "officially exclusive," and it's been a complete whirlwind. After the success of dinner with my family, I began to relax into being a girlfriend for the very first time.

There are definite highs and lows that I'm trying to navigate without making Nate too crazy.

The highs are obvious. I have unfettered access to an insanely hot, sexy, athletic man who has an unquenchable desire to fuck me in every way imaginable. In those first few weeks, we continued Nate's education into all things sexual. We try things that push even my limits.

One night, I present him with my largest butt plug and a bottle of lube and tell him I want him to fuck me in the ass. Nate almost breaks his neck trying to take his pants off as quickly as possible, making me roll around on the bed laughing hysterically as he stumbles toward me with his pants tangled around his ankles. Unfortunately for Nate, it takes me an age to stop thinking about how ridiculous he looks, and I keep cracking up, giving him performance anxiety. Needless to say, I don't get to pop his "butt stuff" cherry that night.

I make the happy discovery Nate has a thing for making me come in public. He buys me a pair of panties with a built-in vibrator he can control with an app on his phone, and tonight he begs me to wear them to O'Connell's.

The first few times he hits the vibrate button, I jerk like I'm being electrocuted. It elicits some very peculiar looks from Cam and Mila as we chat alongside the bar.

I throw Nate some shitty looks over my shoulder as he watches Ford and Matt play pool while fondling his phone. Suddenly, I feel the panties vibrate again, but this time, he has it on a slower, rolling setting, and fuck me, it feels incredible. A slight sheen of sweat breaks out on my top lip as I squirm and press my thighs together, trying to control what's happening in my panties.

When I look over at Nate again, his eyes are locked on me, a wicked smile on his face, his fingers poised over his phone. Mila and Cam continue to talk, completely oblivious to my torture as I feel the tension in my lower belly growing and rolling and building. My nipples harden, and I can feel how wet I am, so wet I think there may be a chance I can be electrocuted.

As I'm about to reach my peak, Mila asks me how much she owes for the utilities before she moves out, and I can't answer her. I just turn away and try my hardest not to give the game away, biting my lip hard.

However, Mila and I were roommates for a long time in college, and I see the horrified recognition dawn on her face as my orgasm washes over me. I close my eyes and rest my forehead on the bar, moaning quietly as the vibrating panties do their job.

"Beth, are you having an orgasm?" she hisses at me, taking a step back.

"Oh god," I groan, slamming my balled up fist against the sticky mahogany bar. "Um, oh god!"

"What's wrong with her?" Cam asks as she reaches out to rub my back.

"I wouldn't do that," Mila laughs, staring over at Nate who begins to blush and fiddle with his phone, thankfully turning off the vibration in my panties so I can slump on a stool.

"What the hell was that?" Cam appears adorably confused when I finally have the strength to lift my head.

I cough to clear my throat and smooth my hair down, trying to look like I haven't just had a powerful orgasm in the middle of a busy sports bar.

"Nate bought me a pair of vibrating panties, and he's been testing them out," I whisper, giggling behind my hand, then taking a large gulp of vodka tonic.

"Ewwwwww," Mila and Cam squeal in chorus, taking bigger steps away from me.

"I can't believe you just came standing right next to me," Cam groans, making a face, but Mila just laughs and shakes her head. During college, she walked in on me rubbing one out often enough to have seen my "O" face more than once.

"I'll need to get Nate to tell Matt where he got those. It looks fun," Mila giggles.

"Believe me, when I agreed to this, I didn't think it through very carefully," I sigh.

This will be the first and last time I wear the vibrating panties to O'Connell's or anywhere else too public for that matter.

I love that Nate is pretty much up for anything, and I feel free to suggest most things to him. Some of the guys I've been with in the past have made me feel slutty or dirty for asking for the things that get me off, but there's none of that with Nate. He makes me feel sexy and desirable at every turn.

Aside from the hot sex, we've settled into the part of a relationship that scares me the most: the day-to-day activities that people do when they share each other's lives. But so far, I feel good about everything we're doing; I love eating breakfast together while I do my sketches and he reads the sports section of the paper. We've taken long walks through my favorite parts of the city, and I've relished showing Nate all the places that have special meaning to me.

He tried to teach me to skate, whizzing me round the rink while I screamed and clung to him like a terrified monkey. I helped him make his apartment a little more "adult" by getting rid of the frat house vibe, buying some new soft furnishings to soften it up, getting a proper entertainment center to house his numerous games consoles, and finally getting him to buy some proper drapes for his bedroom.

The fear I have that all this stuff is boring and mundane is, so far, unfounded. Mila's right—when you share your life with someone you care about, it doesn't feel like a chore; it feels comforting and gives you a sense of security I've only ever felt with my family and platonic friends.

I often find myself wondering why I fought this for so long, but then I come to the conclusion that I must have been waiting for Nate, and that gives me a gooey feeling inside.

So far, I have to say, I really love being Nate's girl.

Nate

We're on a road trip playing the Chicago Rush, Minnesota Mayhem, and Detroit Devils back-to-back, and during the leg in Detroit, I take a nasty check and crash awkwardly into the boards, my left leg twisting painfully under my large body. Of course, having another two hundred pounds of angry Devil on top of that doesn't help the situation any. Once I haul myself back onto my skates, I gingerly push off and make it back to the bench without giving away how much fucking pain I'm in until I hobble down the tunnel and try to walk it off.

Thankfully, we're winning easily, and Coach Casey let me stay on the bench for the last few minutes of the game before sending me straight down to see the athletic trainers for treatment.

My left leg has always been my weakest; my hamstrings give me grief, and after a heavy hit during my high school career, my knee can be a bit tricky. This far into the season, a lot of guys are suffering, and as we get closer to the postseason and playoffs, the trainers are busy tending to injuries and strains. I know Bugs has some back problems, and Matt's been talking to the trainer about his hip flexors. Hockey players are hard men, and we skate with all sorts of injuries, but I know the end of the season hurts like a bitch.

"How does that feel?" the trainer asks me as he bends my left leg at the knee and presses it back toward my chest, testing it.

I grunt in pain and shake my head. "Nope, it's tight, and I can feel my knee grinding."

"Let me get you a heat pad, then we'll sort out a massage to loosen it up before you head back to the hotel," he replies, carefully straightening my leg and allowing me to sit up on the examination table. I drag my hands through my sweaty hair in frustration and huff out a breath.

Shit!

I sit in the treatment room with heat pads on my leg and get worked over by the masseur before I'm allowed to shower and head out to the team bus. Despite our win, the mood is quite sombre because we're all exhausted after the back-to-back. With our next game four days away, management decides we can stay overnight in Detroit before flying back in the morning.

During the journey back to the hotel, there are some rumblings among some of the guys about going out for beers and food, but I'm not in the mood. Although I'm not worried about my leg, I want to keep the weight off it and rest up before having to sit on a flight for five hours.

"You okay, man?" Bugs asks me as we disembark the team bus at the hotel. "Is your leg bothering you?"

"No, it's fine. The massage loosened it up some, but I'm gonna stay in tonight and rest up with an ice pack," I reply, slinging my duffel over my shoulder and wincing slightly as my knee jars. I catch Bugs' concerned expression, but he doesn't ask me about it again.

"Well, if you change your mind, just text me, and I'll tell you where we are. Matt's got a few good bars he wants to hit up." My captain slaps me on the shoulder and moves away to join the guys to discuss their assault on the Detroit bar scene.

After I grab one of the athletic trainers and ask for an ice pack, I head up to my room and strip out of my suit. I'm sharing with one of the rookies, so he'll

be gone for most of the evening which I'm ridiculously thankful for. Once I'm in my athletic shorts and
T-shirt, I grab a beer from the mini-fridge and settle
onto the bed with the ice pack on my knee. It's already
got an ugly black and blue bruise blooming on it and
my lower thigh, but I'm sure the swelling is less than
it was.

Just as I'm scanning the channels for the game
highlights, my phone pings with a message from Beth.

[BETH: Please call me. That was a hard hit.
Are you okay?]

Just seeing the message from my girl makes my
face split into a ridiculous grin. I can just imagine her
watching the game at home, screaming at the screen
when I took my hit. She gets so worked up when I play,
it's completely adorable.

I hit the FaceTime app on my phone and connect
the call, feeling a desperate need in my gut to see her
beautiful face. However, when the call connects, all I
can see is the ceiling of her bedroom.

"Babe, what are you doing?" I laugh. I hear shuffling
and mumbling, but the screen still faces the ceiling.

Beth lets out a huge huff of breath, then I hear her
voice. "I said call me, not FaceTime. I have a face mask
on, so I don't want you to see me. It's got five more
minutes until I can take it off, so if you want to talk
now, you'll just have to deal with the ceiling."

I let out a deep, rumbling laugh at how cute she's
being. "I don't care about that. Let me see you, princess."

"No," Beth moans. "I have a green face like that chick from Wicked. Can I call you back in five?"

I know she doesn't like me catching her doing her beauty stuff, so I relent and give her the time to take the mask off before she calls me back, looking fresh with a beautiful pink stain to her cheeks. How the fuck did I get so lucky to have such a gorgeous woman by my side?

"Hi babe, how are you? That hit seemed bad?" she garbles, squirming on her bed to get into a comfortable position. I notice her shoulders and upper chest are bare apart from thin straps of her tank top. Despite her concerned expression, I can't help feeling my dick harden at the sight of her smooth, silky skin.

"I'm fine. Just some tenderness and bruising. I'm icing it," I explain, shifting around the ice pack. "How's the read through going?"

I love the way her face lights up when she talks about her work. "It's amazing. Andre and I were so starstruck to start with, but after a while, the actors just seem like normal people. I mean, I saw Axel picking his nose the other day." She scrunches her nose up and makes a face which causes me to laugh and miss her so much.

"I'm glad it's going well. Just don't go falling in love with a movie star." I'm only half joking.

Beth hits me with one of her breath-taking smiles, and she cocks her arrogant eyebrow at me. "Who says he hasn't been wooing me already?" she teases, and even though I'm fairly secure in our relationship, I can't help the stab of jealousy that twists my gut.

I must be wearing my feelings on my face because I see Beth's expression change to one of worry. "I'm only joking, cowboy. You're more than enough man to keep me busy." Her voice has taken on that raspy, sexy tone she gets when she's turned on. Does my jealousy get her off? I decide she needs a little reminder of exactly how much of a man I am.

Holding the phone away from me, I reach behind my head and pull my T-shirt over my head, settling back against my pillows, positioning the phone so she gets a clear view of my chest and abs.

"Maybe you need reminding, princess," I growl, enjoying the pinkness in her cheeks and the blush that begins to crawl across her chest.

Beth bites her bottom lip and drags her tongue across it. "I think I do need reminding. How are you going to do that exactly?"

I can tell how turned on she is by the hitch in her breathing and the fact that her pupils are dilated so much I can barely see the rim of ice blue around the edge.

"First, you're gonna get yourself naked, then you're gonna do exactly what I tell you to do," I command, staring straight at her with a wolfish grin on my face. I'm pleased to see the little glint in her eye that tells me she's completely up for what we're about to do.

"What about your roommate?" she asks quietly, nibbling that delectable lip.

"He's out with the rest of the guys. He won't be back for hours," I reassure her. "C'mon princess. I need to see you."

Beth smiles, nods, and repositions her phone so it's propped up on some pillows at the foot of her bed, giving me an unfettered view of her body. She slowly kneels up and grabs the hem of her tank top, peeling it up her body, revealing her smooth, taut stomach, that sexy belly button ring, and finally the smooth, round globes of her naked breasts. My dick is now at full mast as I watch her shake out her loose ponytail and run her hands suggestively over her tits, making her nipples harden.

"Fuck, babe. You look so hot," I moan, sliding down into the pillows and smiling into the camera.

"What should I do now?" Beth asks, biting her thumb as she continues to kneel in front of her phone in only her cute boy short panties.

"I need you to put your fingers in your panties and show me how wet you are," I instruct, moving my free hand under the elastic waistband of my shorts so I can grip my aching dick. I feel it kick back in my hand as Beth's hand slides down over her stomach and into her panties, carrying out my instructions to the letter. I can tell by the hooded look of her eyes and the little moan she releases when her fingers smooth through her wet folds and graze her clit. I can just imagine how plump and swollen it is already. She's so responsive it drives me crazy to not be able to touch her.

I watch, open-mouthed, as her fingers move in rhythmic circles inside her panties while her other hand cups one of her full breasts and tugs on her hard, rosy nipple.

"How wet are you, princess?" I ask in a gravelly voice, giving my dick a few rough pumps.

Beth smirks and removes her fingers from her panties, tracing the wet trail of her arousal up her body and around one of her puckered nipples, making it shimmer.

"I'm so wet and ready for you, Nate," she moans. "I want to take my panties off and show you."

"Do it," I say. "Show me your pretty pink pussy." The pumps and tugs to my dick are becoming harder and faster, and I'm not sure how much longer I can go before I nut all over myself.

Sensing my urgency, Beth pushes her panties over her hips, then sits back so she can slide them down her legs, tossing them carelessly off the bed. She now sits in the middle of her bed, her knees demurely held together and drawn up so I can only see her legs and shoulders.

"I want to see you," she whispers. "Show me how hard I make you."

That's no problem at all. I chuckle and angle the camera so it's near my shoulder, peering down my body so she can see my hard, thick cock gripped in my big hand. I'm extremely satisfied to hear her breathy sigh through the speaker as she catches sight of me.

"Do the camera flip thing so I can see you and you can see me," Beth instructs in a breathless voice. I do as she asks, holding the phone in front of my face and flipping the camera so I can see her, but she can get a look at what's going on below my waist.

"What now?" she asks, still sitting in a position that keeps all her best bits covered up.

I take a deep breath, trying to regain some self-control. "Sit back, spread your legs, and show me how you'd want me to touch you if I was there."

"Only if you do the same," Beth gasps, shuffling back and slowly spreading her long, sexy legs to reveal the glory between them. My breath freezes in my throat as I catch sight of the delicate silver piercing in her clit nestling in the wet folds of her pussy.

Fuck, she's so beautiful it kills me.

"Touch yourself, baby. Get yourself off for me," I moan, finally losing the last shred of control. I begin pumping my hard dick as I watch her fingers slide between her legs and trace circles around her swollen pussy.

"Pump your fingers inside. Imagine it's my dick, fucking you hard," I growl, and we continue to masturbate for each other, my hand pumping furiously. Her fingers do as instructed. She tilts her hips up to give her easier access, and I watch as first one then two fingers sink into her wet, needy pussy.

"How close are you?" I beg, knowing that my control is right on the edge.

Beth lets out a moan of frustration and pumps her fingers faster, rubbing her clit with the heel of her hand. "It's not enough Nate. I need you here. I need your hard dick inside me."

"Oh baby, I know. Just keep thinking about my dick thrusting inside you. When I'm home, I'm gonna fuck you so hard."

I hear Beth's frantic, pained moans as she continues to finger fuck herself, my dirty talk helping her along.

I, on the other hand, am so close I can feel pre-cum dripping onto my fist as I slow my pumps slightly.

"Keep talking," Beth begs. "Tell me something you wanna do to me when you get home."

"I'm gonna come up behind you, push your skirt up over that tight little ass, rip your panties off, and bury my face in your pussy," I groan.

"Oh god yes!" she cries. "Keep going."

"I'm gonna eat you out until you come on my face, then I'm gonna lube your little ass up and push my hard, fat cock deep inside you." I feel my balls pull up tight and begin to throb. "Oh fuck. I'm coming, Beth!"

"Oh Nate, I want you to fuck my tight little ass!" She cries out, and I struggle to keep my eyes open as cum spills all over my hand and abs as I watch Beth's pussy throb and pulse out her orgasm. We hold eye contact the entire time, and it makes it so much hotter. Her little whimpers of pleasure cause me to groan loudly and finally close my eyes, letting out a deep shuddery breath.

"Jesus baby, that was so fucking hot," I sigh, grabbing my T-shirt so I can clean myself up.

"It certainly was," Beth gasps. I love that she makes no attempt to cover her body up. She shifts so she's laying on her side, her beautiful face propped up on her palm so she's gazing into the camera. Her breasts and cheeks still show a pretty blush as evidence of her orgasm, and she's never looked more gorgeous. "Are you sure your knee's alright?"

I tuck my dick away and flip the camera so she can see my face again. "It's fine, babe. I promise. Are you working tomorrow? Once we're back in Seattle, I have a free day. I'd love to take you on a date."

Beth's brow creases and she bites her lip. "I have a thing to do tomorrow."

"That's okay. Maybe we can meet afterward," I suggest, trying to hide my disappointment.

"Why don't you come with me?" she suggests, sitting up so quickly her tits bounce and jiggle deliciously. "Hector has set up a beach cleaning event as a team bonding exercise and to get some press shots for the movie. It would be great to have you there. You know how much he fanboyed all over you in L.A."

I've wanted to get more involved in Hector's charity, so this would be a good way in. Plus, if I could persuade some of the guys to come along, it would be great publicity for the team as well.

"Sounds great. How about I see if I can get some of the guys to come along?"

"That would make Hector's day!" Beth says enthusiastically. "We're meeting at Discovery Park by the West Point Lighthouse at one. Will you be back by then?"

"Yeah, we're flying out early, so we'll be back in Seattle by mid-morning," I confirm, feeling that flip of excitement at the prospect of seeing my gorgeous girl.

21

Beth

"I'm expected to pick up trash?" Cleo asks, a horrified look clouding her perfect features.

Hector has just finished outlining the plan for the beach clean, the heads of his charity standing on either side of him while their press people take photos for their website and press releases. A few people stare over at Cleo in amazement and a few others laugh nervously when they see a storm cloud spread across Hector's kindly face.

"Yes Cleo, we're doing a beach clean, so that will involve you picking up garbage and other trash from the beach to help clean it up for the myriad of wildlife that live here," Hector explains with endless patience.

I look at Andre and roll my eyes. The one thing I've learned about Cleo since starting the process of making this movie is that she's a total diva and not a very nice person. I was devastated at first because I expect famous people to be as lovely as they appear on the silver screen. Unfortunately, Cleo is a spoiled brat who treats her poor assistant like a slave and makes Hector and the producers stress out at every opportunity.

When she found out I was going to oversee her makeup, I received a massive email from her assistant listing all her allergies, intolerances, and other quirks that I should be aware of when selecting the makeup for the shoot. Thankfully, everything I use is humanely sourced, hypo-allergenic, vegan, etc. so nothing listed in her ridiculous demands would cause me any problems. However, her demand that I not speak to her during our time together may be a little tougher to achieve. Then again, judging by the kind of person she's turning out to be, we won't have much to say to each other anyway.

Andre and I continue to smirk and roll our eyes as Cleo and her assistant argue about how much trash she'll *actually* have to pick up before she can leave. I keep gazing up the beach toward the parking lot, hoping that Nate will arrive soon. He texted me this morning on his way to the airport, and judging by the time difference he should be back by now.

"Listen everyone, you have your teams and your zones. So please head to the tables and collect your gloves, trash bags, and pickers," the head of the charity says loudly. "Once again, we really appreciate you all taking part in this event. If you can, spend a minimum of one hour cleaning your zone. After that, if you'd like to continue, come back to the tables to get your new assignment. Have fun everyone and enjoy the day."

There's a ripple of applause and some whoops of excitement as people surge forward to gather their equipment. With a slight feeling of dread, I see Hector making a beeline for me, and I know he's going to ask about the whereabouts of my boyfriend and his friends. I've been checking my phone obsessively to see if there are any messages from Nate or Mila, but as yet I've got nothing, so I hope they're on their way.

"That woman will be the fucking death of me," Hector whispers when he reaches us, nodding at Cleo as she pulls on her gloves and continues to bitch at her poor assistant. "Just came over to check on the status of the Whalers. Our press people want some shots of them, but they have another event to get to soon."

Oh god, this is so awkward. I feel my cheeks burn with embarrassment. I felt so smug when I texted Hector with the news that Nate and some of the other Whalers would be coming to the event. But now here I am, standing in front of my new boss with no word as to where my boyfriend and his meathead teammates are.

"Um, I'm not ..." I begin.

"Here they are!" Andre pipes up, putting his hand on my shoulder to stop me babbling.

We all turn around to see a procession of huge hockey players striding down the beach, laughing and goofing around like they don't have a care in the world. I see Mila walking next to Matt, holding his hand and laughing at something he's saying. I also see Cam and Bugs, the rest of Nate's line, plus a few of the rookies that I don't know very well. Finally, my eyes drink in the gorgeous sight of my sexy as fuck boyfriend. He's dressed in dark jeans that hug his thighs perfectly, a Whalers hoodie, and his Mavericks ball cap. As our eyes lock, his smile lights up my world.

Jesus, who even am I?

"Put your tongue back in your head, baby. You're drooling," Andre croons, slapping my ass and chuckling to himself. I hiss at him and elbow him in the ribs, but it's impossible for me to wipe the huge grin off my face as Nate catches my eye and winks.

"Excellent!" Hector cries, rushing over and greeting all the players one at a time, pumping their hands enthusiastically and commenting on their great game last night. When he gets to Nate, they have a long chat about his knee, and when Nate finally comes over to me, I notice he is limping a tiny bit.

"Hey sexy," he growls in my ear, putting his big arms around my waist and lifting me off my feet. My arms loop round his neck, and we kiss so deeply that his cap lifts off his head and falls to the ground. Our tongues mingle, and he tastes like mint and hot man; it's completely addictive.

"Now, now children, this is a family event," Andre laughs. "Keep it clean."

Nate and I untangle from each other, and I feel my cheeks heat with a blush when I realize most of the team are watching our reunion. Thankfully, Hector is oblivious as he chats to the players and guides them over to the press people to get the shots and sound bites they need before heading off to their next event.

"Where were you? I was getting worried," I murmur as we walk along, Nate's arm slung over my shoulder, holding me close against his big body.

"Sorry, the plane was delayed, then we all had to go home to change. I didn't wanna pick up trash in my suit," Nate chuckles, giving me a reassuring squeeze.

Before I can reply, Nate and the others are whisked away by the publicists, and Mila, Cam and I collect our gloves, trash bags, and litter pickers.

"Oh my god, is that Axel Henderson?" Cam gasps grabbing my arm and digging her nails in.

I look over to where she's staring so hard I feel like her eyes are going to pop out of her skull. And sure enough, I see Axel looking totally bad ass in dirty, ripped jeans and a Van Halen T-shirt, his long, dark blonde hair hidden under a ratty beanie and his eyes hidden by his ever-present aviators.

"Yep, that's him," I confirm, prying Cam's death grip from my arm.

"Oh, he's so freaking hot," she breaths.

"He's okay," I shrug. Axel and I have had a few conversations, and of all the actors on the shoot, he's the most down to earth and easy to talk to.

"Okay? Did you see him in that movie where you pretty much see all his ... assets?" Cam gasps, fanning herself. "I mean, he's a talented actor, but his asssssssss ..."

"Hey ladies, I believe we're cleaning the same zone." The deep, Louisiana drawl gets all our attention.

I see the moment Cam strokes out as Axel appears at our little circle—her mouth holds the word "ass" and her eyes bug out of her head. As Mila and I smirk, she seems to come back to herself and takes a huge inhale of breath, spinning around to face Axel, her normal cool demeanor completely dissolving.

"Mr. Henderson, it's such an honor. I'm Cameron Sawyer, the assistant to the GM of the Whalers," she gushes as she pumps Axel's impressive arm in a vigorous handshake.

"Pleasure to meet you, Cameron." He clasps his other gloved hand over Cam's, and I watch as she gasps and flutters her eyelashes. I've never seen her like this before. It's so funny because she's surrounded by famous athletes all day and doesn't bat an eyelid.

"Axel, this is my roommate Mila. She also works for the Whalers, and she's dating Matt Landon," I say trying to take the heat off Cam, who's about ready to pass out.

Axel turns his gorgeous green eyes toward Mila, and they shake hands and chat while Cam regains some of her signature composure. Perhaps I should try to hook them up? I've known her for a while now, and I've never seen her go on a date or even hook up with anyone. Maybe a hot affair with an even hotter young actor will be good for her.

As I ponder my matchmaking options, we get geared up and begin walking along the beach toward our zone. I give a quick look toward the press area and see that Nate and the guys are still talking to the publicists and taking photos with Hector and his charity workers, so I figure he'll come and find me when he's done.

I rub my hands together and giggle evilly, jogging up next to Axel so I can hatch my plan to get Cam laid.

Nate

Jesus, this chick can talk. I thought I was coming here to pick up trash and hang out with my girl, but it seems like we're all getting a lesson in the environmental impact of microplastics. I notice a few of the rookies I guilted into coming along yawning and rolling on their heels, so I should probably do something before we lose them.

"Belinda, it's great hearing about your work here, but I know I speak for us all when I say we're more men of action than big thinkers," I say, clapping my hands together and grabbing a pair of gloves from the table. "I'd say we're gonna be more useful to you picking up trash, so why don't you show us where you want us and set us to work?"

Belinda blushes and flits her eyes around the group of large men who, I'm sorry to say, are on the verge of totally hating me for bringing them to this event and realizes she's about to lose our attention.

"Of course, I'm sorry. I'm just so passionate …" She stumbles over her words.

"And that's awesome! It's why we're all here. Isn't that right, guys?" I reassure her, feeling like a bit of a dick for interrupting her.

I get a rousing chorus of agreement from my team-mates, and one by one they go to Belinda, thank her for everything she does, and set about getting their gear and zone assignments from her assistant.

"I'm going anywhere Cleo is," the rookie Knox mutters, scanning the beach trying to find the famous movie star. "She's hot as fuck."

I laugh and slap the kid's shoulder. Knox is twenty and wet behind the ears. I'd pay money to watch him hit on Cleo. "She's over there. Go for it."

Knox straightens his broad shoulders and puffs out his chest, running his hand over his short, cropped black hair. He's a good-looking kid with his light brown skin and intense green eyes. He told me in one of our roommate late night chats he's got Jamaican, Irish, and Cherokee heritage which gives him a unique appearance. He might just catch Cleo's eye, but then again, she might shoot him down in spectacular fashion. I'm dying to see what happens.

"Did you just send the rookie to hit on the movie star?" Bugs asks, coming up to stand beside me, holding his trash bags and litter picker.

"Sure did," I laugh. "Knox snores like a fucking freight train, so this is my payback. I'm gonna watch him go down in flames."

"You're an evil man, Halsted," Bugs chuckles, but then his laughter dies in his throat as something catches his eye. I follow his gaze across the beach, and my body tenses and coils like I'm about to throw my gloves off on the ice and crack some skulls.

Farther down the beach, I see the other movie star, Axel something, with his arm around my girlfriend. He's whispering something in her ear, pulling away as she dissolves into peals of carefree laughter.

"Is that douche canoe seriously hitting on my girl-friend?" I growl, about to take off at full speed.

"Easy, kid," Bugs whispers, putting his big hand on my forearm, the muscles under his fingers are stretched so tight I feel like they might snap. We've been linemates long enough that he knows exactly when I'm gearing up to fight. "She's just being friendly."

"Friendly?" I snarl. "He needs to take his fucking hands off my woman." And before he can stop me, I take off down the beach. In skates, I can cover two hundred feet in a matter of seconds, but I quickly realize sand is much trickier. I stumble and trip my way over to my girl, my sneakers filling with sand which I fucking hate.

However, my progress is halted by a tall redhead. "Hey, Nate," Mila says with a smile. But the smile quickly slips from her face when she sees the expression of murder on mine. "What's up?"

"Nothing," I growl trying to slip past her, but her hand falls on my arm and stops me in my tracks.

Mila tugs me toward her and gives me a knowing smile. "I know it looks bad, but she's just being friendly. She's always been the same. It doesn't mean anything. Don't go charging over there like a bull in a china shop and make yourself look like a dick," she warns, staring me down.

Mila's warning takes some of the wind out of my sails where Beth is concerned, but it doesn't dull the anger I have toward the dude with his hands on my girlfriend. Why isn't she pushing him away? My inner caveman is beating his chest and roaring inside my head, desperate to burst free and flatten the guy into the sand. But I realize that if I cause a scene in front of her new work people, Beth will never forgive me, so I take a few deep breaths and allow Mila to talk me back from the edge.

"Now go over there, introduce yourself to him, and give Beth a kiss she'll never forget. That's the quickest way to nip this in the bud and won't involve anyone ending up in the emergency room," she chuckles, slapping my bicep and indicating for me to go.

When I get over to them, I can't seem to stop myself clasping Beth's delicate wrist, pulling her against my body, and turning on my heel so I become an impenetrable wall between her and the movie dick.

"Hey man. I'm Beth's boyfriend, Nate Halsted," I say in my gruffest, deepest voice, pulling myself up to my full height, puffing my chest out in a blatant show of strength and size. It's something primal inside me that I've never felt before.

Axel's not a small guy. He's six feet tall and obviously takes care of himself in the gym, but next to me, he might as well be a pre-pubescent pipsqueak. I feel a little shiver of smugness when he has to pull off his sunglasses and look up at me to complete the introductions.

"Nice to meet you, Nate. I'm Axel," he stretches his hand out and I clasp it. Hard. "Beth mentioned she's dating a hockey player."

Again, I feel a pull of smugness when I feel Axel's hand bones grind together under my grip. While this show of manliness ensues, Beth is wriggling behind me, trying to get free from me. I can hear her growling like an angry kitten, and it makes me want to throw her over my shoulder and carry her away from this scene. However, I know that'll earn me even more time on her shit list, so I release her wrist and allow her to come round my body and re-join the conversation.

"Axel really loves hockey," she says, slightly breathless from her struggle. "He was just telling me he supports the Gators."

"Oh yeah?" I reply in a disinterested voice. I catch Beth's glare and feel her sharp elbow in my side, but I continue to glare at Axel.

"Yeah, I grew up in New Orleans …" he begins to drone, all the while keeping his eyes on Beth and that just flares my anger again.

"Babe," I interrupt, cutting him off mid-sentence. "Will you grab me a bottle of water? I'm dehydrated from the flight." I turn to her and give her one of my best panty melting smiles, but she just glares at me.

Instead of doing as I ask, she shoves her bottle of water into my stomach and storms off toward Cam and Mila, who have been watching our exchange with grimaces on their faces.

Shit, I'm such an asshole.

I'm about to go after her when the fucking movie star laughs. He actually laughs and shakes his head.

"What the fuck is so funny?" I can barely contain my fury now, my fists ball at my sides and I'm tense and ready to pounce.

"I don't mean no harm, man," he chuckles in his warm Southern drawl. "She's a spunky little thing. She's been trying to set me up with her friend over there. That's all." Axel nods his head in the direction of the girls, and when I turn around, I see Beth gesticulating wildly while Mila listens and Cam makes puppy eyes at Axel.

Suddenly, my caveman turns on his heel and drags his club back into his cave with his head hanging in shame. I'm so stupid. I feel the panic twist in my gut–have I fucked this up with my jealousy?

I should probably examine this aspect of our relationship another time because right now I need to do some serious damage control. I may be a meathead, but I have good manners, so I stick my hand out toward Axel and offer it in apology.

"I'm sorry, man," I mutter. "She makes me fucking crazy."

Axel laughs kindly and shakes my hand good-naturedly. "No sweat. We're all good. Go kiss your woman. I've got trash to pick up." He ambles off down the beach toward some of the other Whalers, and I release my breath.

Now for the hard bit. I look over at Beth. Her cheeks are red, her jaw is tense, and she looks ready to kick my ass all over this beach.

"Fuck my life," I grumble as I limp slightly toward her. My angry sprint across the sand has made my knee stiff, something I'll regret at practice tomorrow.

As I approach, I see Mila and Cam offer me sympathetic smiles before they scurry off to pick trash away from our little domestic interlude. Beth turns her back to me, and I can tell by the way she's holding her arms around her body, her shoulders tense, that she's pissed beyond belief.

Carefully, I put my hand on the back of her neck and grip it gently, stroking my thumb up and down the sensitive spot below her ear. It's a place she likes to be kissed, and I hope it'll ease her tension. However, I couldn't be more wrong. Beth lunges forward and spins around, slapping my hand away, glaring at me with her icy eyes.

"What the fuck, Nate?" she hisses, stepping up to me and shoving my chest. Despite the fact she barely clears my pecs, she's got the fury of a typhoon, and it's quite intimidating. "How could you embarrass me like that?"

"Hey, that dude had his hands all over you. What did you expect?" I growl back. I'm pissed again. Did she expect me to let that shit slide?

"I work with these people; you can't just go all alpha on every man I talk to! That's not what I signed up for."

"I thought he was hitting on you," I argue back, feeling like this fight is getting out of control.

"So, what if he was?" Beth yells, drawing a few stares from nearby volunteers. "Just because someone hits on me doesn't mean I'm going to immediately run off and fuck them."

"That's not what I thought …" I begin in a quiet voice, reaching out to cup her beautiful, angry face in my hand, but she bats it away again.

"It's what your actions are saying. Your actions speak volumes. They say you don't fucking trust me."

Jesus, her eyes are so full of sadness and regret I feel the bile rise in my throat, and I think I'm going to barf. I'm supposed to make her feel like a queen, but I've achieved the complete opposite. I need to fix this before I lose the best thing that's ever happened to me.

"I do trust you, baby," I say quietly, staring deeply into her eyes. It's time to lay my cards on the table. "I'm falling in love with you, and I'm fucking terrified you don't feel the same way."

There. I've told her the thing that's been consuming my waking moments since she agreed to be mine. I fucking love her, and I've been dying to say the words out loud for weeks.

Beth looks at me with wide and unblinking eyes, her mouth opening and closing like a fish. All the fight seems to drain from her face, and her eyes fill with tears.

"You love me?" she whispers, finally finding her voice, even though it's raspy with emotion.

I manage to cup her gorgeous face in my rough hands, and I smooth a lone tear from her cheek, stepping into her so our bodies are flush.

"I've been in love with you since we danced together at the benefit in L.A.," I confess, pressing my forehead against hers and kissing her nose. "I love you, Beth."

I pull away so I can see her face. The tension in my body is wound so tight I feel like if she doesn't return my words, I'll never recover. I watch Beth sweep her tongue over her lips and swallow hard.

Fuck, she's not going to say it back. Have I just made a massive fool of myself saying it too soon?

"Jesus, princess. Please say something," I finally beg, unable to take it any longer.

My breath punches out of my chest, and I stumble back as Beth suddenly launches herself into my arms, wrapping her legs around my waist and smashing her lips against mine. Her perfect ass fills my palms, and I open my mouth to allow her tongue to stroke mine, the feeling of pure bliss filling me up.

"I've never said this before to someone in a romantic sense," she whispers against my lips, pulling away so her gaze traps mine.

I can sense her battling with the words. I know what a massive step this is, and I'm so close to telling her she doesn't need to say it back. But before I can, she utters the most beautiful words I've ever heard.

"I love you, Nate. I really do."

Now it's my turn to claim her mouth, making her gasp as I grind her pussy against my throbbing cock, sliding my tongue against the seam of her mouth, vaguely aware of a loud round of applause happening somewhere near us.

I really don't care; I've got the most gorgeous woman in the world in my arms, and I want everyone to know she's mine.

22

Beth

I still can't believe I said those words out loud for the very first time to someone I'm romantically involved with. I never in a million years thought I'd say it just five weeks into a relationship and that the words would come so easily and feel so right. I felt like my chest was going to burst open when Nate told me he loved me, and I couldn't hold my own declaration inside.

Obviously, I would prefer it to happen over a romantic, candle-light dinner and not on a blustery beach in front of my friends and his teammates, but when you have to say it, it doesn't really matter where you are.

It's pure torture having to stay at the beach clean when all I want to do is drag him home and make love to him. But we do our duty, sack off drinks with the team and race back to my apartment where we literally rip our clothes off in the hall, Nate taking me against the wall, thrusting into me with urgency and animalistic passion.

Later, in bed, we make love for what feels like the first time. Nate makes me come with his tongue and fingers first, getting me so worked up I beg him to enter me. But he isn't in a hurry; he rolls me onto my front and kisses every star on my tattoo while his fingers work my pussy from behind, sliding through my slick folds until I whimper with need. Then he sits up against my headboard and pulls me into his lap, holding my hips so he can drag the blunt head of his huge cock around my entrance, teasing me into a sloppy mess.

Finally, he lowers me down, filling me to the max, both of us sighing in relief. As I move on top of him, Nate captures my hard nipple in his mouth, rolling it between his teeth and licking away the sting. Nate's hands grasp my ass and help me move up and down, my clit rubbing deliciously against his cock and abs as I ride him to a slow, throbbing release that makes me clench and ripple around him.

Afterward, we sit there, his seed ebbing out of me, our arms around each other, gentle kisses and caresses eventually leading to more lovemaking that ends with Nate and me gasping our declarations of love for each other at the moment of our release.

The steady, thumping of Nate's heartbeat against my cheek is the most comforting sound I can think of at this moment. I'm lying sprawled across his huge, naked body and have been for most of the night, allowing the rhythm of his heart to lull me to sleep.

Now I can see the slash of morning sun through the gap in my drapes, and lifting my head gently so as not to wake Nate, I check the clock on my nightstand.

It's eight am, and I know that Nate has practice in a few hours, so I decide to get up and make him some breakfast.

I carefully slide off him and climb out of bed, Nate grumbling in his sleep, rolling over into the space I've just vacated. I'm momentarily distracted when the sheet falls off his gloriously tight butt, but the rumbling of my stomach wins out. I pull on Nate's discarded T-shirt and quietly slip out into the hall, grabbing the rest of our clothes from the floor and throwing them into my room.

Mila's door is open, and the apartment is quiet, so she obviously stayed at Matt's again last night. I guess I should start getting used to this. Loss twists in my gut when I think about her moving out, but I'm so happy for them. I know how she feels now; the love crap she's spouted for all those years finally makes sense to me. I know what it feels like to love someone completely and with my whole heart—and it feels amazing.

Smiling to myself, I quickly check the fridge and am thankful to find eggs, cheese, and spinach so I decide to make omelettes. After whisking up the eggs and cheese, I pour the mixture into the skillet and sprinkle the spinach on top, setting the coffee maker up while it cooks, putting some slices of bread into the toaster.

"What smells so good?" I feel large hands circle my waist and hot breath on my neck as Nate comes up behind me.

"I'm making omelettes," I sigh, pushing back against him, pleased with the hard ridge I feel against my butt.

"Nope, that's not it," Nate huffs against my neck and runs his lips across the sensitive place below my ear. "I think it's you that smells good. You smell like us."

Fuck me, this guy is unbelievable. His simple words make me so wet. I squirm in his arms and tilt my head so he can continue dragging his lips across my skin.

Suddenly, the acrid smell of burnt toast hits my nose. "Shit, the toast!" I pull away from him, grab the burned slices out of the toaster, and dump them in the sink.

"Sorry, baby. Didn't mean to distract you. Let me put more in while you do the omelettes," he laughs, taking more bread from the bag on the counter.

"You're very distracting," I grumble, flipping the omelette in half and sliding it onto a plate, sprinkling more cheese on top. "Here, eat this."

Nate stares at the food hungrily and sits at the counter, adding cream to his coffee and digging in. Before I can even make my own omelette, he's finished his and eaten four slices of wheat toast with peanut butter.

We talk easily over our food, making plans for me to come to the next home game and go for drinks afterward. I've agreed to help Mila pack up for her move to Matt's new place, so that's going to take up some of my time. Plus, things with the movie are about to pick up once rehearsals begin.

While we stack the dishwasher, Nate's phone vibrates on the counter, and I look over to see "Mom" calling on the display. He leans over me, brushing his hard body against mine and igniting my libido at the most inappropriate time. He grabs his phone, kisses my lips, and swipes the screen.

"Hey mom, what's up?" he answers, with the biggest grin on his face. He's completely adorable as I watch him chat to his mom, pacing around my living room wearing only his low-slung jeans. It's totally wrong to be having the thoughts I'm having about his delicious chest and abs while he's talking to his mom. Perhaps I should go and have a cold shower.

"So, your flight gets in at seven. I don't have a game that night, so I'll come pick you up, and we can go for dinner," Nate says, glaring at me hungrily. "Yeah, Beth'll be there. She's dying to meet you."

I smile back at him and decide to be a little bit naughty. Slowly, I lift up my T-shirt, revealing my naked body to his lusty stare. I toss it on the floor at his feet, lick my lips, and saunter toward the bedroom.

"Mom, sure, yeah. I'll email you the flight confirmations. No, it's fine. I've gotta go. Something came up. Love you." I smirk at Nate's hastily ended phone conversation, and I squeal with delight as I hear him charge down the hall, scooping me up and depositing me on the bed.

"You made me hang up on my mom, you naughty girl," he growls as he rips off his jeans and swiftly covers my body with his. "You know what happens to naughty girls, don't you?"

Let's just say Nate spent the next hour showing me exactly that.

Nate

"Halsted! How's the knee?" Coach Casey yells at me from the blue line as I power round the net and intercept the shot Knox aimed at our second-string goalie.

"Feels great, Coach," I shout back, throwing Knox a shit-eating grin as I skate past him with the puck. He plows to a stop, pulls his glove off, and flips me off before talking to the goalie about something.

Once I deliver the puck into the net at the other end of the rink, I skate over to Coach, and he questions me about my fitness. To be honest, my knee is still tight, but other than that, I feel fucking amazing. It's been a few days since the beach clean, and I've yet to go home for anything other than to grab an overnight bag and my hockey gear. It's been excellent spending time with Beth; I even got her to go on a classic date of dinner and a movie. Although halfway through the action movie I'd chosen, I felt her lips graze my neck and her hands started to roam under the massive tub of popcorn on my lap. Needless to say, I didn't find out whether they stopped the nuclear reactor from exploding, but I did give Beth an explosive orgasm in the back of my truck in the parking lot.

I'm going to have to go home today though, because I need to get my apartment ready for my mom's visit. She flies in tonight, and I need to put sheets on the spare bed and get some food in. I'm not sure she'll want to eat my pre-prepared meals that the nutritionist delivers to me once a week. In fact, I'm pretty excited to have some of my mom's home cooking.

Coach and I talk for a few more minutes, then he sends me off to work with Knox some more while he skates to the side to talk to Mila about something. When I look back, I see them talking intensely, Mila holding her phone against her chest while she speaks quickly, her eyes flicking to me and back to Coach several times.

"Are we gonna do this thing or what?" Knox grumbles, skating up to me, his helmet under his arm, his black hair glistening with sweat.

"Nate, come on over, son!" Coach yells suddenly, and I feel a trickle of icy cold sweat crawl down my spine. I skate a little too quickly over to the boards and immediately see that Mila's eyes are shiny and wet.

What the fuck? Is it Beth? Has something happened to her?

"What's going on?" I rip my bucket from my head and shuck my gloves, dropping them onto the bench, trying not to let panic consume me.

"Son, Mila just took a call from your father," Coach begins, his large hand resting on my arm. "He's been trying to call you all morning."

"What's wrong? Is there a problem with my mom's flight? She's coming to see me for a few days," I ramble. "He'd better not be stopping her from coming. She needs a vacation."

Suddenly, I'm pissed at my father. It would be just like him to stop her coming. But I see the expression that passes between Coach and Mila, and I realize that's not the problem.

"Someone had better start talking," I growl, the feeling of dread settling over me like a fog.

Mila coughs and clears her throat, reaching out to put her hand over mine; however, I don't feel her touch. I'm ice cold.

"Nate, your dad is at the hospital. It seems your mom had a bad headache this morning while she was packing. He got her to lie down and rest, and when he came back to check on her, he couldn't wake her up." Mila's lip begins to wobble, and her eyes fill with tears.

Coach squeezes my arm and I turn to him; everything seems to be moving in slow motion and I blink dumbly while he continues.

"Your dad called an ambulance, and they took your mom to the hospital. It seems her headache was an aneurysm, and she's in surgery to try and fix it." Coach smiles at me kindly, making sure I understand what he's saying. "Mila's working on getting you a flight that leaves in two hours, so get yourself to the locker room and get changed. Do you understand what I'm saying?"

"Nate," Mila whispers. "You need to hurry. Matt's dressed and waiting if you need him to drive you."

I shake my head to try and clear the ringing in my ears. My mom is in surgery, and I need to get to Oklahoma to see her before ... No! Not before anything. I just need to go and help her.

"I'll get changed," I mutter stepping off the ice and heading toward the locker room at a shambling run. Suddenly I remember we have a game tomorrow. "What about the game ..." I yell back over my shoulder.

"Don't worry. You're excused for as long as you need. The GM approved it. Just get yourself home, son," Coach Casey says sadly, shooing me away before huddling close to Mila and talking quietly.

The next two hours seem to pass as if I'm moving through water. People keep hurrying me along, but I can't seem to make myself move any quicker. Matt packs up my duffel while I shower and dress, Mila follows us out to the parking lot as she babbles about my flight, telling me my boarding pass is in my email, then Matt and I jump into my truck. Luckily, I have my overnight bag in the back from the nights I've spent at Beth's so at least I have a toothbrush.

Shit. Beth! I need to let her know what's happening.

"You doing okay, man?" Matt asks as we weave through the Seattle traffic toward the airport.

"I need to call Beth," I say quietly as I bring up her contact. When I hit the call button, her gorgeous smiling face fills the screen of my phone, and it eases some of the crippling pain I feel.

However, that feeling soon fades as my call goes unanswered and bounces to voicemail. Shit, she's in closed rehearsals today so her phone is probably off.

"Fuck!" I yell, thrusting my phone into my pocket and gripping my hair.

"Easy, Nate. Mila and I will tell Beth what's going on. She'll be fine. You just concentrate on getting to your mom," Matt calms me, his big hand gripping the back of my neck a little too tightly.

"What if I'm too late?" I whisper, the sting of tears in my eyes and nose feel weak and alien to me.

"Don't think that. Stay positive," Matt growls as we pull up to the departure gate. "I'll take your truck back to the arena so it's safe while you're gone. If you need anything, you call one of us. I don't fucking care what time it is. If we're on the ice, you call Mila."

All I can do is nod my head up and down. The words I want to say are stuck in my throat, and I don't trust myself not to cry like a fucking pussy.

"And we'll take care of Beth. Just go and be with your family." He slaps my arm, and I stare over at my teammate and one of my best friends with gratitude.

"Thanks, man," I manage to grind out, jumping out of the cab and grabbing my overnight bag from the back seat. Matt doesn't drive away until I'm in the terminal building, and by the time I see he's gone, I'm flicking through my phone looking for the email with my flight information.

23

Nate

The coffee in the take-out cup balanced on my knee is cold and sludgy, and it hasn't given me the caffeine boost I'd been hoping for. All it's managed to do is make me realize I don't like coffee from vending machines.

I've been sitting on the hard plastic chair in the ICU waiting room for three hours. Pretty much since I charged into the Mercy Hospital. The nurse brought me back here and told me to wait because my mom was still in surgery.

That was fucking hours ago, and I've still not seen my father anywhere. I assume he's with my mom, so I just sit, pace, and try to drink coffee while I wait. I've still not been able to get a hold of Beth, and that's driving me crazy. I need to hear her sweet, lyrical voice. I need her to tell me it's going to be okay. I need to hold her body against me, so I know I'm still here and I'm still human because at the moment I feel like an empty shell.

As if sensing my desperate need to speak to her across half a continent, my phone begins to vibrate in my pocket. I quickly drop the shitty coffee into the trash can and fumble my phone out of my jeans, huffing out a relieved breath when I see her name.

"Hey princess," I sigh, feeling my heart stutter back to life.

"Nate, oh my god! Mila just called. Are you alright, baby?" Beth shrieks down the line. Her breath sounds like she's running.

"I'm fine. I'm at the hospital, but no one will tell me anything. Mom's still in surgery, and I haven't seen my father yet," I say, pacing up and down the waiting area.

"What can I do? What do you need?" she gasps, and I hear her car door slam.

"I need you to not drive while you're on the phone, princess," I warn, picturing her trying to do a hundred things at once. "How about I call you when I've spoken to the doctors and we go from there?"

"I'll be home in about twenty minutes." I hear her start up the engine of the VW Bug and exhale a huge breath. "I love you, Nate. I'm so sorry." Her voice has a wobble that I've never heard before, and it just about breaks me.

"Love you too, baby. I'll call you soon." I hang up and take a deep breath. I feel a new surge of resilience pulse through my body now I've spoken to my girl. I know she has my back one hundred percent, and as I spot my father walking toward me down the corridor, I realize I'm about to need every ounce of strength she's just given me.

It's been two years since I've seen my father in person, and I'm a little shocked by his appearance. He's always been a solid, hard man with a military haircut and faded tattoos decorating his forearms and chest. He holds his body in a manner that screams discipline and hard work, but as I watch him walk toward me, I notice a huge change.

His hair is longer than I've ever seen it and a snowy white instead of the salt and pepper I was used to. His hard, military body seems softer under his sweater, and his strong jaw has weakened around the jowls. My father seems to have aged ten years in the last two, and if I was more familiar with him, I'd say he's probably aged even more in the last ten hours.

"You made it then," he says when we're finally face to face. Maybe it's my imagination, but he even seems smaller than before, his neck craning up to look me in the face. One thing that hasn't left my father in the last two years is the arrogant sneer he wears.

"I've been here for a few hours. No one would tell me anything," I reply, standing my ground while my father checks me out.

"Yeah well, your mom was in surgery, so there was nothing much to tell," he grumbles. "I know you're a big shot in Seattle and are probably used to getting everything when you ask for it, but we're a bit slower out here in the sticks." Disapproval emanates off him in waves, and it's clogging up my throat.

"That's not what I meant," I growl, taking a deep breath and pinching the bridge of my nose. "Where's mom now?"

"They've taken her back to her room in the ICU. She's still unconscious. The docs told me to come find you, so they can give us the news." He begins to march back in the direction he came from without a backward glance. "Keep up, hot shot. You're getting slow in your old age."

Jesus, even at this shitty time he can't resist busting my balls. I stride after him and catch up quickly as we reach her room.

"Be real with me. It's not good, is it?" I whisper before we enter.

"She'll be fine." My father has nothing else to say.

It's another hour before a doctor comes to my mom's room. In that time, I've had a small nervous breakdown but managed to hide it from my father. The sight of my mom lying in that hospital bed hooked up to all sorts of wires and monitors almost made me stroke out. She has a breathing tube in her throat, and her head is bandaged. Her skin has a sickly pallor that makes her blend in with the sheets and gown, almost like she's disappearing before my very eyes. The steady beep from the monitor at least gives me comfort that her heart is still beating.

My father goes straight to her side and sits in the only chair in the room, taking her hand and kissing it. It's the most shocking thing I've ever seen him do; they're not that sort of couple. They've never been affectionate with each other, and to see my father display heart and compassion completely throws me.

As I lean against the wall and watch them, I feel like an intruder on their private moment. It's uncomfortable, and I decide I'll go and find a chair when the doctor comes in, followed by a young nurse in blue scrubs. She immediately goes to mom's side and begins to fiddle with the equipment around her and take her stats.

"Mr. Halsted, I'm Dr. Miranda Todd, your wife's neuro-surgeon," she extends her hand to my father, they shake, and she nods at me. Dr. Todd looks to be in her forties with short red hair and a face full of freckles.

"What's the prognosis, doc?" my father asks, returning to the seat. I can't believe how fucking calm he's being. The guy who used to scream in my face if I missed a shot is now chatting over his wife's unconscious body as if she's just got the flu. It's taking every ounce of my self-control not to yell and beat his stupid face to a pulp, but the doctor is speaking, and I need to listen.

"The medical term for an aneurysm that develops inside the brain is an intracranial or cerebral aneurysm, and it's probably been developing in your wife's brain for years. As blood passes through the weakened blood vessel, the blood pressure causes a small area to bulge outwards like a balloon. The headache your wife experienced today is what we call a 'thunderclap' headache, and this is when the blood vessel ruptures and causes the bleed on the brain."

Dr. Todd has a very calming tone, and as I listen to her explain what's going on inside my mom's brain,

I feel comforted but still terrified that there's a pretty massive "but" on the way.

"Why did this happen?" I ask, my father's head snapping round as I speak. If he thinks he's got the monopoly on asking questions, he's got another thing coming.

"No one knows why the blood vessels weaken and rupture, but we can put the weakness down to a few factors like family history, being a smoker, or high blood pressure," Dr. Todd replies.

"Well, my wife has never smoked, and I've not heard of anyone in her family having this problem," my father barks. "It must be her blood pressure. She's been incredibly stressed over the years what with the death of our son and ... other factors." He glares at me and I get the distinct impression he's trying to lay this at my door.

"Whatever the cause, we did a procedure called neurosurgical clipping to repair the blood vessel ..." Dr. Todd goes on to explain the procedure, but I can't take it in once she describes cutting a hole in my mom's skull.

"The procedure went well, but we'll be monitoring your mom very closely over the next twenty-four hours," Dr. Todd says, putting her hand on my arm and smiling kindly. "I'm not going to lie to you about the risks. There are no guarantees, but this was the best course of action we could take."

"Thank you, doctor," I croak out, shuffling my feet, afraid that if I look her in the eye, I'll completely lose my shit.

"If you have any more questions, please just ask."

Dr. Todd smiles kindly and leaves me and my father alone, glaring at each other across my mom's unconscious body. She's often been the buffer between us, so the thought of her not being here anymore is more than my muddled brain can come to terms with.

24

Nate

"I need to make a call," I say after a few awkward moments where neither of us speaks.

"That's right. Go and call your whore," my father mutters under his breath, leaning over and kissing my mom's hand.

The hairs on the back of my neck stand on end, and I feel words rise in my throat and burst out before my brain even catches up.

"What the fuck did you just say, old man?" I sneer, balling my fists and bracing my stance the way I do on the ice.

"If checking in with your slam piece is more important than staying with your mom, then go and do it," he growls, not meeting my eyes. "You've always been the same. Putting pussy before everything else."

"Are you fucking kidding me?" I yell, finally losing my cool. "Jenna and I were in love, and you couldn't stand it, so you ruined us. And then you made me so scared of fucking up my hockey career, I didn't have another serious girlfriend until I met Beth. You have no right to make any comments about my relationship, so keep your goddamn nose out of my business."

My father moves more quickly than I can fathom, and before I understand what's happening, he has the collar of my shirt bunched up at my throat, and he's pressing me against the wall. Suddenly, I'm fifteen again and my body freezes, my throat closes, and I breathe in noisy gasps.

"Your mother is lying there in a fucking coma, and all you can think about is your little whore," he growls, spit flying from his lips and dotting my cheeks. "You don't need to be here. We've managed just fine without you."

"I'm here for her, not for you," I reply, shoving his hand away. "And if you wanna know why I've stayed away, you should look at the way you treated me for all those years."

I feel the panic subside as I remember Beth's words about my situation with my father. I realize he only has the power I give him, so I decide in that moment to take his power away.

"Oh, the big man's finally grown a pair," he scoffs, shaking his head and moving away with one final shove to my chest. However, I'm not done with him, so I shoot my large hand out and grip him by the shoulder. The rage on his face as he turns around could sour milk, but I hold my nerve and say what I need to say.

"I'm here to support mom. I'm not here to get into this shit with you," I say in a calm but menacing voice. "I don't wanna have to kick your ass, so if you wanna remain by mom's side, I suggest you cut this shit out and just be a husband and father. And just so you know, if you call Beth a whore or anything other than her given name, I will fucking end you."

The expression on my father's face is one for the family scrapbook (if we had such a thing), and I watch his Adam's apple bob up and down in his throat as he weighs up his options. His blue gaze holds mine for what seems like hours as he decides whether to back down or try to beat my ass.

The loud beeping of one of the many machines behind us breaks the moment, and both of us spin to look at my mom. Before either of us can make a move, several medics and Dr. Todd come running into the room and start swarming around the bed.

"Gentlemen, could you please give us room to work," Dr. Todd says in a calm voice as she begins to press buttons and lower my mom's bed into a flat position.

"What the fuck is happening?" my father bellows, trying to get to my mom's bedside. I make a grab for his arm, but his other arm swings round and socks me in the chest. "Let go!"

"We need to leave. Let them help her," I yell, pulling my father to the back of the room near the door, but just like him, I can't quite seem to leave. My eyes are fixed on the flurry of activity around the bed, and I'm trying to understand the complex commands and medical jargon the medics are shouting to each other.

With a dawning horror and a realization I've gained from watching too many medical dramas on TV, I notice the heart monitor isn't beeping anymore. It's making a continuous shriek that as far as I know means there's no more heart activity. Dr. Todd begins heart compressions while the nurses ready the AED machine; my father has stopped struggling and just watches with unblinking horror as they work tirelessly to resuscitate his wife.

Finally, one of the nurses moves us out of the room, and she talks quietly, explaining what's going on, but I don't hear a word. I watch helplessly through the window as they shock my mom's lifeless body again and again while the heart monitor continues to show no activity.

I gaze slowly at my father who is yelling at the poor nurse and fighting to get back in the room, but even in my state of disbelief, I'm still holding him back in my iron grip. The sting of tears is hurting my nose and eyes as I realize the activity in the room has ceased, and Dr. Todd is checking her watch and speaking words I can't hear because suddenly the loud bark of my father's voice comes screaming back into sharp focus.

"What the fuck is going on? Let me in there!"

Dr. Todd appears at the door, and I know what that look means. I saw that same look on the paramedic's face the night they came to help Max.

My mom is gone, and I'm totally alone.

Beth

I've almost worn a hole in the rug in our living room with all my pacing, and I think Andre is about to run out and find a tranquilizer gun to take me down.

"Jesus, Bee, will you sit down and stop pacing?" he grumbles from the couch. He looks like shit, gnawing on his thumb nail while his eyes track my incessant pacing.

"It's been hours since we spoke," I cry. "He told me he'd call back when he spoke to his mom's doctors. I know Oklahoma is the ass-end of nowhere but still …"

Andre rises from the couch and puts his hands on my upper arms, stopping me in my tracks. "Baby, you need to stop," he coos softly. "He's going through a terrible experience and even though the pair of you are so cute I could puke, he might not be thinking straight and calling you back might have slipped his mind."

"But I want to help him," I sob, leaning forward and resting my forehead against Andre's chest. "He sounded so alone and all the stuff with his dad…he needs someone there to be on his side."

I feel completely lost. I want to be by Nate's side so badly but rushing off to Oklahoma on a whim isn't smart. I've got no idea what I might be walking into, so I need to wait for him to contact me no matter how frustrating and heart-breaking it is.

"Come on. Let's order some sushi and watch a movie until he calls," Andre suggests, giving me a comforting hug.

Later, while Andre eats our take-out and I push a spicy tuna roll round my plate, Mila comes home with Matt. She dashes over and pulls me into a tight hug while I retell everything I know all over again. This time I don't even attempt to hold the tears back. Mila hugs me and cries as well while Matt and Andre talk about practical things like flying me out to Oklahoma City and what will happen about my commitments to the movie.

As the evening turns into night, Andre hugs me tight and heads home with strict instructions to call him as soon as I hear anything. Matt follows shortly afterward because the Whalers have a game the next day, and staying up all night with a pair of weeping women isn't going to help him play well. As I sit curled up on the couch, I hear Mila talking in hushed tones and then there's the sound of them kissing goodbye. It makes my chest ache with longing for Nate; I just want to hold him and kiss him and comfort him, but he's so far away.

"Come on, Bee. Let's go to bed," Mila says softly when she returns, her lips swollen and pink from her goodnight kiss. "You're dead on your feet, and if you have to fly out to Oklahoma City, you want to be rested."

"What if he calls?" I ask quietly, gripping my phone in my hand, checking the screen for the millionth time.

"We'll both keep our phones on." She holds her hand out and I look up, taking it so she can haul me off the couch. "I'll stay with you."

After we both wash up and change into our pjs, we snuggle up in my bed with the TV on quietly, watching some crappy reality show. I bury my face in the pillow and breathe in deeply. It still smells faintly of Nate's body wash, and that's both comforting and pure torture. Mila gently strokes my hair, and despite everything going on, I manage to drift into a fitful, dreamless sleep.

The rumbling vibration of my phone rips me from my slumber. I sit up and grab it from my nightstand while Mila moans and rolls over to turn on the light on her side. I see Nate's name and photo on the display, and after several panicky attempts, I manage to answer the call.

"Nate?"

"Hey, princess." Oh god, he sounds completely broken. This can't be good. I quickly check the clock. It's four in the morning which means it's six o'clock in Oklahoma. "Did I wake you?"

"Yeah. No. It's okay. I was waiting for you to call all night," I reply, sitting up against the headboard while Mila does the same. "What's happening? How's your mom?"

There's a deafening silence and I'm certain I can hear Nate's ragged breathing over the line. "She died."

I feel my chest constrict, and my heart begins to pound way too fast, my eyes fill with tears, a strange, strangled noise comes out of me, and I feel Mila's hand go to my shoulder.

"Oh baby, I'm so sorry," I sob, unable to control my emotions. "What happened?"

Nate takes a huge breath. "She was recovering from surgery when her heart stopped. They tried to resuscitate her, but they couldn't get her back. The doctor says she probably had a secondary bleed, but they won't know until they do an autopsy."

I can't stop the sobs from wracking my body, and I have to clap my hand over my mouth to prevent Nate from hearing them. He doesn't need to deal with my emotional breakdown along with everything else he's going through.

"Babe, are you there?" he asks quietly.

"Yeah, I'm here. What do you need? What can I do?" I cover the phone and take a deep breath, trying to compose myself so I can help the man I love.

"I don't know yet. I've been up all night, so the doctors told us to go home and come back later so we can arrange to have her body released to her church. Then we can arrange the funeral," Nate says in a surprisingly steady voice. He sounds like he's taking charge, and it makes me wonder where his dad is.

"Do you want me to come?" I ask, making eyes at Mila who grabs her phone and logs on to a travel website.

Nate huffs out a sigh. "Not yet. Things are ... complicated. I really don't want you caught up in all this shit. If I need you to come, I'll let you know. I have a lot of phone calls to make in a few hours. I need to call Coach and let him know I won't be back for a while, so I want to get some sleep first."

His rejection feels like a knife in my heart, and my hand reflexively goes to my chest as if I've been physically struck.

"If that's what you want," I whisper. "But I'll come whenever you need me. I love you, Nate, and I'm so sorry."

"Thanks. I've gotta go." And the line goes dead.

A strangled sob erupts from my throat, and I drop my phone on the comforter. Mila drags me toward her and holds me tight. I sob uncontrollably—I'm not a crier, I never have been, but I just can't seem to stop it.

I'm crying for Nate's mom, dying so young. I'm crying for Nate, and I guess I'm crying for myself. Nate hung up without saying I love you. He just cut me off, and as selfish as it seems, I'm heart-broken that he didn't return my words. They've been so hard for me to say and just as they feel right and natural, he dismisses me.

I cry until I've soaked Mila's tank top, my face is swollen, and my throat is raw. I can tell by the shuddering of her body that she's sobbing too, and as we comfort each other, we cry ourselves back into a restless sleep.

25

Nate

There's something about the smell of your childhood home that should elicit all kinds of warm, comforting memories. However, the smell of my parent's house does nothing of the sort—all I can smell is pipe tobacco, boot polish, and the faint floral scent of my mom's homemade potpourri. This never felt much like a home to me, especially after Max died, and everything changed. It was just a place for me to eat, sleep, and avoid my father's sharp slaps and disapproval.

We've been home from the hospital for a few hours, and my father hasn't spoken a word to me. The ride from the hospital was silent and full of crackling hostility, and once we arrived at the house, he retreated to their bedroom and slammed the door. I was left wandering around like an abandoned visitor, not sure what to do or where to go.

The sun is just beginning to rise, and it occurs to me I haven't called Beth back. Jesus, she must be going out of her mind. I quickly bring up her contact, but my finger hovers over the call button. What the fuck am I going to say to her? How am I going to explain what happened without completely losing my shit? She didn't sign up for this. We're supposed to be light and fun—this is way too intense. What if Beth can't cope and she bails?

I press the call button, and after four rings, a sleepy Beth answers. The sound of my name in her sweet voice breaks my heart. Why would this angel want to be with a man like me? A man who can't take care of his own mother? Why the fuck didn't I insist she see a doctor about her headaches? I asked Dr. Todd whether they could've detected the weakened blood vessels, and she confirmed that if they'd been looking for it specifically, it could have been detected. That made me feel like I completely failed her. I had the money and means to get her the best doctors in the world, but I hadn't followed up. After our conversation where she told me her headaches were getting bad, I didn't check in on her again or insist she make the appointment. I'd been so caught up in Beth and everything going on with us, I'd taken my eye off the ball.

I'm a selfish asshole.

"Hey, princess," I say in a voice that doesn't even sound like me. "Did I wake you?"

"Yeah. No. It's alright. I was waiting for you to call all night," she replies. "What's happening? How's your mom?"

I take a deep ragged breath. "She died."

The wretched sob that comes down the line makes my throat constrict and my nose sting.

"Oh baby, I'm so sorry," Beth sobs. "What happened?"

I recite the events of the night in a robotic, dead voice.

I can hear Beth breathing and gasping down the line, but it's muffled so it sounds like she's holding back. I knew this would be too much for her; she doesn't deserve to have this laid at her door in her first serious relationship.

"Babe, are you there?" I ask quietly.

"Yeah, I'm here. What do you need? What can I do?"

"I don't know yet. I've been up all night, so the doctors told us to go home and come back later so we can arrange to have her body released to her church. Then we can arrange the funeral," I say steadily. I don't want her to worry, so the stronger I sound, the better.

"Do you want me to come?" she asks.

God, that's the last thing I need—and the only thing I want. If she turns up, my father will annihilate her, and there's no way I'll subject her to his hate and grief. That's my burden to bear alone.

"Not yet. Things are … complicated. I really don't want you caught up in all this shit. If I need you to come, I'll let you know. I have a lot of phone calls to make in a few hours. I need to call Coach and let him know I won't be back for a while, so I want to get some sleep first."

I've got so much to do I don't even know where to begin.

"If that's what you want," she whispers, and I hear my rejection in her voice. "But I'll come whenever you need me. I love you, Nate, and I'm so sorry."

Fuck, I can't say those words back to her. If I'm going to let her go, I should start as soon as possible.

"Thanks. I've gotta go." There, I ripped off the Band-Aid, and it's the right thing to do to save her from more pain.

So why do I feel like I'm dying inside?

The days after the tense phone call with Beth are a combination of frantic activity and mind-numbing silence. Later that day, my father emerges from his room showered, shaved, and dressed impeccably. I, on the other hand, have two days' worth of reddish blonde scruff on my face, bags under my eyes, and wrinkled clothes that could smell better.

"We're going to the hospital at sixteen hundred hours. Clean yourself up!" he barks at me as he puts on the coffeemaker.

After camping out on the couch for the last few hours, I finally retreat to the childhood bedroom that holds absolutely nothing of me. I remember going to Beth's room when I visited her house—her parents' refusal to touch her teenage room, allowing her happy childhood memories to remain. In contrast, my room is now a generic guest room with a floral comforter and an exercise bike in the corner. The closet contains my father's dress uniforms, towels, and spare bed linen. However, on the very top shelf, I find a box of my peewee hockey trophies and some clippings from my high school team. I guess that says everything I need to know about my place in this family–I'm relegated to a dusty box hidden away in a closet.

After a shower and change of clothes, we head back to the hospital, riding in silence yet again. I literally have no idea how to communicate with my father. I understand the man has lost his wife, and for that I'm incredibly sorry, but I don't know how to offer any kind of comfort. He's made no attempt to offer comfort to me, so for the time being we exist in our own private bubbles of grief.

At the hospital, Dr. Todd meets us in her office and talks us through the events that led to my mom's death. She confirms that the autopsy showed a secondary bleed in a different part of the brain, and this one was catastrophic and probably killed her instantly. I gain a little comfort from this information, especially when Dr. Todd reassures us that she would have felt little pain, and she wouldn't have been aware during either event.

My father is all business and wants to know when her body can be transferred to the Chapel of Rest at her church and other highly practical arrangements. One thing I do know about my father: he's all about order and planning, so the fact he's taking this in his stride should make me thankful. However, as he questions Dr. Todd about these things, I just glare at him and wonder if he has a heart beating inside his chest. I can't help the seething resentment I feel toward him.

"Do you have any questions, Nate?" Dr. Todd asks, jolting me from glaring at my father.

"Um, no. You explained everything really clearly," I reply. "And thank you for what you did. I know it didn't turn out for the best, but I know you took excellent care of my mom in her final moments."

"Of course," she says sadly. "I'm just sorry I didn't get to meet your mother. It's obvious that she was very well loved and highly thought of."

My father lets out a dismissive snort that only I hear, and he stands, thanking Dr. Todd with a firm handshake before we take our leave.

"You just can't let it go, can you?" I growl as we walk out toward the parking lot.

"What? You playing the devoted son? It's a fucking joke," he snorts. "You've got all this money and power. Why didn't you get a doctor to see her? She told me she told you about her headaches."

The fury and my guilt finally burst through the surface, and I charge at my father, ramming my shoulder into his back and slamming him against the car, setting off the alarm. I bring my huge fist into his ribs and feel a satisfying crunch and a gust of breath leave his body. My father squirms in my grip and manages to turn his body around so we're facing each other. I draw my fist back to deliver a punch to his face, but he's quick as a cat and manages to sock me in the chin with a bruising upper cut that rattles my teeth. The roar of fury that leaves my body doesn't even sound human as we wrestle and deliver blows to each other, blood filling my mouth and dripping into my eye. I'm an animal, and all I want to do is rip and destroy everyone in my path.

Finally, I feel several pairs of hands grabbing at my body and arms, and we're pulled apart by some security guards, both of us nowhere near finished thanks to the years of built-up resentment and fury.

"Don't even think about coming back to the house, and if you know what's good for you, you'll go back to Seattle and forget you even have a family!" my father yells from the other side of the still beeping car.

"Don't worry! I forgot that years ago. Mom was the only family I had, and now she's gone. I might as well be a fucking orphan," I shout back, struggling against the hands holding me. "But I will be at the funeral, so don't even think about stopping me."

"Sir, I think you should come back in and have a doctor look at your eye," the security guard holding me says, leading me away from the scene. I allow him to lead me back toward the ER, all the fight flooding out of my body. Suddenly I'm bone tired.

26

Beth

"**H**eels or flats?" I ask Mila, holding up the two pairs of black shoes.

"Wear the flats but take the heels just in case," Mila replies, standing in the doorway of my bedroom, her carry-on bag clutched in front of her, her foot tapping impatiently. "Bee, come on. If we miss the plane, we'll be on our own getting to Oklahoma."

"I'm nearly done," I growl, shoving the heels into my carry-on and following that with my makeup case and several pairs of panties. I've got no idea how long I'm going to stay in Oklahoma because Nate has pretty much ghosted me for the last few days. We've spoken a few times, but each time, he's been more tense and distant. I'm terrified to push him because I've got no idea how to deal with his grief, so I just tell him I miss him, and I love him and pray he says the words back. However, each time we end our calls he just says, "and you" and hangs up. The absence of the words cuts me deeper each time, but I suck it up and realize he's just trying to cope with his loss, and I shouldn't make it about me or us.

Mila's phone pings, and she huffs out a frustrated breath. "Matt's downstairs. We need to go."

"For fuck's sake, I'm ready," I yell, grabbing my black coat from the hanger and stomping toward the door. As I pass Mila, I press a kiss to her cheek. "I'm sorry," I whisper.

"I know, sweetie," she replies, following me out of the apartment.

I've been completely blown away by the support the Whalers organization has shown to Nate at this time. The GM has allowed the team to use their plane to fly out to Oklahoma for the funeral, and I was overwhelmed when Mila told me that all but a few of the injured players, the coaches, the trainers, and the GM himself will all be attending. Because of the game schedule, it'll only be a day trip, but I plan on staying as long as Nate needs me there.

The Whalers released a statement on their website and social media platforms and the outpouring of love from the fans has been incredible. I sent Nate some links to show him how much people are supporting him, and I just received a "thanks" in return. Every time we communicate, it seems to get colder and colder, and the worry twisting in my gut won't ease up. I need to hold him in my arms as soon as possible.

The flight is uneventful, luxurious, and quiet. Mila's told me stories about the pranks and raucous behaviour of the players on their away series, but everyone is somber and quiet, talking in hushed tones in their small groups. Most of the players are already wearing their suits so they don't have any luggage which means once we land, we can board the bus immediately and head straight to the cemetery. The local AHL team has offered us the use of their team buses which is generous and shows what a tight knit family the hockey world is.

Mila has been an absolute rock; instead of sitting with Matt, she sits next to me and holds my hand the whole flight. We don't really talk; she just feeds me little details about what will happen when we land and the information she's received from the pastor about the funeral. My only concern is how quickly I can be with Nate, desperate to hold him in my arms and comfort him.

I'm almost vibrating with need by the time we land and board the buses for the thirty-minute journey to the cemetery. I send Nate a text to give him our ETA and watch as the three typing bubbles appear and disappear for several minutes. It makes me think he's writing me a long, lovely text, but all I receive is "OK." The feeling of dread and fear twists my insides again, but I take a deep breath and push them away.

Nate

Even though I wear suits a lot for my job, the one I'm wearing today is fucking choking me. Obviously, I didn't think I'd be attending a funeral, so I didn't bring any of my custom-made suits to Oklahoma with me. Instead, I had to go to a mall and buy an off the rack, shitty black suit that's too tight across my chest and feels like if I sit down my ass is going to bust the seams. I intend to rip the fucking thing to shreds with my bare hands once this day is over.

I've been standing next to my father and Aunt Sue, greeting the mourners for the last half an hour, shaking hands with people I don't know and a few I do recognize from my childhood. I smile and nod, accepting their condolences, and I'm thankful that no one asks me about hockey or requests an autograph. I don't need to give my father anymore reasons to hate me right now.

Since our fight, I've been staying at a hotel. Apart from going to the house to retrieve my bag and seeing him at the church to arrange the service, we've avoided each other completely. When Aunt Sue arrived, she came to my hotel and we had dinner. Even though I've not seen her since I was in my early teens, it was nice to talk about my mom and hear stories about her. The sisters had grown apart when my mom married my father because before I came along, they'd travelled extensively with the Army.

She lays a reassuring hand on my arm as more people approach us. "You're doing great, honey. Keep smiling," she whispers as my father gruffly greets more people. I know my teammates are on their way following Beth's text and the thought of seeing them gives me a strength I didn't know I needed.

But then, as the next mourner presents themselves to me, my whole world implodes.

"Hi Nate, I'm so sorry for your loss."

That sweet, quiet voice belongs to only one person. My Jenna.

I look up from the hand that's extended toward me into the soulful, grey eyes that seem huge behind her glasses. Her pale blonde hair is cut in a choppy, shoulder length bob that makes her seem older than the teenager I remember. She's wearing a black shift dress that barely hides her swollen, pregnant belly. But the one thing that hasn't changed is her sweet, shy smile.

"Wow, peanut. Look at you," I stammer, raking my eyes up and down her body, taking in all the changes and all the things that will never change about the first girl I ever loved.

Before I know what I'm doing, I take a step forward and draw her into a hug, her small body fitting against mine just like it always did, except now there's a bowling ball sized bump between us.

"I'm so sorry, Nate. My mom saw the announcement in the paper, and she called me. I knew I had to come," she whispered into my neck as we hug for a little too long.

A loud cough draws us apart, and I notice the large roughneck standing next to my Jenna. He thrusts his hand out to me as I let her go, suddenly feeling a little awkward.

"Hey man, I'm Daryl. Jenna's husband. I'm sorry for your loss," he says in a gruff Texan drawl. "She's been real cut up about it, made me drive all night to be here."

I swallow loudly and realize that Jenna is all grown up. She's no longer the girl of my childhood–she's married and about to become a mom. It's what she always wanted, and my father stole that dream from us having it together.

"Thanks, Daryl. I appreciate you both being here." I nod numbly at them. "We'll catch up afterward, for sure."

Jenna takes this as her cue to move on and speak to my Aunt Sue, and she nods sadly at me, giving my arm one more squeeze. Her touch has me coiled tight as a spring, and I have to excuse myself to get some air. I push past a few more mourners and stagger outside, gulping down huge gasps.

Shit, that was intense. I had no clue she'd show up, especially married and pregnant. I don't even know how to process this.

27

Beth

I'm ridiculously nervous when the bus pulls up outside the church. I changed into my black dress in
the very cramped and not overly clean bathroom at the
back of the bus and applied a quick sweep of waterproof mascara and pale lipstick. Today is not the occa-
sion for my signature red.

"Whalers!" Coach Casey stands at the front of the
bus, addressing the team, dignified in his black suit.
"We are here to support one of our brothers in his time
of need. You will show the utmost respect to Nate and
his family and conduct yourself like gentlemen. We
have three hours in Oklahoma before we have to board
the plane and return to Seattle. Anyone that misses the
bus will be left behind and fined. And to make myself
clear, this is a dry event. None of you will let a drop of
alcohol pass your lips. Am I understood?"

"YES, COACH!" the team agrees in strong voices,
and everyone begins to disembark. Mila and I wait
until the end before we leave, and I remember to get
my bag because I don't plan on returning with the team.

I've managed to agree with Hector that Andre and the assistants can cope with rehearsals until I return.

"Come on, Bee. Your man needs you," Mila coaxes as I stumble up the path in my ridiculous heels. I should've stayed in my flats.

We follow the procession of hockey players into the church, and it looks like the service is about to start. Their entrance causes quite a stir, and there are gasps of awe and surprise from the congregation as the players line the walls of the church because there are no seats available. They stand like a guard of honor in dark suits, tall and respectful.

When I finally make it into the church, I see that Nate has left his seat at the front and is shaking hands and exchanging bro-hugs with Coach and some of the players. My heart skips when I see him, tall and masculine in his ill-fitting suit. His face is clean shaven and his hair is a little too long. All I want to do is run to him, but I stand patiently and wait for him to approach us.

"Hey Mila, thanks so much for organizing all of this," Nate says quietly.

"Oh, it was mostly Cam. She's so sorry she couldn't be here," Mila says as she pulls Nate in for a hug. She whispers something in his ear, and he smiles weakly at her.

Finally, after what feels like a hundred years, it's my turn. I expect a smile, a kiss, and a hug, but all I get is a hand on my upper arm and a watery smile. "Thanks for coming, Beth."

What the actual fuck? That's all I get? Even Mila got a hug.

I feel my eyes fill with tears, and I try my best to pass them off as tears for him.

"Nate, I'm sorry," I step toward him, hoping to initiate some contact, but he steps away.

"The service is about to begin. I need to get back to the front. We'll speak afterward." And then he's gone, striding back down the aisle toward the only empty seat at the front.

I'm completely shell-shocked. He's treating me like a vague acquaintance, not his girlfriend. He hasn't saved me a seat next to him so I can hold his hand and support him through this. He's essentially dismissing me, and as the first hymn begins, I feel my heart shatter into a million tiny pieces while the tears slide down my cheeks.

I float through the funeral in a fog of despair. I itch to go to Nate and hold him, especially when he, his father, and other male members of the church carry his mom's coffin down the aisle at the end of the service. He's got a determined, dignified expression on his beautiful face as they proceed past us, but not once does he glance at me or even acknowledge my presence.

I can feel Mila looking at me all the way through the service, but I can't bring myself to return her gaze for fear of bursting into noisy, snotty tears. She grabs my hand tightly as we follow the funeral procession out into the cemetery toward the graveside. The men place the coffin down carefully, and the mourners gather around as the pastor begins the final committal.

I can't help but steal glances at Nate from across the grave site. He's holding his head high, but at no point does he meet my heated gaze. I just want to catch his eye and offer him a kind, supportive smile, but he never looks at me.

I'm so confused. Is he pissed that I didn't come sooner? Is something going on with his dad that's upsetting him or is his grief just so deep that he's lost? I need to find out what's going on with him, and after the coffin is lowered and people start to disperse, I take my chance.

"Nate." I put my hand on his arm, and he turns away from speaking to a pretty, pregnant woman and her tall male companion. "Can we talk for a minute?"

"Jenna, I'll catch up with you later." Nate addresses the woman, and I feel an iron fist around my heart as I realize this must be *his* Jenna. I shouldn't feel any jealousy because she's obviously with the guy she's holding hands with, and she's very pregnant, but I can't help the feeling of betrayal that he's talking to her and not me.

When Nate turns to me, it feels like a cold chill sweeps over me. He's not looking at me with love and fondness like he always has. There's distance and nonchalance that freezes my blood.

"Baby, what's going on?" I ask quietly. I will not cause a scene at his mom's graveside. "Have I done something to upset you?"

Nate releases a huge breath and shakes his head. "No," he laughs unkindly. "I'm standing at my mom's grave Beth; this really isn't about you."

His words are like a slap in the face, and I stumble back on my high heels and almost fall, but I regain my balance and step up to him.

"Why are you being like this?" I grind out through gritted teeth. "I know this is a terrible time for you, but

I'm trying to be supportive and be here for you. Why won't you let me?"

I can see the muscles in his jaw twitching as he grinds his teeth; I've literally never seen him so tense.

"My mom told me she had headaches, you know," he confesses in an angry voice. "I took that call just as you and I were starting up. I told her to go to the doctor and get it checked out, but I didn't follow that up. Do you know why?" He cocks his head to emphasize his angry question.

"No, I don't," I whisper, tears threatening to spill down my cheeks again.

Nate leans in close, so close I can smell the whiskey on his breath and feel the heat emanating off his coiled body.

"I didn't follow up because I was too busy fucking you," he growls nastily. "If I hadn't been so distracted trying to make you come, I'd have made sure my mom made that appointment."

I gasp and slap my hand across his face, the tears falling as I stumble away from a man I don't even recognize.

Nate

I watch as the woman I love staggers away from me, her heels sticking in the earth, my cheek stinging from her vicious slap. I see Mila grab hold of her elbow, throwing me a confused look over her shoulder as she helps her away from the graveside.

I've done the right thing; she doesn't need all the shit's that's gonna come with helping me get over this.

Then why do I feel like I've taken a puck to the chest?

"What's going on with Beth?" Bugs asks as he, Matt, and Thor come up to me, offering me more handshakes and hugs.

"I just ended things," I grumble, kicking some turf with my ill-fitting dress shoe.

"What the fuck, man?" Thor growls. "You dump your girl at your mom's funeral? Who the fuck does that?"

I turn on our enormous goalie who matches me in height but must outweigh me by twenty pounds of hard, Swedish muscle.

"I did what's best for her. She's a good time girl; she doesn't need to nurse me through this shit. Better I cut ties now than end up ghosting her when I don't feel like hanging out at O'Connell's."

"Sorry to say this at your mom's funeral, but you're a fucking idiot," Matt says menacingly. "That woman has done nothing but worry about you and try to help you and you've just pushed her away. Do you know how hard it was for her to take a chance on you? And this is how you repay her?" He shakes his head and stalks away.

"He's right. You've just made a huge mistake," Bugs adds, following Matt and Thor toward the rest of my teammates.

The whiskey I drank this morning is heating my blood, and I feel like I want to fight and destroy, but before I can stomp over to my team and pick a fight, I feel a soft familiar hand slip into mine.

I turn and see Jenna standing next to me. She looks up with her kind, grey eyes, and I feel an immediate calm settle my raging blood. She always managed to do that with just a look.

"You and I need to talk," she says quietly but with the dogged determination I always loved about her.

"I can't believe they haven't bulldozed this place and built a Starbucks," I grumble as Jenna and I sit at a picnic table in the park we used to frequent as kids. I had suggested we sit on the slide for old times' sake, but she cocked her eyebrow at me and pointed to her huge belly. Enough said.

Jenna doesn't react to my attempt at lightening the mood and just fixes me with her determined grey eyes. After she confronted me at the cemetery, she got Daryl to drive us here to talk. He's currently sitting in his truck with a coffee and the paper. I'm glad Jenna has found herself a good man.

"Wanna tell me what that was about back there?" she finally asks, and I know there's no way in hell I can lie to her.

I take a big, steadying breath and roll my neck. The tension I've felt since arriving in Oklahoma City is starting to make me crazy.

"That was Beth, the woman I've been seeing in Seattle. It wasn't working out, so I ended it." *Lies, lies, all fucking lies.*

I can tell from her expression that Jenna sees right through me. I exhale and drop my head, pressing my forehead to the rough surface of the picnic table. The whiskey in my stomach is roiling, and I feel like I'm going to throw up.

"I call bullshit, Nate." Jenna's hand rests on my shoulder. I look up at her and realization strikes. My father caused us to break up all those years ago, and now I'm letting him interfere in this new relationship. I'm giving him all the power again.

"Oh, shit. I've totally fucked up, haven't I?" I groan, looking up to see Jenna nodding in agreement at my stupidity.

"Yes, you have, you big dope. I heard everything you said to Beth, and I can't believe you were so cruel," she growls at me. "Those weren't the words of the boy I know."

"Well, I'm not that kid anymore," I argue back, glowering at her.

"Yes, you are, Nate. I've followed your career, and you care deeply about others; you never do anything to hurt people on purpose unless it's on the ice. And even then, you do what you do to protect your brothers. Don't you dare try and make yourself out to be an asshole. You're hurting, and that is totally understandable, but that woman flew across the country to be by your side, and you spoke to her like she's trash." Jenna slaps my chest just the way she used to when I pissed her off. "Your mom would be so ashamed of you."

And that just about kills me. It's a low blow but a necessary one. I know I've been unfair to Beth, but I still think being apart is best for both of us while I come to terms with all this.

"I just need some time, Jenna," I explain. "I do love Beth, but I can't be with her while I deal with this."

"I understand. I just hope she's willing to forgive you when the time's right."

Before Jenna and her husband head back to Texas, she makes me promise to keep in touch.

"I miss you, peanut," I whisper into her hair as we hug goodbye. "We were always best friends before everything else."

"I know, honey. Let's try and get back to that, okay?" She reaches up and caresses my cheek. "I want my baby to know he has a kick ass godfather."

28

Beth

"**I**'m not letting you leave here without eating something," my mom scolds as I sit at the family table, spinning cold, uneaten spaghetti around my fork.

Mila and my sister are washing up, and my dad has retreated to his office. Heartbreak must have been designated as mom's territory.

And I am heartbroken.

I had no idea pain this acute and deep was survivable, and I'm still debating whether I will get through it. In the week since Nate crushed my world, I've floated through the days, barely eating, only showering when forced to by a slightly disgusted Mila, and totally avoiding work. Mila fielded a few angry phone calls from Andre until he finally came by and yelled at me for fucking up our big break. Then he held me for an hour while I cried and snotted all over his cashmere sweater.

I now realize that this is why I've protected my heart for all these years. This is why I've never allowed myself to fall head over heels in love because I always knew it would end, but I had no comprehension how badly it would hurt.

The fact that Nate pretty much blamed me and our relationship for his mom's death just about ended me. He'd never mentioned the headaches to me. If he had, I would have encouraged him to follow up and make his mom get an appointment. But he kept that to himself, so blaming me just feels like an excuse. He obviously just wanted the conquest of getting the closed off, love-phobic girl to fall for him, so he could brag to all his hockey buddies about it.

I tried to call off Sunday dinner, but Mila made me shower and wash my hair and even drove me over here in my car. Of course, my mom was thrilled to see her, so she ended up staying, helping to keep the conversation going while I sat and sulked over my uneaten dinner.

Now I guess it's time to explain everything to my mom.

Mila and Katie make themselves scarce, and my mom joins me at the table with two large glasses of red wine.

"Talk to me, honey," she says quietly, stroking my arm.

I take a huge gulp of wine and blink back the tears. "He dumped me at his mom's graveside, and he blames me for killing her."

My mom gasps and almost spits her wine out. Once she stops choking, she says, "I need more information."

So, I tell her my sad tale of heartbreak, drinking two more glasses of wine before I finish, not even feeling the effects.

When I'm done, I look expectantly at my mom and wait for her opinion, both professionally as a therapist and personally as someone who loves me unconditionally. She huffs out a breath and finishes her wine, thinking carefully before she speaks.

"This isn't about you, mi amore," she finally says. "From what you've told me about Nate's past and the abuse he suffered at the hands of his father, he's pushing you away because he's afraid."

"Afraid of what? He's been the one chasing me, telling me to take a chance on love," I cry. "And I did that, and he shit all over me!"

"The only way Nate knows how to deal with grief is what he's seen at home. When his brother died, his mom retreated into her grief and left him alone, and his dad took it out on him. It's no wonder he's pushing you away. He feels like he has to deal with this alone. And I wouldn't be surprised if he's afraid he'll hurt you in the process." She reaches out and smooths my cheek. "I believe that if you're patient, he will come back to you once he's had time to process his grief. If you want to wait for him, then you need to tell him so, but if you want this to be over, you have to move on."

God damn it. I sometimes wish I didn't have a therapist for a mom.

"I don't know what I want yet. I'm still too hurt."

"That's completely your choice, but can I please give you one piece of advice?" my mom asks.

I nod.

"If he comes to you before you've made your decision, make sure you listen to him, no matter how mad you are. You can be quite hot-headed sometimes, so don't let anger cloud things. Remember he's hurt and confused too."

I feel more tears spill down my cheeks when I think about how hurt Nate is, and I pull my mom into a tight hug.

"I love you, momma," I sob as she rocks me and strokes my hair.

"I know, sweetie. I just wish we'd had this conversation years ago. Heartbreak gets so much more difficult the older you get," she chuckles, stroking the tears off my cheeks while I roll my eyes.

Nate

"Good to have you back, Halsted," Knox says as we bump fists in the locker room.

"Thanks, man," I reply, lacing up my skate.

It's my first practice back in preparation for our game tomorrow afternoon. It's the game that will declare us winners of the Pacific Division and guarantee our road to the postseason playoffs. The L.A. Pumas are also set to take the division, and their game is also tonight. If they win, we *have* to win our game. The guys have arranged to go to Bugs' place to watch the game tonight, and I'm conflicted about whether to go. Mila and Cam are likely to be there, and I can't deal with more earache from my female friends.

I've already been chewed out by Jenna and my Aunt Sue for the way I treated Beth at the funeral, so I really don't need more chicks telling me I've been an asshole.

Things with my father didn't get any better after the funeral. Aunt Sue hung around for a few more days to help clear out some of my mom's things, and we had dinner again before I left. She told me she'd spoken to my father about what was going on with us, and he'd told her in no uncertain terms to mind her own business. I thanked her for trying, but I've pretty much written our relationship off. I will not reach out to him again. If he wants a relationship, he'll need to come to me.

Speaking of relationships, things are distinctly chilly in the locker room today. Knox is the only guy who approaches me directly. The rest of the guys have given me uncomfortable nods of acknowledgement and gone about changing into their gear.

Matt looks particularly pissed when he comes into the locker room, and besides a brief greeting, he keeps his distance. To be fair, I can't blame him. I've totally fucked over his girl's best friend. He must be getting it in the neck from all angles.

"Right, guys. We play the biggest game of the season so far tomorrow night. Let's get out there and work hard for the win!" Coach Casey shouts from the door to his office.

"YES, COACH!" we yell, banging our skates, helmets, and sticks against the benches.

I spot Mila standing behind Coach, giving me daggers, and I turn away from her, shame washing over me.

"You're coming over tonight, right?" Bugs asks as we dress after practice. I scrub my hair dry with a towel and drop it into the overflowing hamper. It's been a brutal practice, not just because Coach has pushed us to our limits, but the vibe in my line is off. I can feel the hostility radiating off Matt like heatwaves, and we've made some dumbass plays because of it. Tonight will be a good opportunity to clear the air so we can get back to winning hockey games.

"Sure," I agree, looking over sheepishly at Matt. "Will the girls be there?" I ask quietly.

"Mila's coming, Cam's busy, but if you're asking about Beth, I don't know," he replies. "You're gonna have to face her sometime. You might as well get it over with."

I take a deep breath through my nose and nod, the thought of seeing her beautiful face twisted in anger is more than I can take. But Bugs is right. I need to man up and face her, at least try to apologize, and explain what happened in Oklahoma.

I just hope she'll listen.

29

Beth

"**N**o, absolutely not!" I huff, folding my arms across my chest and standing firm.

"Please Bee, you need to get out and see people. You're turning into a recluse," Mila begs.

She's trying to persuade me to go to Bugs' tonight to watch the Puma's game, but the thought of a) watching hockey and b) hanging out anywhere Nate might possibly be is too much for me to deal with. He's been back in Seattle for three days, and he hasn't reached out once to me—firmly cementing my heart to the fact he doesn't want to reconcile, and it's really over.

"If you can guarantee he won't be there, I'll come, but otherwise I've got a date with Brad Pitt and a pound of M&Ms," I grumble.

"After the daggers I gave him at practice and the fact hardly any of his line are talking to him, I doubt very much he'll be there," Mila says, throwing my purse at me. "Matt just texted. He'll be here in five, so get your damn coat on and let's go."

"You're the bossiest roommate ever. When are you moving out again?" I sass, cocking my eyebrow at her.

"Ah, there's my favorite bitch," she laughs, pulling on her boots and heading for the door.

Damn, I love that girl. I'm going to miss her so much when she abandons me for love. Perhaps I should get a cat, especially if I'm destined to be alone for the rest of my life. I might as well start my crazy cat lady collection sooner rather than later.

"Beer in the fridge, hard liquor on the counter, and if there's anything you don't see, just ask," Bugs says as we arrive at his place, slinging his thick arm around my shoulder and leading us through to his huge living area.

I quickly scan the room looking at all the hockey players and thankfully I don't see Nate, so I feel some of my anxiety flow away.

"I'll take a soda if you have one. I'm not drinking at the moment," I reply, forcing a smile even though I'm so unbelievably sad.

"In the fridge, babe. Help yourself." Suddenly Bugs shoots his arm out and points an accusing finger at the rookie called Knox. "Rookie, I said no shooters. We have a fucking game tomorrow!"

With that, he stomps across the room to wrestle the shot glass out of Knox's hand, clipping him round the ear like a naughty kid.

After a few pre-game drinks, we settle down to watch the make-or-break game. The tension in the room is thick, and I can see how nervous all the guys are. It must be awful to have your fate in someone else's hands; the outcome of this game determines how easy the Whalers will have it tomorrow.

I feel the tension in my body melt away the further into the game we get. If Nate hasn't shown up for the puck drop, it's likely he's watching alone at home. I feel a pang of guilt that he's not with his teammates because of me, but then I steel myself against that feeling. He dumped me; he made this mess, so he can suffer the consequences.

"Jesus, that soda is running right through me," I mutter to Mila just before the end of the first period. The score is still tied at zero, so I feel like it's safe to pop to the bathroom before the guys descend on it during the interval.

I jump up off the couch and scoot out of the great room to use the bathroom I know is nestled by the front door under the stairs. After washing my hands, I head out of the bathroom and freeze.

"Hey, princess."

Nate is standing by the front door, just closing it. He looks tired but so very handsome, my heart stutters in my chest. He's wearing his worn blue jeans that hug every curve of his thighs and a red lumberjack shirt with the sleeves rolled up. He's had a haircut since I saw him at the funeral, but he's grown a lot of scruff on his face. I hate myself for thinking that he's never looked more handsome.

"Hey," I squeak, coughing to clear the lump in my throat.

"How are you?" he asks, keeping a respectful distance from me, as if I'm a scared animal he's trying to pacify.

"Fine. You?" I can barely string two words together, terrified my traitorous voice will give away how much I'm hurting.

He takes in a huge breath and scrubs his hand over his short hair, rubbing it back and forth. God, I used to love those hands on me.

He locks me with that sky blue gaze, and I feel my resolve to stay mad at him crumble away. Damn him.

"I'm not good, baby," he says simply. "I was an asshole in Oklahoma. What I said to you was unforgivable."

"Yes, it was," I growl, putting my hands on my hips, giving him my most sassy self even though I feel anything but.

"Will you let me explain?" he asks, his eyes imploring me.

"I'm listening."

The expression on Nate's face shows me he wasn't expecting to get his chance that easily, so he takes a minute before he speaks.

"I thought I was protecting you," he says quietly. "When we got together, you didn't sign up to help me through this type of situation, so I didn't wanna be a burden to you."

"Jesus, Nate, isn't that what you've been trying to teach me about relationships?" I yell, my frustration erupting. "You told me that being with someone in a committed relationship was so great because you always had each other's backs. I was ready to have your back, and you pushed me away."

His face shows shame and regret.

"Everything okay out here?" Bugs pops his head around the corner and looks between us.

"We're fine," I reassure him, and he quickly disappears back to the others.

"I'm sorry about what I said to you, I'm sorry I destroyed what we had, and I hope one day we can be friends again," he declares, imploring me with his eyes.

I try to hold my shit together. I will not give him anymore of my tears. I need to be a strong woman and not let those dreamy eyes hypnotize me.

"I accept your apology, but as far as being friends, I'm still not there yet. You really hurt me Nate. I need time before I can be around you."

Suddenly, this hallway is too small, and we're too close. I can smell his body wash and the special scent that will always be Nate. It's choking me, and I need some fresh air.

"Can you tell Mila I left? I'm sure she'll be going home with Matt anyway," I stammer, trying to scoot around his large frame.

"Let me give you a ride. I didn't see your car," he offers, ever the gentleman.

"No, no. I'll get a cab. It's fine," I literally fly out of the front door and flee down Bugs' drive, bringing up the Uber app as I march down the street.

"Beth! Wait! Your purse," I hear Nate calling after me as he sprints down the street to catch up. Of course, he manages this in a few strides because I'm a short-ass, and he's a professional athlete.

I stop and spin around as he approaches, both of us breathing hard and staring at each other, the heat and electricity zapping between us.

"Here," he holds out my purse and coat, his hungry eyes trained on my mouth.

Fuck, he's so sexy when he's hot and panting, like he's just come off the ice. Despite the fact I'm still mad as hell at him, I don't resist when he lunges at me, grabbing the back of my neck and claiming my mouth. I ball my fists and slam them into his chest, but I can't stop the rest of my body sinking against his and my mouth opening for his insistent tongue. Jesus, he tastes so good, like home and sex and everything I'll ever need for the rest of my life. I feel the hard push of his arousal against my stomach, and I can't help but moan into his mouth as his hand grips my ass and hauls me up against him.

Just as suddenly, his harsh, cruel words from the funeral invade my brain. The hurt in my chest overwhelms me, and I push him away, taking several steps back. I put my fingers to my swollen lips and plead with my body to obey.

I will not kiss him again.

"No!" I cry. "You don't get to do that. You don't get to just kiss me and make it all better. You made a total fool out of me."

"Shit, I'm sorry, Beth. I didn't mean ..." he stutters.

"I need to go. Please let me go Nate," I plead, grabbing my purse and coat from the ground where I dropped them, running off toward the security gate at the entrance to Bugs' gated estate. The feel of Nate's lips is still fresh, my heart more confused than ever.

Nate

"Halsted, you've got a visitor," one of the assistant coaches yells across the noisy locker room. "Make it quick."

My head snaps up from taping my knee, and I give the coach a quizzical look. Who the hell could that be? I pull my jersey on. I don't want to be caught by a pap in just my pads, and I head to the locker room door.

This is a huge game, a must win game because the L.A. Pumas won last night, so if we lose, they take the division. I should have my head in the game. Whoever this is had better have a fucking good excuse for showing up at the locker room door.

As I exit into the hall, I scan the area searching for a familiar face, and my breath catches in my throat. My father stands like a sentry on duty against the cinderblock wall, looking as serious and glum as ever.

What the fuck is he doing here?

We lock eyes, and I see something I've never seen before. Am I imagining it, or is he nervous?

"What do you want?" I ask in a tight voice. "If it's not obvious, I'm kinda busy."

My father swallows hard and pushes away from the wall, approaching me. I tower over him in my skates and gear, and for the first time since I was a child, I have no fear of this man. In fact, the only emotion I have is pity. Pity that he's now alone and the responsibility for that falls at his door.

My father looks at me, and I think he sees me for the first time; he sees the man I've become and not the teenager he bullied for so many years, and it makes me stand a little taller.

"I've had some time to think after everything that happened, and I owe you an apology," he says in his usual strong voice, but this time there's something missing. The arrogance and poison have gone.

"For what?" I ask. I'm not letting him get off that easily. I want specifics.

He blows an exasperated breath and closes his eyes. "I had a chance to speak to your Aunt Sue, and she told me some things about what happened with … Beth. And I feel like I have to take responsibility for some of that."

I can't stop my eyes from bugging out of my head a little, and I wait for more. He definitely has more to apologize for.

"She also got me thinking about how things have been with us. I'm not a sensitive man. I don't do feelings and all that shit, but I realize that when … we lost Max, you were hurting too. The way I chose to deal with it was okay for me, but taking my hurt and frustration out on you was wrong. In my own way, I wanted all this for you." He reaches out and grabs the badge on the front of my jersey. "I wanted you to succeed so badly I lost sight of everything else. I should've been your dad, not your drill sergeant and not your coach."

I can see him struggling with the emotion of what he's saying, and it causes a lump to form in my throat that I just can't shift.

"I know the road to forgiveness will be a long one, but I hope we can travel it together and have some kind of relationship." I notice his eyes become a little shiny. "I've lost the love of my life, but I know now that I still have a little part of her still in you, son."

Fuck me, I feel like I'm going to lose it if he keeps going. I can see from his eyes that he means what he's saying, but everything is still raw and painful. He's right about it being a long road, but every journey begins with a single step, so I decide to be the bigger man and take it.

"Do you wanna stay for the game? I can get you a ticket," I reply in a gruff voice filled with emotion. I see relief on my father's face at my olive branch, and his shoulders seem to relax for the first time.

"I'd like that. I've not seen you play hockey for such a long time." He extends his hand, and I look at it for a few seconds before I grasp it in mine—small steps.

"I'll have a ticket sent to Will Call for you to collect. And a jersey if you'll wear one."

"I'll wear it with pride." His hand rises and instead of clipping my ear or slapping my face, he grips my arm and squeezes it in support. "One more thing," he says sternly.

"Yes?" Shit, here it comes. I knew this was too good to be true.

"You'd better make things right with that girl of yours. She spoke to me at the funeral, and despite everything I'm sure you've told her about me, she was gracious and kind. Love doesn't happen for everyone, and you'd be a fool to let that go."

With that pearl of wisdom, my father marches off up the corridor toward the main concourse, and I feel like I've just had an out of body experience.

"Kid, get your ass back in here. Team talk in five," Matt yells from inside the locker room, breaking the shock I'm currently in.

So much has just happened, but the main thing I'm taking from this moment is that I need to win Beth back, right after I help my team win this fucking game!

30

Beth

"**O**h my GOD!" I squeal, leaping off the couch, covering Andre in popcorn as the buzzer sounds to end the game. The Whalers won with a shutout and have taken the Pacific Division from the L.A. Pumas. We hug and watch as the players swarm the ice and leap on top of each other, celebrating with back slaps and a dog pile. My eyes scan the screen, and I see Nate powering down the ice and barrelling into Thor, sending the goalie flying into his own net and several more players bundle on top of the goalie who is obviously going to be named MVP for the game. Thor did an incredible job keeping the deluge of shots out of the net, and I'm so proud of the whole team.

But none of the players make my heart flutter and my panties melt like a certain number seventeen. I eat up the shots of him, his hair sweaty and plastered to his head, his face bruised from a brutal slam into the boards in the second period, but his smile is so huge I can't help but mimic it.

Then my heart literally stops when Nate skates over to the family area and tosses a puck over the glass. The man that catches it seems so familiar, but it can't possibly be.

"Shit!" I hiss as Andre and I finally stop jumping around.

"What?" he asks, brushing popcorn off his shirt.

"I think that's Nate's dad," I gasp as the camera pans away from Nate to focus on some of the other players.

"Are you sure? Why the hell would he be at the game? He lives in Ohio, right?"

"Oklahoma," I correct. "Fuck, Nate must be freaking out."

"It didn't look like that to me. He gave him a puck and the guy was wearing Nate's jersey," Andre says.

I have to check so I grab the remote and rewind the game to the part where Nate throws the puck. When I pause it, I can see very clearly that the recipient is none other than his dad. And he's tossing him a puck, not launching one at his head, so I guess he's there at Nate's invitation.

"I'm confused," Andre muses. "Doesn't Nate hate his dad?"

"Yeah, I guess something happened," I reply, completely confused by the whole scene. Suddenly I'm desperate to speak to him.

"Well, I have a feeling some drama is gonna go down in this apartment tonight, so I'm hitting the road," Andre laughs, kissing me on the cheek and heading for the door. "I want to hear *everything*!"

I laugh and slap his ass as he leaves. "I'll only tell you what you need to know."

"Thank god. I don't need the gory details, that's for sure."

"Ugh, you're disgusting. Get out," I laugh, shoving my bestie out the door and returning to the couch.

I grab my phone and see I have a few frantic, screaming caps messages from Mila about the win but nothing from Nate. Should I message him? Does he want to hear from me with all this other stuff going on? The kiss we shared last night sure as shit felt like he wanted me. My fingers hover over his contact, but I hesitate. Do I really want to jump back in so blindly? He really hurt me, and my heart is still bruised. I need to protect myself and not be stupid again.

"Rein it in," I grumble at myself and at my vagina in particular. She was extremely interested during the game and literally purred every time Nate came on the screen. I will not be ruled by my heart or my pussy. My head will be in control, and my head is telling me to turn my phone off and go to bed.

So, for once I listen and do the sensible thing.

Nate

The roar of jubilant hockey players echoes round the locker room as beers are cracked open and gear is tossed around in sheer joy. We're going to the motherfucking playoffs! So much has happened in such a short space of time I can't even process it. The reconciliation with my father is still new and delicate, but after the game, he comes to the locker room door again and looks prouder than I've ever seen him. He grasps the puck I'd tossed him and tells me he can't wait to show the guys at the base.

"I'm flying out first thing, so would it be okay if I called you in a few days when you wake up from your hangover?" he asks tentatively.

"Sure. That would be good," I shake his hand and watch him disappear into the crowd, a feeling of peace settling over me.

After that, things get kind of crazy; there is beer and celebration, followed by drinks at O'Connell's and an after party at Ford's that includes too many puck bunnies for my liking. I've been itching to call or message Beth all night, and the drunker I get, the more I want to speak to her. But the last thing she needs is a drunken booty call from me. I need to think of a grand gesture to win her back, and I'm pretty sure Knox and I do some sort of brainstorming on how I'm going to do that. I vaguely remember dragging my sorry ass into an Uber sometime around three am, and thankfully I wake up alone around noon feeling like a rhino took a shit in my mouth.

Moaning loudly, I reach for my phone and am thankful to see it's powered off. When I turn it on, I'm even more pleased to see no calls or messages made to Beth's number. The next time I speak to her, I want to be in control of my facilities.

I do notice, however, a very cryptic message from Knox.

[KNOX: The plan is a go. The guys are on board. We'll do it at the housewarming tomorrow.]

I scratch my head and squint at the screen. What the fuck is the plan, why are the guys on board, and why are we doing it at Matt and Mila's housewarming? I must still be hammered because I have no clue what this is about. Before I can even start to deal with this, I need to re-hydrate and shower the beer smell off my skin.

Half an hour later, I have showered, brushed my teeth, chugged several bottles of water, and choked down some scrambled eggs and toast. I'm just braving a coffee when my phone rings, and I see Matt's contact flash up.

"Matt, what's up?" I ask, hitting the button on my coffeemaker, the smell of super strong espresso filling the kitchen.

"Not much. How's the head, kid?" he chuckles, sounding a little hungover himself.

"Not bad. I'm a bit confused though. Got a weird message from the rookie about some plan, but I've got no fucking clue what it's about," I confess, hoping Matt can shed some light on it.

He laughs loudly, and I pull the phone away from my ear, the sound making my head throb. "Oh shit, you don't remember."

"Remember what?" I growl, suddenly terrified I've done something really stupid.

"Jesus, this is gonna be fun. You held a little brain-storming session in Ford's TV room last night. You called us all in and did a presentation about how you intend to win Beth back and we all shouted ideas at you. The rookie came up with a stellar plan."

"What is it? I have no clue," I beg, certain that whatever that cocky rookie came up with will have me looking like a total dick in the quest to win back my woman.

"Let me fill you in," Matt replies, and I hear him slap his hands together.

Shit, this is gonna be bad. So very bad.

31

Beth

"I can't believe we lived together for less than a year before you abandon me for a boy," I grumble, clinking my glass with Mila's. We're sitting on the kitchen island in Mila and Matt's new house drinking a very well-earned martini. We've spent the day moving her stuff to the house and directing very hungover Whalers where to put it all.

"Not just any boy," Mila laughs. "He's a pretty fucking sexy boy."

"Hey, less of the boy, Red," Matt yells from the living room where he and some of the guys are moving the couch into place. A moment later, he stalks into the kitchen while we giggle at his comment, his muscles bulging in his sweaty T-shirt, a hungry expression on his face. Mila sucks in her breath as Matt positions himself between her knees, takes her martini glass, and plants a deep, lingering kiss on her lips. It's so hot even I'm a little turned on.

"That's how a fucking man kisses his woman, and don't you forget it," he growls before handing a very pink Mila back her drink, heading back to his tasks with a smug look on his face.

"So, are you ready for the party tonight? With this group, it's best to get the party out of the way before you get the place looking nice," I say, jumping down from the counter.

"Yep, it's all good. Bugs is bringing the liquor, and apparently the rookie has some kind of surprise planned," Mila makes a concerned face. "As long as it's not a stripper or a parade of puck bunnies, I'm fine with it."

I look shyly at Mila and finally ask the question that's been burning my tongue since I got here. "Is Nate coming?"

She laughs kindly and hugs me. "Yes, he'll be here."

Several hours later, the house is filled to the rafters with hockey players, coaches, and their partners. The drinks are flowing as the celebrations continue from the night before, and I'm certain a few of the younger players are just topping up and haven't actually been to bed yet.

Mila and Matt spend most of the night curled around each other, talking quietly and kissing. I'm so pleased for my friend, and seeing them makes me yearn to see Nate, but he hasn't shown up. A few of the players have been telling me how hammered he got last night, so perhaps he's too hungover to come.

Suddenly I hear the feedback of a microphone that makes everyone wince. "Listen up, Whalers, the karaoke book is on the dining table. I'm making it mandatory that everyone sings, or you have to do a forfeit which will inevitably end up with you naked somewhere. So, if you wanna keep your junk hidden, get signing up. The first act will be on in ten."

"Ohhhh, I love karaoke," Mila cheers, her cheeks pink from all the kissing and martinis. "We should do a duet!"

Her suggestion makes me think of Nate and our first dates in L.A. He'd been so terrified of singing in front of people, and even though his voice was dreadful, he'd thrown himself into it like he does with every-thing—with heart, courage, and total commitment.

"Come on. Let's go and pick a song."

Nate

"Are you ready for this?" Knox asks as we stand in the garage doing tequila shots.

"I'll need about a million more of these," I grumble, knocking back the shot and allowing Thor to fill it up.

"Don't get too hammered, kid," he laughs. "You don't want to disappoint your lady if this plan works. No one wants whiskey dick during the good make up sex."

There's a rumble of agreement, and Ford sweeps the shot out of my hand, tutting at me and downing it himself.

"I can't believe you've talked me into this," Ford moans, wincing as the shot burns down his throat.

"We're a fucking team, and the kid needs us," Bugs pipes up. "We're brothers, and when one of us needs help, we muck in and do what's needed. So, let's suck it up and do this shit!"

"YES, CAP!" we all chant, forming a huddle and jumping around to pump ourselves up for the upcoming humiliation.

32

Beth

"**W**here have all the guys gone?" I ask searching around the party. The first line has been conspicuously absent for about ten minutes, and I only noticed because Matt isn't stuck to Mila's face.

"I think they had a beer pong table set up in the garage," Mila replies. It might be my imagination, but she appears a little shifty.

"Okay," I say, giving her a suspicious side eye. We've just signed up to sing my favorite Lady Gaga song and are waiting for our names to be called when Knox gets back on the microphone.

"Ladies and goons, I'd like to officially welcome you to Matt and Mila's housewarming party." A massive cheer goes up, and I look around for Matt, but I still don't see him anywhere. Something fishy is going on here.

"Now, our first act of the night is a little nervous, so we need to give him a great big Whalers welcome. Wooooooooooo!" Knox whoops into the microphone so loudly I have to cover my ears, then I hear the music begin.

I recognize the opening bars to The Backstreet Boys "I want it that way," but I don't see a singer. What I do hear is Mila giggling, and I feel her hands on my arms, turning me around to face the kitchen island.

"You are ... my fire. The one ... desire!"

Jesus, this guy has a horrible voice, I think as Mila moves me through the crowd of people and pushes us to the front.

Oh. My. God.

The first line of the Seattle Whalers is sitting on a line of high bar stools like a freaking boy band, and right in the middle is Nate, singing one of my favorite songs really badly. My hands fly to my mouth as I gasp out a slightly hysterical giggle, my cheeks burning red when Nate's eyes lock on mine, but he keeps right on singing.

Suddenly, as the chorus hits, the guys all stand up like any good boy band and join in the song, also in horribly out of tune voices. Mila claps and squeals next to me like a total groupie, and the laughter and heckling coming from the rest of the team almost drowns out their voices. But I only have eyes for Nate as he sings the next verse, slowly walking toward me, all hot sexy eyes and delicious, hard body.

I feel my heart melt as he stands in front of me and sings the next verse, pulling all sorts of funny, thrusty dance moves while the rest of the guys all pick a girl to grind up against. Of course, Matt is all up on Mila, and she's having the best time. Poor Cam chooses that moment to arrive, and Bugs makes a bee line for her, causing her to gasp and blush.

As the final verse begins and I think this can't get any more embarrassing, all the guys reconvene in front of me and drop to their knees. Nate takes my hand and sings the last bit slowly and sexily before the key change hits, he kisses my hand, and all the guys pop up and start dancing around like total idiots to the delighted shrieks of the women and the loud chants of the men.

In the end, I can't keep the delighted smile from my face. The man I gave my heart to is making an absolute fool of himself in front of all the people he respects most in the world, and it's all to show how much he loves me. I finally let myself go, dancing along to the final chorus, singing along with the rest of the crowd and clapping wildly when the song comes to an end.

People flock around the guys to chirp them and slap them on the back, but I only have eyes for Nate as he pushes past everyone to reach me.

"Did I make a big enough fool of myself for you, princess?" he asks, slightly breathless from his performance.

"Well, I don't know," I say, rubbing my chin and looking thoughtful. "Perhaps one more song?"

"You've got to be fucking kidding me," he growls, pulling me against his hard body. "That's the last time I ever subject people to my singing voice."

"Shame, it's quite a turn on watching you gyrate like that," I giggle, putting my arms around his neck and pressing my pelvis against him, closing my eyes when I feel his hard length.

"So, I need to know—am I forgiven? Are you my girl again?" he asks, his playful tone replaced with seriousness.

This is the moment where I choose my future. Do I forgive Nate for the horrible things he said to me in his moment of grief, or do I go back to being alone? I've never been afraid to be alone, but I finally realize I don't need to be. I've got a chance to share my life with the most incredible, kind, sexy man I've ever met, and I'd be a fucking fool to pass up this chance.

So, I do the only thing I can think of to seal the deal. I crush my lips to his and pour everything I have into our connection, wrapping my legs around his waist and climbing him like a tree.

"I love you, you big, sexy jock," I giggle against his lips as I feel Nate's hands grasp my ass.

"I love you too, princess."

"Get a room!" Thor yells, and I must be honest—that sound like a fucking excellent idea.

EPILOGUE

Cameron

Shit, I'm late. I really hate being late for things. It's one of my little OCD quirks. Whereas most of my friends are ten minutes late for everything, I'm usually ten minutes early. I've never missed a flight or an appointment; the very thought gives me hives.

As I push my way through the double doors that lead into Matt Landon's new house, I hear deep male voices. This is what I expect to hear since I'm entering a house full of NHL hockey players. However, the actual sound that assaults my ears is one similar to a bag of cats being drowned.

Is that supposed to be The Backstreet Boys?

Matt's housewarming/moving in with his girl-friend party is in full swing, and I soon realize that the horrible singing is due to the karaoke happening in the main room. I greet several of the players as I work my way toward the terrible singing, and before I know what's happening, a large, calloused hand grabs my wrist and pulls me into the commotion.

The hand belongs to the captain of the Seattle Whalers, Warren "Bugs" Parker, and he seems to be singing in my face.

"What the fuck, Warren?" I growl as I try to look round his huge shoulders to see what's happening. However, Warren is determined to serenade me, moving his muscular body against me, his fern green eyes twinkling with mischief, his face split in half by that breath-taking grin.

As the song slows down, Warren turns and saunters away from me, and I get a clearer view of what's happening; I see the entire first line of the Whalers down on their knees in front of my good friend Beth. They continue to sing to her while our defenseman, Nate, holds her hand. I can see her light blue eyes are filled with tears, and she's smiling and nodding like a woman in love.

I see what this is all about—Nate has obviously roped in his pals to help him win Beth back. And it looks like it's working.

As the song picks up for the big finale, all the guys leap to their feet and begin to dance around like fools. I see Warren making a beeline for me again, and I try to back away into the crowd, but I feel several pairs of large hands pushing me forward. Before I can protest, I'm pulled into Warren's large arms and we're dancing. Actually, dancing isn't the right word; we're grinding against each other, and suddenly all I can see are his dazzling green eyes.

"Hey Cam," he whispers as his hands move down my back to the top of my ass.

Wow, Warren's hands are on my ass!

It feels like all the air has been sucked out of the space, and it's just the two of us. We've been friends for years, and I thought I'd filed him securely in the Friend Zone. However, the way we're pressing against each other is definitely beyond friendly, and suddenly I'm unbelievably confused.

This is definitely a complication I don't need in my life at the moment. But it's been so long since I've been wanted and desired in the way I know Warren does—what harm can it do? I work hard so I have no time to date, and my last serious relationship was over a year ago.

Perhaps I can allow myself one little taste of this deliciously sexy man ... one little taste is all I need.

Read the rest of Cam and Bugs' story in All She Needs – Coming September 2021.

Acknowledgments

Dear Beauties

Thank you again for joining me and my crazy hockey crew on this rollercoaster ride. I'm sorry if Nate's journey was a little hard going, I know how much you all love him and his sweet, sensitive nature. It all worked out in the end though. I absolutely loved writing caveman Nate, he's so hot!

I'd like to thank everyone who helped me get my second book baby out there. The Team at 4 Horsemen Publications have made another gorgeous book. JM, Valerie, Erika and Brandon—thank you for all your help and support.

To my wonderful Insta family, you support me so much, I really couldn't do this without you.

@annapsbooknook, @tatted_book_freak, @claire. reads.romance and me_myself_and_romance_books are only a few of the wonderful bookstagrammers who share and review my books.

Yet again, I've had amazing support from my author friends. You've helped me to navigate this crazy game and given me so much invaluable advice—Emma Creed, Lulu Moore, Melissa Ivers, Danica Flynn, Mae

Harden, Kat Baxter and Fern Fraser are just some of my amazing author lovelies.

Lana, yet again you have read everything I've sent you and kept me writing even when I've been so tired it hurts. I can't wait to write Thor for you, you've been so patient!

My wonderful Street Team and ARC readers. Thank you for your support, honesty and suggestions. You make this process so exciting, I love hearing what you think.

My family and friends have been incredible. You have whole-heartedly supported me on this new adventure and haven't taken the piss out of me (too much!). The fact that my mum has been promoting my books to my old school teachers has caused me a few blushes, but they have all been incredibly proud.

Of course, I love all the members of Bunney's Beauties. You happily indulge and participate in my love of hot men, the Dallas Stars and Tyler Seguin and you keep me writing.

And to you, my wonderful reader, thank you again for buying my book and revisiting characters who I hope are becoming like old friends. Don't worry, there's plenty more to come. Bugs and Cam's story will be released in September 2021.

Lots of love   *Emily*

Author Bio

Emily began reading romance novels in 2019 and became instantly hooked. She was inspired to write her own during the 2020 lockdown and first self-published it on Wattpad. With the help of Instagram, she gained a loyal following and eventually secured a publishing contract. Emily is a recent but enthusiastic follower of the Dallas Stars and in particular the delicious Tyler Seguin. She loves an espresso martini, dirty-talking alpha heroes with tattoos, and a lazy Sunday breakfast. Emily lives with her husband and extremely old feline fur baby.

www.emilybunney.com

INSTAGRAM
@emilybunneyauthor

TWITTER
@ emilybunneyaut1

FACEBOOK
https://www.facebook.com/emilybunneyauthor

BUNNEY'S BEAUTIES FACEBOOK GROUP
https://www.facebook.com/groups/96708790038369

Book Club Questions

1. What part of the book did you enjoy the most?

2. What part of the book do you think could have been improved?

3. Who were your favourite characters? Which characters would you like to see get their own book?

4. Which character gave you the strongest emotional response (either good or bad)?

5. If you were making a movie of this book, who would play the lead characters (they don't have to be actors)?

6. Share a favourite quote from the book. Why did this quote stand out?

7. What did you think of the book's length? Too long or too short? Are there any parts you wanted to be developed more?

8. What songs does this book make you think of?

9. If you had the chance to ask me anything about the book or being an author what would it be?

10. Which characters would you like to invite to a dinner party and why?

11. How realistic were the hockey scenes? Is there any way I can improve these?

12. Did you like the slow burn or do you prefer insta-love?

**Discover more at
4HorsemenPublications.com**

10% off using HORSEMEN10